Erle Stanley Gardner and The Murder Room

>>> This title is part of The Murder Room, our series dedicated to making available out-of-print or hard-to-find titles by classic crime writers.

Crime fiction has always held up a mirror to society. The Victorians were fascinated by sensational murder and the emerging science of detection; now we are obsessed with the forensic detail of violent death. And no other genre has so captivated and enthralled readers.

Vast troves of classic crime writing have for a long time been unavailable to all but the most dedicated frequenters of second-hand bookshops. The advent of digital publishing means that we are now able to bring you the backlists of a huge range of titles by classic and contemporary crime writers, some of which have been out of print for decades.

From the genteel amateur private eyes of the Golden Age and the femmes fatales of pulp fiction, to the morally ambiguous hard-boiled detectives of mid twentieth-century America and their descendants who walk our twenty-first century streets, The Murder Room has it all. **>>>**

The Murder Room
Where Criminal Minds Meet

themurderroom.com

T0352436

Erle Stanley Gardner (1889–1970)

Born in Malden, Massachusetts, Erle Stanley Gardner left school in 1909 and attended Valparaiso University School of Law in Indiana for just one month before he was suspended for focusing more on his hobby of boxing that his academic studies. Soon after, he settled in California, where he taught himself the law and passed the state bar exam in 1911. The practise of law never held much interest for him, however, apart from as it pertained to trial strategy, and in his spare time he began to write for the pulp magazines that gave Dashiell Hammett and Raymond Chandler their start. Not long after the publication of his first novel, *The Case of the Velvet Claws*, featuring Perry Mason, he gave up his legal practice to write full time. He had one daughter, Grace, with his first wife, Natalie, from whom he later separated. In 1968 Gardner married his long-term secretary, Agnes Jean Bethell, whom he professed to be the real 'Della Street', Perry Mason's sole (although unacknowledged) love interest. He was one of the most successful authors of all time and at the time of his death, in Temecula, California in 1970, is said to have had 135 million copies of his books in print in America alone.

By Erle Stanley Gardner
(titles below include only those
published in the Murder Room)

Perry Mason series

The Case of the Sulky Girl
(1933)
The Case of the Baited Hook
(1940)
The Case of the Borrowed
Brunette (1946)
The Case of the Lonely
Heiress (1948)
The Case of the Negligent
Nymph (1950)
The Case of the Moth-Eaten
Mink (1952)
The Case of the Glamorous
Ghost (1955)
The Case of the Terrified
Typist (1956)
The Case of the Gilded Lily
(1956)
The Case of the Lucky Loser
(1957)
The Case of the Long-Legged
Models (1958)
The Case of the Deadly Toy
(1959)
The Case of the Singing Skirt
(1959)

The Case of the Duplicate
Daughter (1960)
The Case of the Blonde
Bonanza (1962)

Cool and Lam series

The Bigger They Come (1939)
Turn on the Heat (1940)
Gold Comes in Bricks (1940)
Spill the Jackpot (1941)
Double or Quits (1941)
Owls Don't Blink (1942)
Bats Fly at Dusk (1942)
Cats Prowl at Night (1943)
Crows Can't Count (1946)
Fools Die on Friday (1947)
Bedrooms Have Windows
(1949)
Some Women Won't Wait (1953)
Beware the Curves (1956)
You Can Die Laughing (1957)
Some Slips Don't Show (1957)
The Count of Nine (1958)
Pass the Gravy (1959)
Kept Women Can't Quit (1960)
Bachelors Get Lonely (1961)
Shills Can't Count Chips (1961)

Try Anything Once (1962)
Fish or Cut Bait (1963)
Up For Grabs (1964)
Cut Thin to Win (1965)
Widows Wear Weeds (1966)
Traps Need Fresh Bait (1967)

Doug Selby D.A. series

The D.A. Calls it Murder (1937)
The D.A. Holds a Candle (1938)
The D.A. Draws a Circle (1939)
The D.A. Goes to Trial (1940)
The D.A. Cooks a Goose (1942)
The D.A. Calls a Turn (1944)

The D.A. Takes a Chance (1946)
The D.A. Breaks an Egg (1949)

Terry Clane series

Murder Up My Sleeve (1937)
The Case of the Backward
   Mule (1946)

Gramp Wiggins series

The Case of the Turning Tide
   (1941)
The Case of the Smoking
   Chimney (1943)

Two Clues (two novellas) (1947)

Gold Comes in Bricks

Erle Stanley Gardner

An Orion book

Copyright © The Erle Stanley Gardner Trust 1940

This edition published by
The Orion Publishing Group Ltd
Orion House
5 Upper St Martin's Lane
London WC2H 9EA

An Hachette UK company
A CIP catalogue record for this book is available from the British Library

ISBN 978 1 4719 0880 4

www.orionbooks.co.uk

CHAPTER ONE

BERTHA COOL SIGHED DEEPLY and overflowed the edges of the collapsible wooden chair. She lit a cigarette, and her jeweled hands became semicircles of brilliance in the bright lights which beat down on the padded canvas. Against the gloom of the big deserted gymnasium, her glittering diamonds sparkled like drops of ocean spray in the sunlight.

The Japanese, naked except for a breechclout and a light-colored coat of the texture of heavy linen, braced his feet and looked me over. His face was expressionless.

I was cold. The coat which he had given me was too big. I felt naked in my short trunks, and there were goose pimples on my legs.

"Give him the works, Hashita," Bertha said.

There were just the three of us in the big, barnlike room. The Japanese smiled at me with his lips, and I saw white rows of glistening teeth. The pitiless lights, imbedded in the trough-shaped cradle of tin which was suspended over the padded canvas, beat down upon me. The Japanese was well fleshed, firmly muscled. When he moved, I could see his muscles ripple beneath skin that was like brown satin.

He said to Bertha, "First lesson please. Not too severe."

Bertha inhaled a deep drag from her cigarette. Her eyes grew hard as her diamonds. "He's a smart little runt, Hashita. He learns fast, and it's *my* money. I want to get value received."

Hashita kept his eyes on me. "Jujitsu," he explained in a swift monotone, "is like lever please. Other man furnish power. You only change direction."

I nodded, because in the silence which followed his remark, I knew I was expected to nod.

Hashita reached in his loincloth and pulled out a short-barreled revolver. The nickel plate was peeled, the barrel

1

rusted. He opened the cylinder to show me the gun was unloaded.

"Excuse please," he said. "Honorable pupil take gun, hold in right hand, raise gun, and pull trigger. Quickly please!"

I took the gun.

Bertha Cool's face held the expression which I have sometimes thought must adorn the faces of women at bullfights.

"Quickly please," Hashita repeated.

I raised the gun.

He reached smoothly forward and contemptuously pushed my hand down. "Not so slow please. Pretend I am very bad man. You raise gun. Very quickly you pull trigger before I move."

I remembered reading somewhere that the Western badman had been at his most deadly efficiency when he was cocking the gun while raising it. It was a double-action revolver, and I started pulling the trigger as I snapped the gun up.

Hashita was standing in front of me, a broad target. I could feel the hammer coming back as I jerked my wrist.

Suddenly, Hashita wasn't there at all. He had simply dissolved into motion. I tried to move the revolver to follow that streak of human agility. It was like trying to keep pointing at a lightning flash.

Thick brown fingers coiled around my wrist. Hashita was no longer in front of me and no longer facing me. He was under my arm, with his back turned toward me. My arm was over his shoulder. He jerked my right wrist down. His shoulder smacked under my armpit. I felt my feet leave the floor. The bright lights in their tin cradle and the canvas mat reversed position. I seemed to hang suspended in the air for several seconds, then the padded canvas rushed up to meet me.

The jar made me sick.

I tried to get up, but couldn't make my muscles respond. There was a quivering in my stomach. Hashita leaned over, caught my wrist and elbow, and lifted me to my feet so quickly it seemed I'd bounced up off the canvas. His teeth were now flashing in a wide grin. The gun lay behind him.

"Very simple," Hashita said.

Bertha Cool's diamonds flashed back and forth, up and down, as her hands moved in applause.

Hashita took my shoulders and pushed me back, raised my right arm. "Hold very steady please. I show you."

He laughed—the nervous, mirthless laugh of a Japanese. I seemed to be standing still in the center of a room which was swaying back and forth on a huge pendulum.

Hashita said, "Now watch closely please."

He moved slowly, but with such perfect rhythm there was no jerk to his motions. It was exactly as though I'd been watching his image projected on the screen in a slow-motion-picture shot. His left knee bent. His weight slid forward and on his left hip. As he dipped, he turned. His right hand moved forward. The fingers slowly clamped about my wrist. He twisted the ball of his left foot on the canvas. His left shoulder started coming up under my right armpit. The tension of his fingers increased. My right arm was twisted so I couldn't bend the elbow. He exerted pressure, making a lever out of my own arm. The fulcrum rested on his shoulder, back under my armpit. He tightened the pressure until I could feel pain, and then feel my feet lifting from the canvas.

He relaxed his grip, turned smoothly back into position, and stood smiling! "Now," he said, "*you* try. Slowly at first please."

He stood facing me with his right arm extended.

I reached for his arm with my right hand. He pushed me back. There was impatience in his gesture. "Honorable pupil remember left knee please. Bend left knee at same time reach with right hand, then turn foot at same time as twist on right arm, so elbow cannot bend."

I tried it again. This time it was better. He nodded his head, but there was no great enthusiasm in the nod.

"Now try quickly please, with gun."

He took the gun in his hand, raised his arm, pointing

3

the gun at me. I remembered my left knee and flashed out my hand for his right wrist. I missed it by a good two inches and stumbled forward off balance.

He was too polite to laugh, which made it a lot worse.

I could hear the thud of steps along the bare board floor of the gymnasium.

Hashita said, "Excuse, please," straightened, and turned. His slanting eyes were squinted as he strove to peer out from under the glare of the lights into the darkness of the big room.

I could make out the man coming forward. He was smoking a cigar; a short man in the forties with glasses and brown eyes. His clothes had been carefully tailored to emphasize his chest and minimize his stomach, but, even so, the narrow slope of the shoulders and the watermelon stomach dominated the suit.

"You the wrestling instructor?" he asked.

Hashita flashed his teeth, and walked toward him.

"My name's Ashbury—Henry C. Ashbury. Frank Hamilton told me to look you up. I'll wait until you're not busy."

Hashita wrapped sinewy fingers around Ashbury's hand. "Very great pleasure," he said with a hissing intake of the breath. "Will honorable gentleman please be seated?"

Hashita moved with catlike swiftness, picked up one of the collapsed wooden chairs, jerked it open so swiftly that it sounded as though the chair had exploded in his hands. He placed it beside Bertha Cool's chair. "Wait for fifteen minutes?" he inquired. "So sorry, but have pupil taking lessons."

"Sure," Ashbury said, "I'll wait."

Hashita bowed and apologized to Bertha Cool. He bowed and apologized to me. He bowed and smiled at Ashbury. He said, "Now we try again."

I looked over to where Ashbury was sitting beside Bertha Cool. His eyes were fastened on me with mild curiosity. It had been bad enough putting on a private exhibition for Bertha. The presence of a stranger made it unbearable.

"Go ahead," I said to Hashita. "I'll wait."

"You'll catch cold, Donald," Bertha warned.

"No, no. Go right ahead," Ashbury said hastily, placing his hat on the floor by the side of his chair. "I'm in no hurry at all. I-I'd *like* to see it."

Hashita faced me, teeth glittering. "We try again," he said, and picked up the gun.

I saw his arm coming up. I gritted my teeth and lunged. This time I caught him by the wrist. I was surprised to find how easy it was to pivot. My shoulder came up under his armpit. I jerked down.

Then unexpected things happened. I knew, of course, that Hashita had given a little leap as I pulled, but the effect was spectacular. He came up over my head. I saw his feet fly up and his legs silhouette against the blazing brilliance of the lights. He twisted suddenly in the air like a cat, wrenched his arm free, and came down on his feet. The gun was lying on the canvas. I was certain he'd dropped it purposely. But that didn't detract from the effect on the audience.

Bertha Cool said, "I'll be damned! The little shrimp!"

Ashbury glanced swiftly at Bertha Cool, then stared at me, startled respect in his eyes.

"Very good," Hashita said. "Very, *very* good."

I heard Bertha Cool say casually to Ashbury, "He's working for me. I run a detective agency. The little runt is always getting beaten up. He's too light to make a good boxer, but I thought the Jap could teach him jujitsu."

Ashbury turned to take a good look at her.

He saw only Bertha Cool's profile. She was watching me with hard, glittering eyes.

There was nothing soft about Bertha. She was big and well-fleshed; but it was hard flesh. She had a big neck, big shoulders, a big bosom, big arms, and a good appetite. Her face had that placid look of meaty contentment which comes to women who have quit worrying about their figures and feel free to eat what they want as often as they want it.

"Detective did you say?" Ashbury asked.

Hashita said, "Now I show you slowly please."

Bertha Cool kept her eyes on us. "Yes. B. Cool Confidential Investigations. That's Donald Lam doing the wrestling."

"He's working for you?"

"That's right."

Hashita took a rubber-bladed dagger from his loincloth and presented the hilt to my fingers.

"He's a little runt, but he's brainy," Bertha Cool went on, talking over her shoulder. "You wouldn't believe it, but he was a lawyer, got admitted to the bar. They kicked him out because he told someone how to commit a murder and go scot-free. Smart as a steel trap—"

Hashita said, "Stab please with knife."

I grabbed the knife and doubled my right arm. Hashita stepped smoothly in, caught my wrist, and the back of my arm, pivoted, and I went up in the air.

As I got to my feet I heard Bertha Cool say, ". . . guarantee satisfaction. A lot of agencies won't handle divorce cases and politics. I'll handle anything there's money in. I don't give a damn who it is or what it is, just so the dough's there."

Ashbury was looking exclusively at her now.

"I suppose I can trust your discretion?" Ashbury asked.

Bertha Cool seemed to have lost interest in me. "Hell, yes. Absolutely! Anything you say to me stops right there. . . . Don't mind my cussing."

"Advisable not to light on head please," Hashita said. "Honorable pupil must learn to twist in air, so to come down on feet."

Bertha Cool flung over her shoulder, without even looking at me, "Get your clothes on, Donald. We've got a job."

CHAPTER TWO

I SAT in the outer office, waiting. I could hear the low hum of voices coming from Bertha Cool's private office. Bertha never liked to have me listen in while financial arrangements were being made. She paid me a monthly guarantee, which she kept as low as possible, and sold my services for as much as she could get.

After about twenty minutes she called me in. I knew from the expression on her face the financial arrangements had gone to suit her.

Ashbury was sitting in the client's chair, touching it at only two points—the base of his neck and his hip pockets. That posture caved his chest in and pushed his neck forward. Looking at him, I knew where his watermelon stomach came from.

Bertha oozed sweetness and good will. "Sit down, Donald." I sat.

Bertha's jeweled hand glittered as she scooped a check off the top of the desk and dropped it into the cash drawer before I could even get a glimpse of the figures. "Shall I tell him," she asked Ashbury, "or will you?"

Ashbury had a fresh cigar in his mouth. His head was bent forward so that he had to look at me over the tops of his glasses. Ashes from the old cigar had dribbled over his vest. The new one was just getting started. "You tell him," he said.

"Henry Ashbury," Bertha Cool said with the precision of one compressing facts into a concise statement, "married within the last year. Carlotta Ashbury is his second wife. Mr. Ashbury has a daughter by his first wife. Her name is Alta. On the death of Ashbury's first wife, half of her property was left to our client, Mr. Ashbury," and Bertha indicated him with a nod of the head, like a schoolteacher pointing out a figure on a blackboard, "and one half to their daughter, Alta."

7

She looked at Ashbury. "I believe," she said, "you didn't give me even the approximate amount."

Ashbury rolled his eyes over the top of the glasses from me to her. "I didn't," he said without taking the cigar from his mouth, and the motion dribbled more ashes down on his necktie.

Bertha covered up that one with fast conversation. "The present Mrs. Ashbury had also been married before—to a man named Tindle. She has a son by that marriage. His name is Robert. Just to give you the whole picture, Donald, Robert was inclined to take life a little too easy, following his mother's second marriage. Is that right, Mr. Ashbury?"

"Right."

"Mr. Ashbury made him go to work," Bertha went on, "and he has shown a remarkable aptitude. Because of his winning personality and—"

"He hasn't any personality," Ashbury interrupted. "He didn't have any experience. Some of his mother's friends took him in on a corporation because of his connection with me. The boys hope to stick me one of these days. They never will."

"Perhaps *you'd* better tell Donald about that," Bertha said.

Ashbury took the cigar from his mouth.

"Couple of chaps," he said, "Parker Stold and Bernard Carter, control a corporation, the Foreclosed Farms Underwriters Company. My wife has known Carter for some time—before her marriage to me. They gave Bob a job. At the end of ninety days, they made him sales manager. Two months later, the directors made him president. Figure it out for yourself. *I'm* the one they're after."

"Foreclosed Farms?" I asked.

"That's the name of the concern."

"What does it handle?"

"Mines and mining."

I looked at him, and he looked at me. Bertha asked the question. "What in the world would a Foreclosed Farm Underwriters Company have to do with mines and mining?"

8

Ashbury slumped lower in his seat. "How the hell should I know? I can't imagine anything which causes me less concern. I don't want to know Bob's business, and I don't want him to know mine. If I ask him any questions, he'll start trying to sell me stock."

I took out my notebook, jotted down the names Ashbury had mentioned, and added a note to look up Foreclosed Farms Underwriters Company.

Ashbury didn't look at all like he had up at the gymnasium. He rolled his eyes over his glasses to look at me again, and reminded me of a chained mastiff. His eyes seemed to say that if he could get a couple more feet of chain, he'd snap my leg off.

"What do you want *me* to do?" I asked.

"Among other things, you're going to be my trainer."

"Your *what?*"

"Trainer."

Bertha Cool flexed her big arms. "Build him up, Donald. You know—sparring work, jujitsu lessons, wrestling, boxing, road work."

I stared at her. I'd be useless in a gymnasium; I couldn't chin myself with a block and tackle.

"Mr. Ashbury wants you to be in the house with him," Bertha went on to explain. "No one must suspect you're a detective. The family have known for a long time that he's intending to do something about getting in shape. He wanted to arrange with Hashita to come to the house and give him lessons. And he'd been thinking about hiring a good detective. As soon as he saw your work in the gymnasium, he realized that if he could plant you as his trainer, that would solve his problem."

"What," I asked Ashbury, "do you want detected?"

"I want to find out what my daughter's doing with her money. Find out who's getting chunks of her dough—and why."

"Is she being blackmailed?"

"I don't know. If she is, I want you to find out about it."

"And if she isn't?"

"Find out what's happening to her dough. She's either

9

being blackmailed, is gambling, or Bob has inveigled her into financing him. Any of them are dangerous to her and distasteful to me. Not only do I have her welfare to consider, but I'm in a very delicate position myself. The first breath of financial scandal in my family would raise merry hell with me. And I'm talking too damn much. I don't like it. Let's get this over with."

Bertha said, "He took a fancy to you as soon as he saw you throw that Jap around, Donald. Isn't that right, Mr. Ashbury?"

"No."

"Why, I thought—"

"I liked the way he acted while the Jap was throwing *him* around. We're *all* talking too damn much. Let's get to work."

I asked, "Why do you think your daughter is being—"

"Two checks in the last thirty days," he interrupted, "each payable to cash. Each in the sum of ten thousand dollars, and each deposited by the Atlee Amusement Corporation. That's a gambling outfit—restaurants downstairs for a blind, gambling upstairs for profit."

"Did she lose the money gambling in those places?" I asked.

"No. She hasn't been in either place. I found that out."

"When," I asked, "do you want me to go out to the house with you?"

"Now. I don't want any snooping. Win Alta's friendship. Get her to confide in you—capable—dependable—athletic—aggressive."

"She'd hardly pick on a physical culture trainer as one in whom to confide."

"Wrong. That's just what she *would* do. She isn't a snob, and she hates snobs. Try to cultivate her, and she'll snub you. You're wrong— No, wait a minute. Maybe you're right— All right, let me think. . . . Tell you what. You aren't a professional trainer. You're an amateur—but a topnotch amateur. I'm figuring on backing you in a business proposition. I'm figuring on opening a string of private, exclusive gymnasiums where businessmen who are out of shape can be put in first-class condition at so much per. You're going to manage the whole string for me, salary· and bonus. You're not a trainer. You're a business partner who knows the game. Putting me in shape will be incidental. Leave it to me."

"All right. That end of it's up to you. Now I'm only supposed to find out about your daughter's financial drain. Is that all?"

"All! Hell's fire, that's the biggest job you ever tackled. She's steel spring and dynamite, that girl. If she ever finds out you're a detective, I'm sunk and you're fired. Get that?"

"But how about your stepson? Why did you want to tell me about his business and—"

"So you can keep out of his way, and keep Alta out of his damn business. He's a stuffed shirt with a wilted collar. His mother thinks he's a genius. He thinks so, too. Don't get fooled. If he's inveigled Alta into putting dough into his business—Well, I'll fix *that*. I want the facts, that's all. I told him, and I told his mother, I'd be damned if I gave him another cent. If he's getting it through Alta, it's the same as though he were getting it through me. I won't have it. And I'm talking altogether too damned much. I'm finished. When'll you be out?"

"Within an hour," Bertha answered for me.

Ashbury rippled his back in a contortion which enabled him to get his hands on the arms of the chair. Using his arms, he pushed himself up and to his feet. "All right, come in a taxicab. Mrs. Cool has the address. I'll go out and pave the way. Now remember, Lam. No one's to know you're a detective. The minute anyone finds *that* out, your goose is cooked." He spun to Bertha Cool, and said, "*You* remember that, too. Don't make any false moves. Alta's nobody's damn fool. She'll find out if you make a single stumble. One boob play, and you've kicked a hundred dollars a day out the window."

So Bertha was getting a hundred dollars a day, plus expenses. She was paying me eight when I worked, with a monthly guarantee of seventy-five bucks.

Ashbury said, "Get there in an hour, Lam, and you can

meet the family tonight—all except Alta. She'll be out somewhere, won't get in before two or three o'clock in the morning. We have our workout at seven-thirty, breakfast at eight-thirty. And I'm not kidding about having you show me some of that jujitsu stuff. I want to get my muscles built up. I'm too flabby."

He wiggled his narrow shoulders inside the padded coat, and it was surprising to see, when the tips of his shoulders touched the cloth, how much the tailor had been able to do with padding.

"Donald will be there," Bertha Cool said.

After he went out, Bertha said, "Sit down."

I sat on the arm of the chair.

She said, "There's a lot of expenses in connection with running this business that you don't know a damn thing about: rent, secretarial salaries, social security, income tax, occupation tax, stationery, bookkeeping, lights."

"Janitor service," I suggested.

"That's right. Janitor service."

"So what?"

"Well, this is a pretty good job, Donald, and I've decided to raise your wages to ten dollars a day while you're working on it."

"That'll be ten dollars," I said.

"What will?"

"One day."

"What do you mean?"

"That's as long as I'll last. How can I teach anyone physical culture?"

"Now don't be like that, Donald. I've got it all worked out. We'll make arrangements with Hashita to give you your lessons every afternoon. I told Mr. Ashbury you'd have to get off every afternoon between two and four in order to come up here and make reports. What you'll really do is go to Hashita and get lessons in jujitsu. Then you'll give Mr. Ashbury a rehash of those lessons. Don't let him develop too fast."

"He won't," I said. "What's more, I won't."

"Oh, you'll take to it like a duck to water, Donald."

12

"How do I get back and forth? How far is it?"

"It's too far to go on a streetcar, but because he thinks you're coming up to the office to make reports, I've made him agree to pay taxi fare."

"How much?"

"You don't need to bother," Bertha Cool said. "We aren't going to spend all our profits on taxicabs. I'll drive you out to within a block of the place tonight. You can walk the rest of the way. I'll be waiting every day at two o'clock with my car. We may just as well have that extra profit as not."

"It's a foolish chance to take, just to knock down a taxi fare, but it's your funeral," I said, and went out to pack my suitcase.

CHAPTER THREE

BERTHA COOL DROPPED ME within a block of Ashbury's place at ten twenty-five. It was drizzling a bit. I walked the block with my suitcase banging against my legs. It was a big place out in millionaire row with a gravel driveway, ornamental trees, roomy architecture, and servants.

The butler hadn't heard any taxicab drive up. He looked at the rain which had fallen on the brim of my hat and asked if I was Mr. Lam. I told him I was.

He said he'd take my suitcase up to my room, that Mr. Ashbury wanted to see me right away in the library.

I went in. Ashbury shook hands and started performing introductions. Mrs. Ashbury was considerably younger than her husband. She had the big-breasted, big-hipped, voluptuous type of beauty. She was carrying about fifteen pounds too much weight to make the curves smooth and voluptuous. Here and there the contours broke into bulges. Apparently she couldn't keep still. Her body was always in motion, little undulations, swayings and swingings. Her eyes sparkled with animal vitality. She looked me over, and I felt as though she'd rubbed her hands over me. She gave me her hand and started pouring out words. "I think it's the most wonderful idea Henry has ever had. I suppose *I* should do something like that, too. I've really been putting on far too much weight the last two years. I wasn't like that until this high blood pressure came along, spells of dizziness, and a pain over my heart. The doctor told me I shouldn't exercise. But if the doctors can ever get this condition cleared up, I'll exercise, and I lose weight very rapidly. You seem to be in marvelous shape, Mr. Lam. You don't have any weight at all."

She stopped talking long enough to let Ashbury introduce a man named Bernard Carter. He was a fat, jovial chap in the middle forties. He had fish eyes which were badly filmed, fat, pudgy hands, and a back-slapping manner. He was nicely tailored and was the sort of salesman who would show a customer a sample, tell him a smutty story, show him another sample, tell him another story, and get the order. Keep them laughing was his motto. He had three chins, and when he laughed they all quivered with mirth. The fat on his cheeks would push up under his eyes so that you could only see narrow slits when he was laughing, but if you watched those slits closely, you saw that the eyes behind them hadn't changed expression a bit. They were filmed and watchful and fishy. Mrs. Ashbury watched him with beaming approval. He was very attentive to her.

I gathered Carter must be related to Mrs. Ashbury in some way. They seemed to have a lot in common—a pair who liked the good things in life, who lived to enjoy themselves.

Mrs. Ashbury couldn't seem to take her eyes off me. She said, "You don't seem to have an ounce of fat on you. You're little, but you must have a wonderful body."

"I try to keep in shape," I said.

Carter said thoughtfully, "Henry, I guess I'll have to become one of your first clients. I weighed myself the other day—wouldn't believe how much weight I'd put on."

Mrs. Ashbury said, "You're all right, Bernard. Of course, a little exercise would tone you up a bit. Yes, it's a splendid idea, and as soon as my blood pressure goes down, I'm going to exercise. It must be wonderful to be slim and hard like Mr. Lam—only you're rather light for a professional wrestler, aren't you?"

"Instructor," I corrected.

"I know, but you must be good. Henry tells me you took on a Japanese jujitsu wrestler and made him look like thirty cents."

Henry Ashbury stared steadily at me.

"I'm afraid it wouldn't be modest for me to comment," I said.

Her throat, shoulders, and diaphragm rippled as she gave a high-pitched, delighted laugh. "Oh, I think that's priceless. That's just absolutely priceless! Bob would get an awful kick out of that. Bob's modest, too. Did Mr. Ashbury tell you about Robert?"

"Your son?" I asked.

"Yes. He's a wonderful boy. I'm so proud of him. He started in right at the bottom, and through diligent application and hard work, he's been made president of the corporation."

I said, "That certainly *is* remarkable!" Ashbury's eyes stared at me over the tops of his glasses.

Bernard Carter said, "I'm not just throwing any bouquets when I say that Bob's a business genius. I've never seen a man who could grasp things as quickly."

"Doing all right, is he?" Henry Ashbury asked noncommittally.

"All right!" Carter exclaimed. "My God, he's—" He looked across at Mrs. Ashbury, became silent, spread his palms in a little gesture, as much as to say, "Oh, what's the use," and exhaled his breath slowly.

"Glad to hear it," Ashbury said without any show of enthusiasm.

Mrs. Ashbury had a low-pitched, throaty, seductive voice, but when she became excited, it jumped up an octave and bounced off the roof of her mouth as easily as hail off a tin roof.

"I think it's absolutely *mar*velous, and, with it all, he's just as modest as he can be. He hardly *ever* talks about his work. He feels that Henry isn't interested in it. I'll bet you don't even know about their latest strike, Henry, or what Bob—"

"I have enough business at the office," Henry interrupted.

"But you should get together more with Bob. You know, after all, in his position as president of the Foreclosed Farms Underwriters Company, Bob has opportunities to learn a lot of what's going on in the business world. Some of that knowledge might prove very valuable to you, Henry."

"Yes, my love, but I'm too tired when I get home to talk business."

She sighed. "Oh, you businessmen! Bob is the same way. You just can't get a word out of him."

"Where is he now?" I asked.

"Down in the billiard room with his sales manager, Parker Stold."

Ashbury nodded to me. "Come on, Lam. We'll go meet Bob and Stold."

I said conventional things to Mrs. Ashbury, and she took my hand and held it for a minute. When I got away, Henry Ashbury led the way down a long corridor, down a flight of stairs, and into another corridor. I could see a playroom on one side, with a long Ping-pong table. On the other side was a room from which came the click of balls and a mumble of conversation.

Ashbury opened the door. A man who had been getting ready to make a shot, with one hip on the table, climbed down and said "Hello, Governor," to Ashbury.

This was Robert Tindle, a chap with a sloping forehead, long, straight nose, and eyes the color of cheap glass marbles—a watery green, covered with a film that was like scum. You felt that if you looked at those eyes closely, you'd see lots of little air bubbles. His face didn't have any particular expression, and all I could think of when I looked at him was the ad for the contented cows.

He wore a dinner jacket and shook hands without enthusiasm.

Parker Stold evidently had something on his mind. He regarded our visit as an interruption, and acknowledged the introduction to me with a quick "Please'-t'-meetcha" and didn't offer to shake hands. His eyes were a little too close together, but his hair was wavy, and he had a nice mouth. I figured he was a little older than Bob.

The butler got me up at seven o'clock the next morning. I shaved, dressed, and went down to the gymnasium. It was a big, bare room on the basement floor just back of the billiard room. It had the smell of never having been used. There were a punching bag, horizontal bars, Indian clubs, dumbbells, weight-lifting machines, a canvas wrestling mat, and, at the far end, a squared ring for boxing. There were boxing gloves hanging on a rack. I went over and looked at them. The price tags, which had turned yellow with age, were still tied by a faded-green string to the laces.

I was wearing a pair of tennis shoes, slacks, and an athletic undershirt. When Henry Ashbury came in, he was bundled up in a bathrobe. He slipped it off and stood with nothing on but some boxer's tights.

He looked like hell.

"Well," he said, "here we are."

He looked down at his watermelon paunch. "I suppose I've *got* to do something about this." He walked over to the weight-lifting machine and began tugging away at the weights and puffing and blowing. After a minute he stepped aside and nodded toward them. "Do you want a workout?" he asked.

"No," I said.

"Neither do I, but I've got to."

"Why don't you try sitting up straighter—get a better posture?"

"I sit down because I want to be comfortable. I'm most comfortable when I'm slumped down in a chair."

"Go ahead and exercise, then," I said.

He flashed me a quick glance and acted as though he was going to say something, but didn't. He went back to the weight-lifting machine and did some more work. Then he went over and weighed himself on the scales.

He walked over to the canvas mat and said, "Do you think you could show me some of that stuff the Jap was showing you last night?"

I met his eyes and said, "No."

He laughed and put on the bathrobe. After that we sat down and talked politics until it was time to take a shower and dress for breakfast.

After breakfast Ashbury went to the office. Along about eleven o'clock I met Alta, who had just got up for breakfast. She'd evidently heard all about me. "Come on in and keep me company while I eat," she said. "I want to talk with you."

It looked like a good chance to get acquainted. I went in and went through the routine of seating her at the table. I sat opposite her, and had a cup of coffee with cream and sugar while she had black coffee, three pieces of Ry-Krisp, and a cigarette. If I could have had a figure like hers by eating that sort of breakfast, I'd have done it myself.

"Well?" she asked.

I remembered what Henry Ashbury had said about being myself, and not trying to force things. "Well, what?"

She laughed. "You're the new physical instructor?"

"Yes."

"You don't look as though you were much of a boxer."

I didn't say anything.

"My stepmother tells me it's not weight but speed. She says you're so fast that you're like a streak of lightning. I must see you work out some day."

"I'm training your father. He isn't doing any boxing."

She eyed me critically and said, "I can see why you go in for jujitsu. That must be interesting."

"It is."

"They say you're so good that it takes the best of the Japanese to give you any sort of a match."

"That's not exactly true."

"But you do wrestle with the Japanese?"

"Some."

"Didn't Dad see you throwing a big Japanese wrestler last night?"

I said, "Can't we talk about something else besides me?"

"What, for instance?"

"You."

She shook her head. "I'm never an interesting subject of conversation at this time in the morning. Do you like to walk?"

"No."

"I do. I'm going to take a long brisk walk."

Instructions had been most explicit. I was to get acquainted with Alta Ashbury, win her confidence, let her feel that I was capable of whipping my weight in wildcats, and get her to open up and tell me what was bothering her. In order to do that, I had to make hay while the sun was shining.

I took a long brisk walk.

I didn't learn anything on the first part of the walk except that she certainly had a swell figure, that her eyes were warm and brown and had a trick of laughing every time her lips smiled. She had the endurance of a marathon runner, a love of fresh air, and a scorn for most of the conventions. After a while, we sat under some trees. I didn't talk. She did. She hated fortune hunters and men who "had a line." She was inclined to think marriage was the bunk, and that her father was a fool for letting himself get roped into it, that she hated her stepmother, that her stepbrother was the apple of Mrs. Ashbury's eyes, and that she thought the apple was full of wormholes.

I felt that was pretty good for one afternoon. I got back in time to ditch her and duck around the corner to where Bertha Cool was waiting. She took me up to the Jap. Hashita showed me a few more grips and holds, and made me do a lot more practicing. By the time I got done with him, the walk, the exercise of the day before, and the tumbles I'd taken made me feel as though I'd just lost a ten-round bout to a steam roller.

I explained to Bertha that Ashbury was wise, so it wasn't going to be necessary to keep up the jujitsu lessons. Bertha said she'd paid for them, and I'd take them or she'd know the reason why. I warned her about continuing to take me back and forth to the house, and told her since Ashbury was paying for it, I'd better get a cab. She told me she was fully capable of running the business end of things, and got me back in time for dinner.

It was a lousy dinner. The food was good, but there was too much service. I had to sit straight as a ramrod and pretend to be interested in a lot of things Mrs. Ashbury was saying. Robert Tindle posed as the tired businessman. Henry Ashbury shoved in grub with the preoccupied manner of one who hadn't the slightest idea of what he's eating.

Alta Ashbury was going out to a dance about ten o'clock.

20

She took an hour after dinner to sit out on a glassed-in sunporch and talk.

There was a half-moon. The air was warm and balmy, and something was worrying her. She didn't say what it was, but I could see she wanted companionship.

I didn't want to talk. So I just sat there and kept quiet. Once when I saw her hand tighten into a little fist, and she seemed all tense and nervous, I reached my hand out, put it over hers, gave it a little squeeze, said, "Take it easy," and then, as she relaxed, took my hand away.

She looked up at me quickly, as though she weren't accustomed to having men remove their hands from hers.

I didn't say anything more.

A little before ten she went up to dress for the dance. I'd found out that she liked tennis and horseback riding, that she didn't care for badminton, that she liked swimming, that if it weren't for good old dad she'd pull out and leave the house flat on its foundations, that she thought her stepmother was poisoning her father's disposition, and that someone should give her stepbrother back to the Indians. I hadn't said anything one way or another.

The next morning Ashbury started to lift weights, found his muscles were sore, said there was no use going at the thing too damn fast, put on his big lap robe, came over and sat down beside me on the canvas mat, and smoked a cigar. He wanted to know what I'd found out.

I told him nothing. He said, "Alta's fallen for you. You're good."

We had breakfast, and about eleven o'clock Alta Ashbury showed up. Mrs. Ashbury always had breakfast in bed.

When we took our walk that afternoon, Alta told me more about her stepmother. Mrs. Ashbury had high blood pressure, and the doctor said she mustn't be excited. The doctor was standing in with her, gave in to her, wheedled her and petted her. She thought her dad should kick Bernard Carter out of the house. She didn't know what there was about me that made her talk so much, unless it was because I was so understanding, and because she was

21

so worried about her dad she could cry.

She warned me that if Mrs. Ashbury ever wanted any-thing, no matter how unreasonable, I wasn't to cross her at all, because, as surely as I did, the doctor would make an examination, find her blood pressure had gone up, blame the whole thing on me, and I'd go out on my ear. I gathered she didn't want me to go out on my ear.

I felt like a heel.

At two o'clock Bertha Cool picked me up, and the Jap kneaded me as though I'd been a batch of bread dough. When I got away from those stubby fingers I felt like a shirt that had been put through a washing machine, run through a wringer, and dried on a mangle.

I staggered in to supper. It was the same as the previous night, only Alta looked as though she'd been crying. She hardly spoke to me. After dinner I hung around, giving her a chance to talk with me in case there was anything she wanted to confide.

Alta didn't make any secret about how she felt about Bernard Carter. She said he was *supposed* to be working on a business deal with her stepmother. She didn't know just what it was. No one seemed to know just what it was. Alta said both of them hated her, that she thought her stepmother was afraid of some woman whom Carter knew, that one time she'd walked into the library just as her stepmother was saying, "Go ahead and get some action. I'm tired of all this dillydallying. You can imagine how much mercy she'd show me if our positions were reversed. I want you to—" Carter had noticed she'd come into the room and had coughed significantly. Mrs. Ashbury had looked up, stopped in the middle of a sentence, and started talking about something else with the swift garrulity of one who is trying to cover up.

Alta was silent for a while after she told me that, and then said moodily she supposed she was telling me things she had no right to, but for some reason or other I inspired confidence, that she felt I was loyal to her father, and that if I was going in business with him, I'd have to watch her stepmother, Bob, and Bernard Carter. Then she added a few words about Dr. Parkerdale. He was, it seemed, one of the fashionable boys with a good bedside manner. Every time Mrs. Ashbury had a dizzy spell from eating too much, Dr. Parkerdale became as gravely concerned as though it were the first symptom of a world-wide epidemic of infantile paralysis.

She told me that much, then clamped her lips shut tightly.

I said, "Go ahead."

"With what?" she asked.

"The rest of it."

"The rest of what?"

"The rest of the things I should know."

"I've told you too much already."

"Not enough," I said.

"What do you mean by that?"

"I'm going in business with your father. He's going to invest a bunch of money. I've got to see that he gets a fair return on his investment. I've got to get along with Mrs. Ashbury. I want to know how to do it."

She said hastily, "You leave her alone. Keep out of her way, and listen. Don't—don't ever—"

"Don't ever what?" I asked.

"Don't ever trust yourself alone with her," she said. "If she wants to take exercise in the gymnasium, be sure to have someone else there all the time she's there."

I made the mistake of laughing and said, "Oh, surely she wouldn't—"

She turned on me furiously. "I tell you," she said, "I *know* her. She's a creature of physical appetites and animal cunning. She simply can't control herself. All this high-blood-pressure business is simply the result of overeating and overindulgence. She's put on twenty pounds since Dad married her."

"Your father," I said, "is nobody's fool."

"Of course he isn't, but she's worked out a technique that no man can fight against. Whenever she wants anything and anyone balks her, she starts working herself up to a high pitch of excitement, then she telephones for Doctor Parkerdale. He comes rushing out as though it were a matter of life and death, takes her blood pressure, and starts tiptoeing around the house until he's created the proper impression. Then he takes whoever is responsible off to one side and says very gently and with his best professional manner that Mrs. Ashbury really isn't herself, that she simply mustn't become excited, that if he can only keep her perfectly calm for a period of several months, he can cure her blood pressure, that then she can start taking exercise and reduce her weight and be her normal self, but that whenever there's an argument and she becomes excited, all the good that he's done is wiped out, and he has to go back and begin all over again."

I laughed and said, "That seems to be a hard game to beat."

She was furious at me because I'd laughed. "Of course it's a hard game to beat," she said. "You *can't* beat it. Doctor Parkerdale says that it doesn't make any difference whether she's right or wrong, that one mustn't argue with her. That means you have to give in to her all the time. That means she's becoming more selfish and spoiled every minute of the time. Her temper is getting more ungovernable. She's getting more selfish, more—"

"How about Bernard Carter?" I asked. "Does he get along with her?"

"Bernard Carter," she snorted. "Bernard Carter and his business deal! He's the man who comes around when Father goes away. She may fool Dad with that business talk, but she doesn't fool me a darn bit. I—I hate her."

I observed that I thought Henry Ashbury was quite capable of handling the situation.

"He isn't," Alta said. "No man is. She has him hamstrung and hogtied before he starts. If he accuses her of anything, she'll throw one of her fits and Doctor Parkerdale will come rushing out with the rubber tube he puts around her arm and take her blood pressure— Oh, *can't* you see what she's doing is simply laying the foundation for filing a suit for divorce on the ground of mental cruelty, claiming that Father was so unreasonable and unjust with her that it ran up her blood pressure and ruined her health and kept Doctor Parkerdale from curing her. And she has the doctor all primed to give his testimony. The only thing Father can do is efface himself as much as possible and wait for something to break. That means he has to give in to her. Look here, Donald. Are you pumping me or am I just making a fool out of myself talking too damn much?"

I felt like a heel again, only worse.

She didn't talk much after that.

Someone called her on the telephone, and she didn't like the conversation. I could see that much from the expression on her face. After her party had hung up, she telephoned and broke a date.

I went out finally and sat on the sunporch. I felt more like a heel than ever.

After a while she came out and stood looking down at me. I could feel her scorn, even though it was too dark to see the expression in her eyes. "So," she said, "that's it, is it?"

"What?" I asked.

She said, "Don't think I'm entirely a nitwit. You, a physical director. I don't suppose it ever occurred to you I'd take the license number of the car that calls for you every afternoon, and look up the registration. B. Cool, Confidential Investigations. I suppose your real name is Cool."

"It isn't," I said. "It's Donald Lam."

"Well, the next time Dad tries to get a detective who's going to pose as a physical director, tell him to get someone who looks the part."

She stormed out of the room.

There was an extension phone down in the basement. I went down and called Bertha Cool. "All right," I said, "you've spilled the beans."

"What do you mean, *I've* spilled the beans?"

"She wondered who was calling for me afternoons, waited around the corner, got the license number of your car, and looked it up. It's registered in the name of the agency, you know."

I could hear Bertha Cool's gasp over the telephone.

"A hundred bucks a day thrown out of the window just so you could chisel a taxi fare," I said.

"Now listen, lover," she implored, "you've got to find some way out of this. You can do it, if you'll put your mind on it. That's what Bertha has you for, to think for her."

I said, "Nuts."

"Donald, you *must*. We simply can't afford to lose that money."

"You've already lost it."

"Isn't there something you can do?"

I said, "I don't know. Drive the agency car out here, park it at the place where you usually meet me, and wait."

CHAPTER FOUR

ALTA WENT OUT about quarter to ten. The butler opened the garage doors, and while he was doing that, I was streaking down the street. That's one thing I'm good at, sprinting.

Bertha Cool was waiting in the car. I climbed in beside her, and said, "Get that motor going. When a twelve-cylinder car streaks past us, give it everything you've got and keep the lights turned off."

"You'd better drive, Donald."

"There isn't time. Get started."

She started the motor and eased away from the curb. Alta Ashbury went past us like a flash. I said to Bertha, "Go ahead. Give it the gun." I reached over and switched out the headlights.

Bertha started groping for the headlight switch. I jerked her hand away, grabbed hold of the hand throttle, and pulled it out all the way. We started going places. Bertha got jittery, and I leaned over to put a hand on the wheel. After a while, Alta came to a cross street just as the light changed. It gave us a chance to catch up and for me to run around the back of the car and let Bertha slide over.

When the light changed, Alta shot ahead as though she'd been fired from a gun. The agency bus rattled on across the street, gathering headway. Somebody yelled at me to put my lights on, but I kept running dark, hoping we'd get into a snarl of traffic. After a while we did. I switched the lights on and started jockeying for position, trying to keep just a little on the left and behind.

Bertha was full of apologies. "I should have listened to you, lover. You're always right. Oh, *why* didn't you *make* me listen to you?"

I had a job to do driving the car, so I didn't say anything.

Bertha kept right on talking. She said, "Donald, I don't suppose I can ever make you understand me. For years

I had to fight my way. Every nickel counted. There were lots of times when I only allowed myself fifteen cents a day for eating money. Do you know, Donald, the hardest job I ever had was trying to learn how to spend money again after I began to make a little.

"I'd draw a hundred dollars every month from my bank account and make up my mind I was going to spend it on myself, and I just couldn't do it. I'd find myself at the end of the month with seventy or eighty dollars I hadn't spent. When you've once been right up against it where money means so damn much to you, it does something to your morale. You never get over it."

"I've been broke," I said.

"I know, lover, but you're young, and you have brains. Bertha didn't have brains, not the kind you have. Bertha just had to stay in there and pitch, and it was tough sledding. You have something I'll never have, Donald. You're resilient. Put pressure on you, and you bend. Then as soon as the pressure is removed, you spring back. I'm different. Put pressure on me, and I put pressure back. If anything happens, and I can't put any pressure back sometime, I won't bend, I'll simply break."

I said, "All right, forget it."

"Where's she going, lover?"

"I don't know."

"What's she going to do?"

"I don't know even that. We've kicked ourselves out of a hundred-dollar-a-day job. There's everything to gain, and nothing to lose. We may as well shoot the works."

"Donald, you've never failed me before. You've always worked out *some* scheme that let us wriggle through."

"Shut up," I said. "I'm trying to do it now."

It was a tough job following her in traffic. All she needed to do was press her foot on the throttle. The motor would whisper a song of smooth power, and the car would whisk through an opening which would close up behind her. I had to keep my foot on the throttle of the agency car and hold it in second gear a good part of the time so I had the pickup I needed for traffic.

She drove into a parking station. I didn't dare go into the same station. The only open parking space was in front of a fire plug. I said, "All right, Bertha, we park in front of the fire plug. If you get pinched, you can charge it to Ashbury for taxi expenses. You go down toward Seventh Street. I'll go up toward Eighth. Wait on the corner. When she leaves that parking lot, she'll either turn toward you or toward me. If she comes toward me, don't try to follow her. If she goes toward you, I won't try to follow. Whichever one isn't elected will come back and move the car."

Bertha was meek as a lamb. "Yes, lover," she said.

It was a job for Bertha to get in and out of the car. She had to twist around and squirm her way out. I didn't wait for her, and I didn't try to help her. I opened the door and walked down the street fast.

Bertha hadn't gone more than twenty yards from the car, when Alta came out of the parking lot. She turned toward me. I ducked in a doorway and waited.

She was considering the possibility of being followed all right. She kept looking behind her as she walked, but after she'd turned the corner, she evidently figured the road was clear. I picked up her trail. There was a cheap hotel midway in the block. She went in there. I didn't dare follow until after she'd got out of the lobby, then I walked in and over to the cigar counter. There was an automatic indicator over the elevator. I watched the hand. It had stopped at the fourth floor.

The girl behind the cigar counter was blond with stiff, wavy hair. I remembered one time when I'd seen a strand cut from the rope used by a hangman in San Quentin. A traveling salesman had it, and he had combed the strands all out. That girl's hair was about the same color, had about the same wave, and looked to be just about as stiff. She had light eyebrows, and big green eyes. She'd managed to get the expression on her face that one associated with virginal innocence back in nineteen hundred and six; mouth puckered up, eyebrows raised, lashes long and curly. It was the expression of a kitten just venturing out of the back closet into the living-room.

I said, "Listen, sister, I'm a traveling salesman. I've got a bill of goods I can sell the Atlee Amusement Corporation, but I have to have an inside track. There's a gambler here in the hotel who can give it to me. I don't know his name."

Her voice was as hoarse and harsh as that of a politician the morning after election. She said, "What the hell do you take me for?"

I took ten bucks of Bertha Cool's expense money out of my pocket, and said, "A girl who knows all the answers."

She lowered her eyes demurely. Crimson-tinted finger-nails slid across the counter toward the ten bucks. I clamped down on it, and said, "But the answer has to be right."

She leaned toward me. "Tom Highland," she said. "He's your man."

"Where does he live?" I asked.

"Here in the hotel."

"Naturally. What room?"

"Seven-twenty."

"Try again," I said.

She pouted and lowered her eyes. Her nose and chin came up in the air.

I said, "All right, if you feel that way about it," and folded the ten bucks and started to put it into my pocket. She glanced at the elevator, leaned across, and whispered to me, "Jed Ringold, four-nineteen, but for God's sake, don't say I told you, and don't bust in on him. His sweetie has just gone up."

I passed her the ten.

The clerk was looking at me, so I fished around a bit, looking over the cigars. "What's the matter with the clerk?" I asked.

"Jealous," she said with a little grimace.

I tapped a gloved forefinger on the counter. "Okay," I said, "give me a couple of those," took the cigars, and walked over to where the clerk was standing at the counter. "Poker game running down the street," I said. "I want to get away for a couple of hours' sleep, then go back. What have you got, something around the fourth floor?"

"Four-seventy-one," he suggested.

"Where is it?"

"On the corner."

"Nothing doing."

"Four-twenty?"

I said, "Brother, I'm funny, but I always get along with the odd numbers. Four-twenty sounds about right, only it's even. Have you got four-seventeen or four-nineteen or four-twenty-one?"

"I can give you four-twenty-one."

"How much?"

"Three bucks."

"With a bath?"

"Sure."

I took three dollars out of my pocket and slid it across the counter. He smacked his palm down on a bell and called out, "Front!"

The boy walked out of the elevator. The clerk handed him a key and said to me, "You'll have to register, Mr.—er—"

"Smith," I said. "John Smith. You write it. I'm going to sleep."

The boy saw I had no baggage and was giving me the fishy eye. I tossed him a quarter and said, "Snap out of it, son, and smile."

He showed his teeth in a grin and took me up. "Work all night?" I asked him.

"Nope. I quit at eleven."

"How about the elevator?"

"Goes on automatic."

I said, "Listen, son, I don't want to be disturbed. I've been in a gambling game and I'm tired."

"Stick the sign on the doorknob, and nobody'll disturb you."

"Got any gamblers in the house?" I asked.

"No," he said, "but listen, buddy, if you'd like a—"

"I wouldn't," I said.

He thought perhaps I might change my mind and hung around digging out the "Please Do Not Disturb" sign for me, pulling down window shades, and turning on the light in the bathroom.

I got rid of him after a while, hung the cardboard sign on the doorknob, locked and bolted the door, turned out all the lights, went over to the communicating door which connected with four-nineteen, got down on my knees, and started to work. I kept my light gloves on.

The proper place to bore a hole in the door of a hotel bedroom is at the corner of the paneling, just at the lower edge of the molding. The door is thinner there, and a small hole won't attract much attention. A knife that has a crescent-shaped blade on it can be sharpened into a good boring edge.

I felt like a dirty snoop, but a man can't argue with his bread and butter. And that goes double when he's working for Bertha Cool. The way I felt didn't keep me from doing a darn good job of boring a hole in the panel, and getting my eye up to the hole.

Alta was sitting on a davenport, crying. A man was sitting back in a big chair, smoking. Her tears didn't seem to mean very much to him. I couldn't see anything except his legs up as far as the hips, and occasionally the hand when it would take the cigarette from his mouth and come to rest on the arm of the chair.

After a while Alta got done crying. I could see her lips move, but couldn't hear what she was saying. She didn't seem to be exactly angry, more crushed than mad.

They talked for a while, then the man moved the hand that held the cigarette. A second later his other hand came into view with an envelope. He held it out toward Alta. She leaned forward on the davenport, took the envelope, and tucked it under her arm without even looking to see what was in it. She seemed in a grand rush. She opened her purse, took out a folded oblong of tinted paper, and handed it to him. He dropped it in the right-hand side pocket of his coat.

Alta got up hurriedly. I could see her lips say "Good night." Then she walked out of the range of my vision.

The man seemed to be hurrying her along. He got up,

and I had a glimpse of his face. He walked across the room. I heard the door open and close. The door was right across from the elevator. I could hear the cage rattling and wheezing up, then the sound of the door opening and closing. The man came back to the room, closed and locked the door.

I got up from my knees, brushed off my trousers with the palm of my hand, and then suddenly noticed the key which turned the bolt on the communicating door. Those are so rigged that when the bolt is closed, the little thumb grip that works it is straight up and down. This one was straight across.

Slowly, so as not to make any sound, I turned the knob of the door. When I had the knob back as far as it would go, I put my thumb up against the jamb and pushed easily against the door.

It opened about a sixteenth of an inch.

The door had been open all the time. That was something. For a moment I thought of opening it up and walking in, then decided against it. I closed the door, and eased the knob back quietly so that the latch wouldn't click. Then I slowly twisted the brass thingumbob on the door so that it shot the bolt back home on my side of the door.

It was a crummy hotel with the carpets worn thin and the lace curtains dingy. The white counterpane on the bed had a rip that had been stitched together. The connecting door between the two rooms was a loose-fitting affair. I stood staring at it. While I was looking at it, the knob slowly turned. Someone was trying to open that connecting door. He tried it once, then quit.

I walked out into the corridor, closed and locked my door behind me, slipped the key in my pocket, went around to four-nineteen, and knocked.

I heard a chair move, then steps on the floor, and a man's voice said, "Who is it?"

"Lam," I said.

"I don't get you."

"Message from the chief."

He opened the door and looked at me.

He was big, and had the lumbering good nature of a
man who's big enough and strong enough to know no one
is going to push him around. The eyebrows were a little
too heavy and came together across his nose. His eyes were
such a deep reddish brown they were almost black, and I
had to hold my neck back against my collar to look up at
him.

"Who the hell are you?" he asked.

"I'll tell you that when I come in."

He held the door open. I walked in. He closed the door
behind me and twisted the bolt. He said, "Sit down," and
walked over to the same chair in which he'd been sitting
while Alta had called on him, put his feet up on another
chair, lit a cigarette, and said, "What'd you say your name
was?"

"Donald Lam."

"You're Greek to me."

I said, "No, you've never seen me before."

"You aren't telling me anything. I never forget a face.
You said you had a message?"

"Yes."

"From the chief?"

"Yes."

"Who do you mean, the chief?"

I said, "The chief of police."

He was lighting a cigarette when I said that, and the
match didn't so much as waver. He didn't look over at me
until after he'd taken a deep drag at the cigarette, then
his reddish-black eyes turned my way.

"Spill it."

I said, "This message concerns your personal health."

"My health is good. It's going to stay good. What the
hell's the message?"

I said, "Don't cash that check."

"What check?"

"The one you just got."

He took his feet down from the chair. "You've got a hell
of a crust," he said.

I said, "Brother, you've cashed twenty thousand bucks in

checks through the Atlee Amusement Corporation. That's just twenty grand too much. You've got another check in that right-hand coat pocket. As soon as you give it to me, I'll get out of here."

He looked at me as though I'd been a funny tropical fish swimming around in an aquarium.

"Now," he said, "you interest me. Who the hell *are* you?"

I said, "I've told you who I was and what I wanted. Now, what are you going to do about it?"

"In about ten seconds," he said, "I'm going to throw you out of this room so hard you'll bounce."

He got to his feet, walked across to the door, unbolted it, opened it, jerked with his thumb, and said, "Out."

I got up and picked my place, a place where I could make a nice pivot, throw his right arm over my shoulder, bear down as I twisted, and send him hurtling over my head.

He walked over to me, very casually.

I waited for him to move that right arm.

It didn't come up the way I'd been practicing with Hashita. It came around from the side. It caught me by the coat collar. His other hand caught me around the hip pockets. I tried to brace myself, and might as well have tried to push a freight train off the track. I went out of that room so fast I could hear the doorjamb whiz as it went by. I threw up my hands to break the force of the impact against the wall on the opposite side of the corridor. I grabbed the edge of the glass mail chute beside the elevator. He tore my grip loose, pivoted, and sent me down the hall at the same time he brought up his left foot.

I know now just how a football feels when a player kicks a field goal.

What with the momentum of the bum's rush and the force of the kick, I went sailing down the hall for twenty feet before I came down flat on the floor.

I heard him go back, close and lock the door. I limped on down the corridor and around a bend, looking for the stairs, made up my mind I'd picked the wrong end of the hallway, and started back.

I was still twenty feet from the L when I heard three shots. A second or two later I heard running steps in the corridor going in the other direction.

I ran around the right-angled turn. The door of four-nineteen was open. An oblong of light was streaming out into the hallway. I looked at my watch—eleven-sixteen. The elevator boy would have gone off duty, leaving the elevator on automatic.

I pressed the call button, and, as soon as I heard the cage start upward, went into four-nineteen on tiptoe.

Ringold's body was huddled in front of the step that led up to the bathroom. His head was doubled back under his shoulders. His arms were twisted out at a goofy angle. One knee was just inside the door to the bathroom. The left arm was pressing up against the connecting door to four-twenty-one.

I dipped my fingers into the right-hand coat pocket and felt the perforated edges of a folded oblong of paper. I didn't take time to look at it. I jerked it out, stuck it in my pocket, turned, and ran for the corridor. The light switch was near the door. I switched the lights out and stood for a moment in the doorway, looking up and down the corridor. The only person in sight was a woman about fifty-five or sixty with her hair done up in curlers who was hugging a red robe around her, and standing in the open doorway of a room down at the end of the corridor.

"Did you hear someone shoot?" I called to her.

"Yes," she said.

I jerked my thumb toward four-twenty-one. "I think it came from four-twenty-one. I'll go see."

She continued to stand in the doorway. I walked over abreast of the elevator, called out, "He's got a 'Do Not Disturb' sign over the door. I guess I'd better go down to the office."

The elevator was waiting. I opened it, rode down to the second floor, got out, and waited.

It seemed as much as a minute before I heard the elevator taken back down to the first floor, and then saw it go rattling back up. The indicator showed that it had stopped at the fourth. I walked down the stairs and out into the lobby. The clerk wasn't behind the desk. The blond girl at the cigar counter was reading a movie magazine. Her jaws were moving slowly with the rhythmic chewing of gum. She glanced up, then back to her magazine.

After I got out on the street I took the folded oblong of paper out of my pocket and looked at it. It was a check payable to cash in the amount of ten thousand dollars. It was signed *Alta Ashbury*.

I put it in my pocket and walked down to the place where Bertha Cool had left the car. It was gone. I stood there for a minute and didn't see any sign of Bertha. I walked three blocks, picked up a taxi, gave the address of the Union Depot. When I got there I dropped the hotel key into a mailbox, picked up another cab, and gave the address of a swanky apartment hotel three blocks from where Ashbury had his residence. I paid off the cab, and, after he drove away, walked down to the Ashbury place.

The butler was still up. He let me in although Ashbury had given me a key.

"Miss Ashbury in yet?" I asked.

"Yes, sir. She came in about ten minutes ago."

"Tell her I'm waiting on the sunporch," I said, "and that it's important."

He looked at me for a moment, blinked his eyes, and said, "Very well, sir."

I went out on the sunporch and sat down. Alta came down in about five minutes. She swept into the room with her chin up in the air. "There's nothing you can say," she said, "no explanation you can make."

"Sit down," I said.

She hesitated a moment, then sat down.

I said, "I'm going to tell you something. I want you to remember it. Think it over tonight and remember it tomorrow. You were tired and nervous. You canceled a date. You went to a movie, but couldn't stick it out. You came back home. You haven't been anywhere else. You understand?"

She said, "I came down here because I want to make a good job of having this over with once and for all. I hate snoops and spies. I suppose my stepmother employed you to find out just how I felt. Well, she's found out. I could just as well have told her to her face, but as far as *you're* concerned, I think you're beneath contempt. I—"

I said, "Come down to earth. I'm a detective. I was hired to protect you."

"To protect *me?*"

"Yes."

"I don't need any protection."

"That's what you think. Remember what I told you. You were tired and nervous. You canceled a date. You went to a movie but couldn't stick it out. You came back home. *You haven't been anywhere else.*"

She stared at me.

I took the check from my pocket. "I don't suppose," I said, "that you bother to keep stubs of such minor cash outlays as ten-thousand-dollar checks, do you?"

Her face went white as she sat staring at that check, her eyes riveted on it.

I took a match from my pocket, struck it, and set fire to one corner. I held it until the flame got close enough to burn my fingers, then I dropped it into an ash tray. I ground the ashes to powder with the tips of my fingers.

"Good night," I said, and started for the stairs.

She didn't say anything until I was going through the door.

"Donald!" she cried—just one sharp cry.

I didn't turn around but closed the door behind me, went up stairs, and to bed. I didn't want her to know he'd been murdered until she read it in the papers or until the cops told her. If anyone around the hotel knew who she was and the cops came out to question her, she could put on a lot better act of surprise, or grief, or relief, or whatever it was going to be, if she wasn't acting a part.

I had a hell of a time getting to sleep.

CHAPTER FIVE

THE SIRENS CAME about three o'clock in the morning. I could hear them coming a long way off. I started to get up and dress, because I wanted to be on hand when things began to happen; then I remembered my own position in the matter and went back to bed.

But it wasn't Alta the cops were after. They banged around on the front door until Ashbury got up. Then it seemed they wanted to talk with Robert Tindle.

I slipped on a pair of pants over my pajamas, put on my coat, and tiptoed to the head of the stairs immediately after Tindle had gone down to the library. The cops didn't lower their voices or try to pull any punches. They wanted to know if he was acquainted with a man named Jed Ringold.

"Why, yes," Tindle said. "We have a salesman by that name."

"Where'd he live? Do you know?"

"No, I don't. It's on the records up at our office. Why? What's he done?"

"He hasn't done anything," the cop said. "When did you see him last?"

"I haven't seen him for three or four days."

"What does he do?"

"He's a stock salesman. That is, he's a scout. He gets prospects located and phones in a tip. Then the other boys close."

"What kind of stock?"

"Mining."

"What's the company?"

"Foreclosed Farms Underwriters Company."

"What kind of a company is it?"

"For any detailed information," Tindle said, and it sounded to me as though it was something he'd memorized, "I must ask you to get in touch with our legal department,

C. Layton Crumweather, with offices in the Fidelity Building."

"Well, why can't you answer the question?"

"Because there are certain legal matters involved, and in my status as an officer of the corporation I might bind the corporation in some pending litigation." His voice got more friendly and he said, "If you can tell me what you want, I can give you more information, but the lawyer has cautioned me not to speak out of turn because anything I say would be binding on the company, and there are a lot of legal technicalities that—"

"Forget it," the cop told him. "Ringold was murdered. Do you know anything about that?"

"Murdered!"

"That's right."

"Good Heavens, who killed him?"

"We don't know."

"When was he killed?"

"Right around eleven o'clock tonight."

Bob said, "This is a terrible shock to me. I didn't know the man intimately, but he was a business associate. Parker Stold and I were talking about him—it must have been right around the time he was killed."

"Who's Parker Stold?"

"One of my associates."

"Where were you when you were doing this talking?"

"At our office. Stold and I were there chatting and making some sales plans."

"All right, what enemies did this man have?"

"I'm sure I know but very little about him," Tindle said. "My work deals mostly with matters of policy. The personnel is handled by Mr. Bernard Carter."

They fooled around and asked a few more questions, then left. I saw that Alta was tiptoeing out of her room. I pushed her back in. "It's okay," I said. "Go to sleep. They wanted to see Bob."

"What about?"

"Seems Ringold was working for Bob."

"But why did they want to see Bob about that?"

I figured it was time to hand it to her. I said, "Somebody killed Ringold."

She stood staring at me without speech, without expression, almost without breath. She had removed her makeup, and I saw her lips grow pale.

"You!" she said. "Good God, Donald, not you! You didn't—"

I shook my head.

"You *must* have. Otherwise, you couldn't have got that—"

"Shut up," I said.

She came walking toward me as though she had been walking in her sleep. Her fingers touched the back of my hand. They were cold. "What did you think he was to me?" she asked.

"I didn't think."

"But why did you—why did you—"

I said, "Listen, dopey, I kept your name out of it. Do you get me? Where would you have been if that had been found?"

I could see she was thinking that over.

"Go back to bed," I said. "No, wait a minute. Go on downstairs. Ask what's happened, and what all the noise is about. They'll tell you. They're pretty much up in the air now. They won't notice your expressions, what you say, or what you do. Tomorrow, they'll be more alert. Does anyone know that you knew him?"

"No."

"Anyone know that you were seeing him?"

"No."

"If they ask you," I said, "avoid the question. Understand? Don't lie—not yet."

"But how can I avoid it—if they ask me?"

I said, "Keep asking questions. That's the best way to avoid answering them. Ask your stepbrother why they were calling on *him* at this hour of the night. Ask anybody anything, but don't put your neck in a noose. Do you understand?"

She nodded.

I pushed her toward the stairs. "Go on down and don't let anyone know you've seen me. I'm going back to bed."

I went back to bed, but I couldn't sleep. I heard people talking downstairs, heard steps on the stairs, low voices in the corridor. Someone walked down the corridor to the door of my room, paused there, tense and listening. I didn't know who it was. I hadn't locked the door. There was just enough vague light in the room so I could make out the door. I waited for it to open.

It didn't.

After a while it got daylight. Then, for the first time, I felt sleepy. I wanted to relax. My feet had been cold ever since I'd walked out into the corridor. Now they got warm, and a heavy drowsiness came over me.

The butler knocked on my door. It was time for me to go and give Henry C. Ashbury his physical culture lesson.

Down in the gymnasium Ashbury didn't even take off his heavy woolen bathrobe. "Hear the commotion last night?" he asked.

"What commotion?"

"One of the men who's been working for Robert's company was killed."

"Killed?"

"Yes."

"Auto accident or what?"

"Or what," he said, and then after a moment added, "Three shots with a thirty-eight-caliber revolver."

I looked at him steadily. "Where was Robert?" I asked.

His eyes held mine. He didn't answer the question. He said instead, "Where were you?"

"Working."

"On what?"

"On my job."

He pulled a cigar out of the pocket of his robe, bit off the end, lit it, and started smoking. "Getting anywhere?"

"I don't know."

"What do you think?"

"I think I'm making progress."

"Find out who's been blackmailing her?"

"I'm not certain she's being blackmailed."

"She isn't throwing checks around like confetti for nothing."

"No."

"I want you to stop it."

"I think I can."

"Think there's any chance she'll make any further payments?"

"I don't know."

"It takes you a long time to make progress," he said. "Remember I'm paying for results."

I waited until the silence had made its own punctuation mark, and then said, "Bertha Cool handles all the business affairs."

He laughed then. "I'll say one thing for you, Donald. You're a little guy, but I never saw a big one who had more guts. Let's go up and dress."

He didn't say anything about the reason for his inquiries about where I'd been or what progress I was making with his daughter. I didn't ask for any explanations. I went up and took my bath and came down to breakfast.

Mrs. Ashbury was all upset. Maids were running in and out of her room. Her doctor had been called. Ashbury explained she'd had a bad night. Robert Tindle looked as though someone had put him through a wringing machine. Ashbury didn't say much. I studied him covertly and came to the conclusion that the guys in this world who have money and keep it are the men who can dish it out and take it.

After breakfast Ashbury went to his office as though nothing had happened. Tindle rode up with him in his car. I waited until they'd cleared out. Then I called a taxi and said I wanted to go to the Fidelity Building.

C. Layton Crumweather had a law office on the twenty-ninth floor. A secretary tried to find out something about me and about my business. I told her I had some money I wanted to pay Mr. Crumweather. That got me in.

Crumweather was a gaunt, bony-faced individual with a narrow, sloping nose down which his spectacles kept sliding. He was big-boned and under-fleshed. His cheeks looked as though they'd sunken in, and that emphasized the big gash that was his mouth.

"What's your name?"

"Lam."

"You said you had some money to pay me?"

"Yes."

"Where is it?"

"I haven't got it yet."

Two deep furrows creased the center of his forehead, and emphasized the length of his nose. "Who's paying it?" he asked.

"Suckers," I said.

The secretary had left the door open a crack. Crumweather looked me over with little black eyes which seemed unusually small for the size of his face. Then he got up, walked across the office, carefully closed the door, came back, and sat down.

"Tell me about it."

I said, "I am a promoter."

"You don't look like one."

"That's what makes me a good one."

He chuckled, and I saw his teeth were long and yellow. He seemed to like that crack. "Go on," he said.

"An oil proposition," I told him.

"What's the nature of it?"

"There's a lot of nice oil land."

He nodded.

"I don't have title to it—yet."

"How do you intend to get title?"

"With the money that's paid in for stock."

He looked me over, and said, "Don't you know you can't sell stock in this state unless you get permission from the Commissioner of Corporations?"

I said, "Why did you think I took the trouble to come here?"

He chuckled again, and teetered back and forth in the squeaky swivel chair back of his desk. "You're a card, Lam," he said. "You really are."

"Let's call me the joker," I suggested.

"Are you fond of jokes?"

"No. I'm usually wild."

He leaned forward and put his elbows on the desk. He interlaced his long, bony fingers, and cracked his knuckles. He did it mechanically as though it was a gesture he used a lot. "Exactly what do you want?"

I said, "I want to beat the Blue Sky Act and sell securities without getting an okay from the Commissioner of Corporations."

"It's impossible. There are no legal loopholes."

I said, "You're attorney for the Foreclosed Farms Underwriters Company."

He looked at me then as though he was studying something under a microscope, "Go ahead."

"That's all."

He unlaced his fingers and drummed with them on the edge of the desk. "What's your plan of operation?"

"I'm going to put some good salesmen in the field. I'm going to arouse interest in the oil possibilities of this land."

"You don't own it?"

"No."

"Even if I could beat the Blue Sky Act and get you the chance to sell the securities, I couldn't keep you out of jail on a charge of getting money under false representations."

"I'll take care of that end."

"How?"

"That's my secret. I want you to beat the Blue Sky Law so I can have something to deliver when I call for the dough. That's all you need to do."

"You'd have to own the land."

"I'll have an oil lease on it."

He chuckled again. "Well," he said, "I don't make a practice of handling such things."

"I know."

"When would you want to start operations?"

"Within thirty days."

He dropped the mask. His eyes were hard and avaricious. He said, "My fee is ten per cent of the take."

I thought that over a while. "Seven and a half," I suggested.

"Don't make me laugh. It's ten."

"All right."

"What's your first name?"

"Donald."

He pressed a buzzer on the side of his desk. After a moment the secretary came in. She had a notebook with her. He said, "Take a letter, Miss Sykes, to Mr. Donald Lam. Dear Sir: With reference to your suggestion that you wish to reorganize a corporation which has forfeited its charter to the State of California, it will be necessary for you to give me more specific data as to the name of the corporation, and the purpose for which you wish it revived. My fee in such a matter will be fifty dollars in addition to whatever expenses are necessary. That's all, Miss Sykes."

She got up without a word and left the office.

When the door had closed, Crumweather said, "I suppose you know how it's done."

"The same way you did it for the Foreclosed Farms Underwriters Company?"

He said, "Let's not talk about my other clients."

"All right. What *do* you want to talk about?"

Crumweather said, "You have to take all the risks. I'll write letters confirming every conversation I have with you. I'll give you letters which you are to sign. I have a list of certain old corporations which forfeited their charters to the State of California for failure to pay franchise taxes. I've carefully checked those old corporations. Naturally, you want one which didn't do any business, against which there aren't any outstanding legal obligations, and where the entire treasury stock—or a large part of the treasury stock—was issued."

"What's that got to do with it?" I asked.

"Don't you see?" he said. "The Blue Sky Act prevents a corporation from issuing its capital stock until it has permission from the Commissioner of Corporations. After stock has once been issued, it becomes private property the same as anything else a man owns."

"Well?" I asked.

He said, "And the state taxes corporations. Whenever they don't pay their taxes, their franchise is forfeited to the state, and they can't do business any more, but those corporations can be revived if they pay their back taxes and penalties."

"Pretty slick," I said.

He grinned—an oily, foxy grin. "You see," he said, "those corporations are just the dead shells of former businesses. We pay the license, taxes, and revive the corporation. We buy up the outstanding stock which has been issued. Never have to pay more than half a cent or a cent a share. Of course, there are only a few corporations which answer our purpose. I've made all the preliminary investigation. I know the corporations. No one else does."

"Then why do you say in your letter that *I'll* have to give you the name of the corporation?"

"To keep my hands clean," he said. "You'll write me a letter giving me the name of the corporation. I'll simply act as your attorney, following your instructions. Understand, Mr. Lam, I'm going to keep in the clear—at all times."

"When do you give me the name of the corporation?"

"When you have paid me one thousand dollars."

"Your letter says fifty."

He beamed at me through his glasses. "It does, doesn't it? Makes it sound so much better, too. Your receipt will be for fifty, young man. Your payment will be one thousand bucks."

"And after that?"

"After that," he said, "you'll pay me ten per cent of the take."

"How will you be protected on that?"

"Never fear." He chuckled. "I'll be protected."

The secretary came in with the letter. He pushed his glasses back up on his nose with the tip of his forefinger, and his glittering black eyes read the letter carefully. He took a fountain pen, signed the letter, and handed it to the secretary. "Give it to Mr. Lam," he said. "Do you have the fee available, Mr. Lam?"

"Not right at the present moment—not the amount you mentioned."

"When will you have it?"

"Probably within a day or two."

"Come in any time. I'll be glad to see you."

He got up and wrapped long, cold fingers around my hand. "I thought," he said, "you were more familiar with the routine procedure in such cases. You seemed to be when you came to the office."

"I was," I told him, "but I always hate to tell a lawyer the law. I'd rather have *him* tell *me* the law."

He nodded and grinned. "A very smart young man, Mr. Lam. Now, Miss Sykes, if you'll bring in that file in the Case of Helman versus Helman, I'll dictate an answer and cross-complaint. When Mr. Lam comes in to pay his fee, I'll see him personally, and give him a receipt. Good morning, Mr. Lam."

"Good-by," I said, and walked out. The secretary waited until I had gone through the door before going after the file of Helman versus Helman.

I went down to the agency office. Bertha Cool was in. Elsie Brand was at her secretarial desk, hammering away at the typewriter.

"Anybody in with the boss?" I asked.

She shook her head.

I walked across to the door that was marked *Private* and pushed it open.

Bertha Cool shoved an account book hurriedly into the cash drawer of the desk, slammed the drawer shut, and locked it. "Where did you go?" she asked.

"I tailed along for a while, saw her into a movie, and came back to look for you."

"A movie?"

I nodded.

Bertha Cool's little glittering eyes surveyed me thoughtfully. "How's the job?" she asked.

"Still going."

"You've managed to keep her from saying anything?"

I nodded, and she asked, "How did you do it?"

"Just kidding her along," I said. "I think she likes to have me around."

Bertha Cool sighed. "Donald, you have the damnedest way with women. What do you do to make them fall for you?"

"Nothing," I said.

She looked me over again and said, "It may be at that. All the competition is trying to appear big and masculine, and you sit back as though you weren't interested. Sometimes I think you bring out the mother complex in us."

I said, "Nix on that us stuff. This is business."

She gave a throaty chuckle, and said, "Whenever you try to get hard with me, lover, I know that you're after money."

"And whenever you start handing me the soft soap, I know you're trying to kid me out of it."

"How much do you want?"

"Plenty."

"I haven't got it."

"You'd better have it, then."

"Donald, if I've told you once, I've told you fifty times that you can't just come in here and hold me up for a lot of expense money. You're careless, Donald. You're extravagant. Mind you, I don't think you pad the swindle sheet, but you just don't have any perspective in money matters. All you can see is what you want to accomplish."

I said, casually, "It's a nice piece of business. I'd hate to see you lose it."

"She knows you're a detective now?"

"Yes."

"I won't lose it, then."

"No?" I asked.

"Not if you play your part."

"I can't play my part unless I have a roll."

"Good heavens, listen to the man. What do you think this agency is, made of money?"

I said, "Officers were out last night—early this morning."

"Officers?"

"Yes."

"Why? What happened?"

"I don't know," I said. "I was sleeping through most of it, but it seems that Robert Tindle—that's the stepson—had a man working with him by the name of Ringold—or did you read the paper?"

"Ringold? Jed Ringold?" she asked, her voice seeming to jump down my throat.

"That's the one."

She kept looking at me for a long time, then she said, "Donald, you're doing it again."

"Doing what?"

"Falling for a woman. Listen, lover, some day that's going to get you in an awful jam. You're young and innocent and susceptible. Women are shrewd and designing. You can't trust them. I don't mean all women, but I mean the kind of women who try to use you."

I said, "No one's trying to use me."

She said, "I should have known better. I thought it was too damned improbable at the time."

"What was?"

"That a girl like Alta Ashbury with a lot of money, swell looks, and a lot of men chasing after her would fall for you. It's the other way around. You've fallen for her, and she's using you as a cover-up. Went to a movie! Movie, my eye! At eleven o'clock at night."

I didn't say anything.

She picked up the newspaper and checked through it before she found the address. "Murdered within a couple of blocks of the place where she parked her car—you tailing along behind—officers out at the house at three o'clock in the morning. She knows you're a detective—and we still have the job."

Bertha Cool threw back her head and laughed—hard, mirthless laughter.

I said, "I'm going to need three hundred dollars."

"Well, you can't have it."

I shrugged my shoulders, got up, and started for the door.

"Donald, wait."

I stood at the door looking at her.

"Don't you understand, Donald? Bertha doesn't want to be harsh with you, but—"

"Do you," I asked, "want me to tell you *all* about it?"

She looked at me as though her ears hadn't been working right, and said, "Of course."

I said, "Better think it over for twenty-four hours, and then let me know."

All of a sudden her face twitched. She opened her purse, took a key from it, unlocked the cash drawer, opened an inner compartment with another key, took out six fifty-dollar bills, and gave them to me. "Remember, Donald," she said, "this is expense money. Don't squander it."

I didn't bother to answer her but walked across the office, folding the fifty-dollar bills. Elsie Brand looked up from the typewriter, saw the roll of fifties, and pursed her lips into a silent whistle, but her fingers didn't quit hammering away at the keyboard.

Going out to Ashbury's place in a taxicab, I read the morning newspaper. Ringold had been identified as an ex-convict, a former gambler, and, at the time of his death, had been employed by "an influential corporation." The officials of the corporation had expressed surprise when they had been told of the man's record. Although his employment had been in a minor capacity, the corporation had used great care in the selection of its employees, and it was assumed that Ringold's references had been forged. The officials of the corporation were making a check-up.

Police were completely mystified as to the motive for the slaying, and the manner in which the murder had been consummated. Approximately fifteen minutes before the killing, a young man with quiet manners and agreeable personality had asked for a room where he could spend a few hours of undisturbed slumber. Walter Markham, the night clerk at the hotel, was emphatic in his statements that the man had made no effort to get room four-twenty-one, beyond mentioning that he preferred an odd number.

He had been assigned to room four-twenty-one, had gone up, hung a "Please Do Not Disturb" sign on the door, and apparently had immediately proceeded to pry off the molding strip which ran along the edge of the door that communicated with room four-nineteen—the room occupied by Ringold. With the molding off, the man had been able to twist the bolt on one side, and, by use of a chisel, pry back the bolt on the other. The communicating door opened into an alcove formed by one wall of room four-nineteen and the door of the bathroom which went with room four-nineteen. It was assumed that Ringold, hearing some noise at the door, had become suspicious and decided to investigate. He had been shot three times. Death had been instantaneous. The murderer had made no attempt either to leave by the room he had rented or to rob his victim. Apparently, he had pocketed the gun, calmly stepped over the body, walked to the corridor, and stood in the doorway masquerading as a guest who had been aroused by the sound of the shots. No one had seen him leave the hotel.

That the crime had been deliberate and premeditated was indicated by the fact that once ensconced in four-twenty-one, the man had bored a hole in the panel of the door so that he could make certain of the identity of his intended victim before opening the door.

Esther Clarde at the cigar stand had remembered that a very personable young man had followed a mysterious woman into the hotel. She described him as being about twenty-seven years of age, with clean-cut, finely chiseled features, an engaging voice, and lots of personality. He was about five feet six in height, and weighed about a hundred and twenty-five pounds.

The clerk, on the other hand, remembered him as being shifty-eyed and nervous in manner, emaciated, and looking like a dope fiend.

I paid off the taxi in front of Ashbury's house and went in. Mrs. Ashbury was reclining on a divan in the library. The butler said she wanted to see me.

She looked at me with appealing eyes. "Mr. Lam, *please*

don't go away. I want you to be here in order to protect Robert."

"From what?" I asked.

"I don't know. It seems to me there's something sinister about this. I think Robert's in danger. I'm his mother. I have a mother's intuition. You're a trained wrestler with muscles of steel. They say that you've taken the biggest and best of the Japanese jujitsu wrestlers and tossed them around as though they'd been dolls. Please keep your eye on Robert."

I said, "You can count on me," and went off to find Alta.

I found her in the solarium. She was seated on the chaise longue. She moved over and made room for me to sit beside her. I said, "All right, tell me."

She clamped her lips and shook her head.

"What did Ringold have on you?"

"Nothing."

"I suppose," I said, "the three ten-thousand-dollar checks were made for a charitable donation. Perhaps he was a collector for the Community Chest."

I saw the dismay come into her eyes. "The *three* checks?"

I nodded.

"How did you know?"

"I'm a detective. It's my business to find out."

"All right," she said with a flash of temper, "find out why I paid them, then."

"I will," I promised, and started to get up.

She caught my sleeve and pulled me back. "Don't do that."

"What?"

"Leave me."

"Come down to earth, then."

She drew up her feet and hugged her knees, her heels resting on the edge of the cushion. "Donald," she said, "tell me what you've been doing, how you found out about —well, you know."

I shook my head. "You don't want to know anything about me."

"Why?"

"It wouldn't be healthy."

"Then why do you want to know about me?"

"So I can help you."

"You've done enough already."

"I haven't even started yet."

"Donald, there's nothing you can do."

"What did Ringold have on you?"

"Nothing, I tell you."

I kept my eyes on her. She fidgeted uneasily. After a while, I said, "Somehow you never impressed me as being the sort who would lie. Somehow I gathered the impression that you hated liars."

"I do," she said.

I kept quiet.

"It's none of your business," she went on after a while.

I said, "Some day the cops are going to ask me questions. If I know what not to tell them, I won't give anything away, but if I don't know what not to tell them, I may say the wrong thing. Then they'll start in on you."

She sat silent for several seconds, then she said, "I got in an awful scrape."

"Tell me about it."

"It probably isn't what you think it is."

"I'm not even thinking."

She said, "I took a cruise last summer down to the South Seas. There was a man on the boat. I liked him very much, and— Well, you know how it is."

I said, "Lots of young women have taken cruises to the South Seas, found lots of men whom they liked very much, and still didn't pay thirty thousand dollars after they got home."

"This man was married."

"What did his wife say?"

"I didn't ever know her. He wrote me. His letters were —they were love letters."

I said, "I don't know how much time we have. The more you waste, the less we have left."

"I wasn't really in love with him. It was a cruise flirtation. The moonlight got me, I guess."

"Your first one?"

"Of course not. I've taken cruises. That's why girls sail on cruises. Sometimes you meet a man whom you really love— That is, I suppose you do. Girls have. They've married and lived happily ever after."

"But you haven't?"

"No."

"But you played around?"

"Well, you try to show yourself a good time. You can tell after the first two or three days if there's anyone on board for whom you're apt to care a lot. Usually you find someone who's attractive enough for a flirtation. But you're not flirting with *him*. You're flirting with romance."

"This man was married?"

"Yes."

"And he's separated from his wife?"

"No. He told me later he was taking a matrimonial vacation while she was taking one of her own."

"What was hers?"

"I have my doubts about that, too. She was working for a big oil company which had interests in China. She had to go over to wind up the books when they were closing the Shanghai branch."

"Why the suspicions?"

"The big boss also went over. He was on the same boat. She was sweet on him."

"Then what?"

She said, "Honestly, Donald, there were some things about him I didn't like—definitely. And there were other things that appealed to me very much. He enjoyed himself so much. He was—fun."

"You came back. You still didn't know he was married."

"That's right."

"He told you he was single?"

"Yes, definitely."

"Then what?"

"Then he wrote me letters."

"You answered them?"

"No. I'd found out he was married then."

"What's his name?"

"I'm coming to that in a minute."

"Why not tell me now?"

"No. You'll have to get the rest of the picture first."

"Was this man Ringold?"

"Good Lord, no!"

"All right."

"I wouldn't answer his letters because I knew he was married, but I liked getting them. They were love letters —I told you that—but they were full of reminiscences about our trip. Some things were so lovely. We sailed into Tahiti late one night—you'd have to see that to realize it—the native dancers waiting around little fires. We could see the red points of light dotting the shore. Then, as the ship came in, we could see the forms of the dancers around the fires. We could hear the drums beating, that peculiar *Tap—tap—TAP! Tap—tap—TAP! Tap—tap—TAP!* Then they threw more fuel on the fires. Someone turned flood-lights down on the quay, and there were these dancers, with nothing on but grass skirts, stamping their bare feet in the rhythm of a dance, then pairing off and facing each other in a sort of hula which became more and more violent. Then, at a signal, they'd all start a running kind of dance around the fires. He reminded me of that—and other things. They were wonderful letters. I saved them and read them over whenever I felt blue. They were so vivid—"

I said, "Sounds like things a magazine would pay money for, but I don't see why *you* should pay thirty thousand dollars for letters you didn't answer."

She said, "Brace yourself, because I'm going to give you a shock."

I said, "You mean that the letters did something to you that he himself hadn't been able to do? That you—"

She colored. "No, no, no! Don't be a fool."

"I can't imagine anything else that would be worth thirty thousand bucks to a young woman who's as independent as you are."

"You'll understand when I tell you."

"Well, go ahead and tell me."

"The man's name," she said, "was—"

She broke off.

"What's his name got to do with it?" I asked.

She took a deep breath, and then blurted, "Hampton G. Lasster."

"That's a funny name to get romantic about," I said. "You seem to think it should mean something. What is he, a—" All of a sudden an idea hit me with the force of a blow. I stopped mid-sentence and stared at her. I saw by her eyes that I was right. "Good Lord," I said, "he's the man who murdered his wife."

She nodded.

"Wasn't there a trial?"

"Not yet. Just a preliminary hearing. He was bound over."

I grabbed her shoulders, spun her around so I could look down in her eyes. "You didn't have an affair with this man?"

She shook her head.

"Did he see you after you got back?"

"No."

"And you didn't ever write to him?"

"No."

"What happened to his letters?"

"Those are what I was buying back," she said.

"How did Ringold get them?"

"Some smart detectives working out of the district attorney's office figured that what they needed to make a perfect case against Lasster was a motivation—one which would prejudice a jury. They checked back on Lasster just as much as they could. He couldn't account for his time covering a period of eight weeks during the summer, while his wife was away. The detectives couldn't find where he'd been.

"Then, in searching a woodshed, they came on an old trunk which had a steamer label on it. They traced that back and found out about the trip to the South Seas, then got a passenger list, and interviewed passengers. Of course, it was a cinch after that. They found out that Lasster had been definitely interested in me while he was on the cruise."

"Still," I said, "if you were reasonably discreet, that didn't give them anything they could work on—not if he kept his mouth shut."

"But don't you understand? It gave them just the lead they wanted. They waited for the right opportunity, managed to break into the house, go through my room in my absence, and— Well, they found the letters. You see what that means. I can swear on a stack of Bibles a mile high that I haven't written Lasster or seen him since I found out he was married. No one would believe me."

"How did it happen you bought the letters in three installments?"

She said, "There were three detectives. After they got the evidence, they did a little thinking. They were drawing a low salary from the county. If they turned the letters over to the district attorney, they wouldn't even get a raise in pay. I was supposed to be a wealthy woman— Of course, they didn't appear in it themselves. They got Ringold to act as intermediary. I don't know how much Ringold was making out of it, but it was arranged that I'd buy the letters in three installments."

I pushed my hands down in my pockets, stuck my legs straight out in front of me, crossed my ankles, and stared at my toes, trying to see the picture, not only as she saw it but to get angles that she didn't know anything about.

Now that she'd started talking, she didn't want to stop. She said, "You can see what it would mean to a woman like me. The district attorney is crazy to get a conviction in that case. In the first place, they don't know whether it was an accident and she fell and struck her head, or whether Lasster hit her with something. Then, even if the district attorney can prove that Lasster hit her, Lasster's lawyer could bring up that Shanghai trip and might be able to make a showing of emotional insanity or whatever it is a lawyer pulls when he's trying to prejudice a jury by making them think that a woman needed killing anyway.

"Well, the district attorney could put a stop to all that right at the start if he could introduce a lot of stuff about me, make it appear that Lasster was infatuated with me, and wanted to get rid of his wife so that he could marry me. I was wealthy and—well, not exactly ugly. He could put me up in front of the jury in a way that would absolutely crucify me, and if he had those letters, he could rip Lasster to pieces the minute he got on the witness stand and tried to deny it, or he could draw the worst sort of conclusions if Lasster didn't try to deny it."

I kept thinking, and didn't say anything.

She said, "When the detectives first got the letters, they thought Hampton's lawyer might buy them off, but Hampton hasn't much money. I think it was the lawyer who suggested they work through Ringold and get the money out of me."

"Who's the lawyer?" I asked.

"C. Layton Crumweather," she said. "He's the lawyer, incidentally, who does the legal work for Bob's corporation, and I've been terribly afraid that he'd say something, but I guess those lawyers can be trusted to keep their mouths shut."

"Are you certain Crumweather knows about the letters?" I asked.

"Ringold said he did, and I suppose, of course, that Lasster told him. I guess when a man gets arrested for murder, he tells his lawyer everything, no matter whom it may affect."

I said, "Yes, I guess he does."

She said, "Of course, Crumweather wants to keep those letters out of the district attorney's hands. Naturally, he wants to get an acquittal in that murder case. The letters would clinch the case against his client. From all I can hear of Crumweather, I think he's very smart."

I got up and started pacing the floor. Suddenly I turned and said, "You didn't open that envelope when he gave it to you last night."

She stared at me with eyes that began to get wider and rounder. "Then you *were* in that room, Donald?"

"Never mind that. Why didn't you open the envelope?"

"Because I'd seen Ringold put the letters in the envelope and seal it. That's just what he'd done with the other letters. He'd show them to me and then—"

"Did you open that envelope after you got home?" I asked.

"No. I didn't. There were so many startling developments and—"

"Did you burn it?"

"Not yet. I was getting ready to, and then you—"

"How do you know this whole thing isn't a trap the D.A. set for you?" I asked.

She stared at me. "How could it be?"

"He wants to use those letters to prove motivation for the murder. It won't do so much good to show letters that Lasster wrote you unless he can show that you answered them, *but* if he can show that you paid thirty thousand dollars to get those letters back, that would be better than anything else."

"But, Donald, can't you see? He won't have the letters. He—"

"Where did you put that envelope?"

"In a safe place."

"Get it."

"It's in a safe place, Donald. It's too dangerous to—"

"Get it."

She looked at me for a moment, then said, "Perhaps you know best," and went upstairs. About five minutes later she came back with a sealed envelope. "I know these are the letters all right. I saw Ringold put them in. Then he sealed the envelope. That was just the way he'd handed me the other letters—showed them to me, then sealed them in an envelope—" I didn't wait for her to finish. I reached across, took the envelope out of her hand, and tore it open. There were half a dozen envelopes on the inside. I shook those envelopes out into my hand, opened each one in turn. They were filled with neatly folded sheets of blank paper bearing the imprint of the hotel in which Ringold had been murdered.

I looked up at Alta Ashbury. If attendants had been strapping her to the chair in the gas chamber at San Quentin, she couldn't have looked any more ghastly.

CHAPTER SIX

BERTHA WAS WAITING in the agency car to take me to my jujitsu lesson. She had an afternoon paper on the seat beside her, and was jumpy.

"Donald, this is one time you can't get away with it," she said.

"Can't get away with what?"

"They'll catch you."

"Not until they get some lead to work on."

"But sooner or later they'll catch you. My God, why did you do it?"

"What else *could* I do? I'd taken the adjoining room. I'd bored a hole in the panel of the door. That connecting door was unlocked on the other side. Win, lose, or draw, I was elected."

"But why did you go in Ringold's room?"

"Why not? I was hooked anyway—if they caught me."

"Donald, you're trying to protect that girl again."

I didn't say anything.

"Donald, you simply *must* give me the facts. My God, suppose the cops should run you in? I'd try to get you out, of course, but what would I have to work on?"

I said, "You can't drive and talk. Get over and let me take the wheel."

We made the switch. I said, "Get this straight. Alta Ashbury was being blackmailed. It doesn't make any difference what for. The person who was blackmailing her was a lawyer named Crumweather—C. Layton Crumweather."

"That doesn't make sense," she said. "She must have gone to see Ringold. The description fits and—"

"The description may fit, and she may have gone to *see* Ringold, but the man who was blackmailing her was Crumweather."

"How do you know?"

"He was interested in getting some dough for the defense of a client of his—a man who was charged with a crime."

"Who, lover?"

"I've forgotten his name."

She glared at me.

"Now then," I went on, "the only way we can handle this thing—to get Alta in the clear and to get me out of it—is to be in a position to put the screws down on Crumweather. He's a crooked lawyer."

"They're all crooked."

"You're cockeyed. About two per cent are crooked—and they're damn smart. They cover a lot of territory. Some of the honest ones are stupid. The crooked ones can't afford to be."

"Stick up for lawyers if you want to, but give me the dope."

"Crumweather," I said, "is making a specialty of beating the Blue Sky Law."

"It can't be beaten. They've tried that before."

"Any law can be licked," I said. "I don't care what it is."

"Well, you studied it. I didn't."

I said, "The Blue Sky Law can be licked. The way Crumweather is licking it is taking old corporations which have forfeited their charters to the state for failure to pay their franchise taxes, reviving those corporations, and letting them engage in an entirely different form of business. In order to do that, he first buys up the stock of defunct corporations. It isn't every franchise forfeiture that gives him just what he needs. He needs a corporation that had nearly all of its stock issued and which has no corporate liabilities. He buys up the old shares of stock which have become private property in the hands of a bona fide purchaser, then he revives the corporation. He finds out what his clients are going to sell the stock for and gives them the certificates at a price which gives him a ten-per-cent profit on every share that's sold. He instructs his clients to avoid the appearance of selling generally to the public, but keeps them in the position of making individual, private transactions."

"Well?" she asked.

"We'll never touch him on the blackmail," I said. "He's too slick and too far removed. The only way to hook him is to get him where we can bust him with some of this corporation crooked work. It isn't going to be easy because he's plenty smart."

"How did you find all this out?" Bertha Cool asked, staring at me steadily.

"By spending expense money," I told her, and that had her stymied.

"How are you and the girl getting along?"

"All right."

"Is she trusting you?"

"I think so."

Bertha heaved a sigh of relief. "Then the agency will continue on the job?"

"Probably."

"Donald, you're a wonder."

I took that opportunity to say, "I've already approached Crumweather as a prospective client. I thought I could handle the situation that way. I can't. He's too wise. He covers his tracks every time he makes a move. There's only one other way to do it."

"What's that?"

"Become an innocent purchaser for value of some of the stock in one of the other corporations he's promoted."

"What makes you think it's Crumweather who's doing the blackmailing?"

"It has to be. It's the only way it makes sense. Earlier today I thought it might have been a trap set by the D.A., but it isn't or they'd have sprung it by this time. Crumweather is representing a client. It's an important case. A lot of public attention is going to center on it. It's a chance for him to make a big grandstand. He could, of course, do it just for the advertising, but Crumweather isn't built that way. He saw there was an opportunity to bring pressure to bear on Alta Ashbury and make her put up dough. He did it. He got twenty thousand of her money. Something went wrong on the last ten."

"Donald, I'm going to ask you something. I want you to tell me the absolute truth."

"What?"

"*Did* you kill him?"

"What do *you* think?"

"I don't think you'd do it, Donald. I don't think there's a chance in ten thousand, but it looks— Well, you know how it looks. You're just the type who would fall head over heels for a girl and do something desperate to save her."

I slowed for a signal light, and managed a yawn.

Bertha shook her head and said, "You're the coolest customer I ever saw. If you only weighed fifty pounds more, you'd be a gold mine to Bertha."

"Too bad," I said.

We drove for a while in silence, then I said, "I'm going to need a secretary and an office. I'll either hire one or have to borrow Elsie Brand."

"Donald, are you crazy? I can't fix you up in an office. That costs money. It costs altogether too much money. You'll have to find some other way of working your plant, and I can't let Elsie Brand go, even for half a day."

I drove along without saying anything, and Bertha got sore. Just before I drove the car into a parking lot in front of the Jap's gymnasium, she said, "All right, go ahead, but don't go throwing money away."

We went up to the gymnasium, and the Jap threw me all over the joint. I think he just practiced with me the way a basketball player practices tossing balls through a ring. He gave me a couple of chances to throw him, and I used everything I had, but I could never get him up and slam him down on the canvas the way he did me. He'd always manage to twist himself around in the air, and come down on his feet, grinning.

I was awfully fed up with it. I'd hated it from the start. Bertha said she thought I was getting better. The Jap said I was doing very nicely.

After the shower, I told Bertha to be sure to get me a suite of offices for a week, be sure the name I gave her was on the door, see that the furniture looked all right, and have Elsie Brand on hand to take dictation.

She fumed and sputtered, but finally decided to be a good dog. She promised to ring me up late that evening, and tell me where it was.

Henry Ashbury got hold of me that night before dinner. "How about a cocktail in my den, Lam?" he asked.

"Fine," I said.

The butler brought us cocktails in a little cubbyhole fixed up with guns hung on the walls, a few shooting trophies, a pipe rack, and a couple of easy chairs. It was one place in the house where no one was allowed to go without a special invitation from Ashbury, his one hideaway from the continual whine of his wife's voice.

We sipped the cocktails and talked generalities for a minute, then Ashbury said, "You're getting along pretty well with Alta."

"I was supposed to win her confidence, wasn't I?"

"Yes. You've done more than that. She keeps looking at you whenever you're in the room."

I took another sip of my cocktail.

He said, "Alta's first check was on the first. The second one was on the tenth. If there was to have been a third one, it would have been on the twentieth. That was yesterday."

I said, very casually, "Then the fourth one would be due on the thirtieth."

He looked me over. "Alta was out last night."

"Yes. She went to a movie."

"You were out."

"Yes. I was doing a little work."

"Did you follow Alta?"

"If you want to know, yes."

"Where?"

"To the movie."

He gulped the rest of his cocktail quickly and exhaled a sigh of relief. He picked up the cocktail shaker, refilled my glass, and poured his own full to the brim. "You impress me as being a young man who has sense."

"Thanks."

He fidgeted around a minute, and I said, "You don't need to make any build-up with me. Just go ahead and get it off your chest."

That seemed to relieve him. He said, "Bernard Carter saw Alta last night."

"About what time?"

"Shortly after the—well, shortly after the shooting took place."

"Where was she?"

"Within a block of the hotel where Ringold was killed. She was carrying an envelope in her hand and walking very rapidly."

"Carter told you?"

"Well, no. He told Mrs. Ashbury, and she told me."

"Carter didn't speak to her?"

"No."

"She didn't see him?"

"No."

I said, "Carter is mistaken. I was following her all the time. She put her car in the parking lot near the hotel where Ringold was killed, but she didn't go to the hotel. She went to a picture show. I followed her."

"And after the picture show?"

"She wasn't there very long," I said. "She came out and went back to the car— Oh, yes. I believe she stopped to mail a letter at a mailbox along the way."

Ashbury kept looking at me, but didn't say anything.

I said, "I think she had a date to meet someone at the picture show, and that someone didn't show up."

"Could that someone have been Ringold?" he asked.

I let my face show surprise. "What gave you that idea?"

"I don't know. I was just wondering."

"Quit wondering, then."

"But it *could* have been Ringold?"

"If he didn't show up, what difference does it make?"

"But it *could* have been Ringold?"

I said, "Hell, it *could* have been anybody. I'm telling you she was at a movie."

He was silent for a minute, and I took advantage of that silence to ask him, "Do you know anything about your stepson's company—the one of which he's president—what it's doing?"

"Some sort of a gold-dredging proposition. I understand they have a potential bonanza, but I don't want to know about it."

"Who does the actual peddling of the stock?"

He said, "I wish you wouldn't call it that. It sounds—well, it sounds crooked."

"You know what I mean."

"Yes, I know, but I don't like it referred to in those terms."

"All right, fix the terms to suit yourself, then tell me who's peddling the stuff."

He looked me over thoughtfully. "At times, Lam," he said, "that restless disposition of yours makes you say things which border on insolence."

"I still don't know who peddles it."

"Neither do I. They have a crew of salesmen, very highly trained men, I understand."

"The partners don't sell?"

"No."

"That's all I wanted to know."

"It isn't all I wanted to know."

I raised my eyebrows.

"Seen the evening paper?"

I shook my head.

"There are some fingerprints in there. They've developed a pretty good set from the door and doorknob in that room in the hotel. I thought that man they're looking for resembles you somewhat."

"Lots of people resemble me," I said. "They're mostly clerks in dry-goods stores."

He laughed. "If that brain of yours had a body to go with it, you'd be invincible."

"Is that a compliment or a slam?"

"A compliment."

"Thanks."

I finished my cocktail and refused another. Ashbury had two after I quit.

Ashbury said, "You know a man in my position has an opportunity to pick up financial information which might not be available to an ordinary man."

I accepted one of his cigarettes, and listened for more.

"That's particularly true in banking circles."

"Go ahead. What is it?"

"Perhaps you are wondering how I found out about Alta's ten-thousand-dollar checks."

"I was able to make a pretty good guess."

"You mean through the bank?"

"Yes."

"Well, not exactly through the bank, but through a friendly official in the bank."

"Is there any difference?" I asked.

He grinned. "The bank seems to think there is."

"Go ahead."

"I got some more information from the bank this afternoon."

"You mean from the friendly official in the bank, don't you?"

He chuckled and said, "Yes."

When he saw I wasn't going to ask him what it was, he said impressively, "The Atlee Amusement Corporation called up the bank and said a check had been stolen from its cash drawer, that it was a check payable to cash, and signed by Alta Ashbury in an amount of ten thousand dollars. They wanted to be notified if anyone should present that check; said they'd sign a complaint, on a charge of theft."

"What did the bank tell them?"

"Told them to ring up Alta and have her stop payment on the check."

"That was a telephone call?"

"Yes."

"The person at the other end of the line said it was the Atlee Amusement Corporation?"

"Yes."

"Man's voice or woman's?"

"A woman's. She said she was the bookkeeper, and secretary to the manager."

"Any woman can say that into any telephone and it sounds the same at the receiving end of the line."

He thought that over, then slowly nodded.

The cocktails began to take effect. He got in an expansive mood. He leaned over and put a fatherly hand on my knee. "Lam, my boy," he said. "I like you. There's a certain inherent competency about you which breeds confidence. I think Alta feels the same way."

"I'm glad I'm doing a satisfactory job."

"I thought you weren't going to for a while. I thought it would be bungled. Alta's rather smart, you know."

"She's nobody's fool," I said, and then, because he expected it, and because he was a cash customer, I added, "A chip off the old block."

He beamed at me, then his face became worried. He said, "I have an idea you know what you're doing, Lam, but if a ten-thousand-dollar check payable to cash has been stolen, and if the person who presented it for payment should get into a jam and make certain statements and—"

"Quit worrying about it. Nothing will happen."

He said significantly, "If you had read the papers, you'd have noticed the witnesses had given a somewhat contradictory description of this mysterious John Smith. The very contradictions of that description are significant to a man who knows human nature. The young woman sketches John Smith in a much more attractive light."

I didn't say anything.

"You know, Lam, I'm trusting very much to your discretion in this matter. I'm certainly hoping that you don't —that you haven't—that no excess zeal on your part has perhaps laid a foundation for a worse evil than that which you were called in to cure."

"That *would* be embarrassing, wouldn't it?"

"Very. You don't open up much, do you?"

"I prefer to play a lone hand wherever I can."

He said, "I could have unlimited confidence in you,

Donald, my boy, absolutely *unlimited* confidence, if I knew one thing."

"What's that?"

"Whether your plans had taken into consideration the danger of that ten-thousand-dollar check showing up."

It was a chance for a grandstand that I couldn't resist. I said quietly, "Mr. Ashbury, I burned up that ten-thousand-dollar check in your solarium last night. I ground the ashes into powder with my finger tips. You can quit worrying about it."

He looked at me with his eyes getting bigger and bigger until I thought they were going to push his spectacles off the bridge of his nose, then he grabbed my hand and started pumping it up and down. I made allowances for the four cocktails, but, even so, it was quite a demonstration. "You're a wonder, my boy, a wonder! This is the last time I shall ask you anything. You go right ahead from here on and handle things in your own way. That's marvelous, simply marvelous."

I said, "Thanks. You know this may cost you money."

"I don't give a damn what it costs— No, I don't exactly mean that, but— Well, you know what I mean."

I said, "Bertha is unduly economical at times. She's penny-wise and pound-foolish."

"She doesn't need to be. You explain that to her. Tell her that—"

"Telling *her* won't do any good," I said. "It's the way she's built."

"Well, what do you want?"

I said, "Has it ever occurred to you I may have to bribe someone?"

"No."

"Well, it's a possibility to be taken into consideration." He didn't seem particularly happy about it. He said, "Well, of course, if you run into an emergency, the only thing for you to do is to come to me and—"

"And tell you who I'm bribing, how much I've got to pay, and why?" I asked.

"Well, yes."

"Then if anything goes wrong and it's a trap, you're the one who's caught."

I saw his face change color. He said, "How much do you want?"

I said, "Better give me a thousand dollars. I'll keep it with me in case I need it. I may come back and ask for more."

"That's a lot of money, Donald."

"It is for a fact," I said. "How much money have you got?"

He flushed. "I don't see what that has to do with it."

"How many daughters have you got?"

"Only one, of course."

I kept silent while he thought it over. I saw the idea soaking in. He pulled a wallet from his inside pocket and counted out ten one-hundred-dollar bills. "I see your point, Donald, but remember I'm not a millionaire."

I said, "A man who has money has an advantage over a man who hasn't. When he gets in a jam, he can buy his way out. You'd be foolish not to play the trumps you hold in your hand."

"That's right," he said, and then after a moment went on. "Don't you think, Donald, that you could tell me a few of the details? I'd like to know them."

I stared at him steadily. "Would you?" I asked.

"Why, why not?"

I said, "The way I play the game, my clients don't know anything."

He frowned. "I don't think I like that."

"And in a way," I went on, "the police can never charge them as being accessories."

He jumped as though I'd stuck a pin into him. He blinked his eyes four or five times rapidly, and then got to his feet hurriedly. "Very wise, Donald, very wise indeed! Well, I fancy that it's about time to adjourn. I'm going to be rather busy after this, Donald. I won't have an opportunity to talk with you. I just want you to know that I'm leaving things in your hands—entirely in your hands."

He busted up the meeting as quickly as though I'd

72

broken out with smallpox. I had. Legal smallpox.

About eight o'clock that night Bertha Cool telephoned. She'd had an awful time, she said, getting an office of the type I wanted, but she'd finally secured one. It was in the name of Charles E. Fischler, and was at room six-twenty-two in the Commons Building. Elsie Brand would be there at nine o'clock the next morning to open up the office, and she'd have keys.

"I'll want some business cards printed," I said.

"That's all taken care of. Elsie will have some. You're the head of the Fischler Sales Corporation."

I said, "Okay," and started to hang up. "What's new?" she asked.

"Nothing."

"Keep me posted."

"I will," I said, and that time got the receiver on the hook before she could think of anything else.

The evening dragged interminably. Alta signaled that she wanted to talk with me, but I figured I knew all she knew. But I didn't know all Bernard Carter knew, and I wanted to be where he could strike up a conversation that would look sufficiently casual in case he had anything he wanted to say.

He did.

I was knocking balls around in the billiard room when he came in. "Feel like a game?" he asked.

"I'm a rotten player," I said. "I came down here to get away from the small talk."

"What's the matter?" he asked. "Something on your mind?"

"So-so," I said, knocking the cue ball around the table and watching it bounce back from the cushions.

"Have you seen Ashbury?" he asked. "You know, had a chance to talk with him?"

I nodded.

"Nice chap, Ashbury," Carter went on.

I didn't say anything.

"Certainly must be nice to be able to keep in first-class physical shape," Carter went on, looking down at his tight waistcoat. "You move as easily as a fish swimming around in water. I've been watching you."

"Have you?"

"Yes, I have. You know, Lam, I'd like to know you better—have you whip me into shape."

"It could be done," I said, knocking the billiard balls around.

He moved over closer. "There's someone else on whom you've made a favorable impression, Lam."

"Indeed?"

"Yes. Mrs. Ashbury."

I said, "She told me she'd like to take off a little weight after her blood pressure got back to normal."

He lowered his voice. "Did it ever strike you there's something a little strange about the way her blood pressure started to mount and she started to put on weight immediately after she married Ashbury?"

I said, "Lots of women keep on a diet while they're husband-hunting, and then as soon as they marry, settle back—"

His face grew purple. "That's not what I meant at all," he snapped.

I said, "I'm sorry."

"If you knew Mrs. Ashbury, you'd realize how utterly uncalled for such a statement is, how far it's removed from the real facts."

I didn't look up from the billiard balls. I said, "You were doing the talking. I thought perhaps that was what you wanted to say, and I'd make it easier for you."

"That wasn't what I wanted to say."

"Why not go ahead and say it, then?"

He said, "All right, I will. I've known Mrs. Ashbury for some little time. Before her marriage she was twenty-five pounds lighter, and she looked twenty years younger."

"High blood pressure can do a lot to a person," I said.

"Of course it can, but what's the reason for the blood pressure? Why should her marriage suddenly run her blood pressure up?"

"Why should it?" I asked.

He waited until I glanced up to meet his eyes. He was almost quivering with rage. He said, "The answer is obvious. The persistent, steady hostility of her stepdaughter."

I put the cue in the rack and said, "Did you want to talk with me about that?"

"Yes."

"All right, I'm listening."

He said, "Carlotta—Mrs. Ashbury—is a marvelous woman, charming, magnetic, beautiful. Since her marriage I've seen her change."

"You said all that before."

His lips were trembling with rage. "And the reason for it all is the hostility of that spoiled brat."

"Meaning Alta?" I asked.

"Meaning Alta."

"Didn't Mrs. Ashbury take that possibility into consideration before the marriage?"

He said, "At the time of the marriage, Alta had abandoned her father, gone off chasing a good time around the world without caring a snap of her fingers about her dad, but the minute he married Carlotta and she started making him a home, Alta came dashing back and started playing the part of the devoted daughter. Gradually, bit by bit, she's been poisoning her father's mind against Mrs. Ashbury. Carlotta is sensitive and—"

"Why tell *me* all this?" I asked.

"I thought you should know it."

"Think it's going to help me get Henry Ashbury in better physical shape?" I asked.

He said, "It might."

"Just what did you expect me to do?"

He said, "You and Alta get along pretty well together."

"So what?"

He said, "I thought it might change Alta's attitude a bit if she realized that her stepmother wanted to be friendly."

"Well?"

"You've talked with Ashbury?"

"Yes."

"You still don't see what I'm driving at?"

"No."

His eyes bored steadily into mine. "All right," he said, "if you want it straight from the shoulder. Carlotta—Mrs. Ashbury—needs only to breathe a whisper of what she knows to the police, and Alta would be put into Jed Ringold's room last night at the time of the murder."

I raised my eyebrows.

"Well," Carter amended hastily, "just before the time of the murder— Did it ever occur to you that the woman who went up to see Ringold answers Alta's description, that it wouldn't take a hell of a lot of detective work to establish the fact that Alta's car was in a parking station within a couple of blocks of the hotel, and that a witness could be called who would testify that he'd seen Alta hurrying toward the parking lot from the direction of the hotel at just about the time the murder was committed?"

"What," I asked, "do you want *me* to do?"

He said, "The next time Alta starts talking about her stepmother you might casually explain to her that Mrs. Ashbury has it in her power to put Alta in a hell of a spot, that she isn't doing it because Carlotta is a square shooter and loyal to the man she's married."

I said, "You seem to take it for granted that Alta's going to discuss her stepmother with me."

"I do," he said, and turned on his heel and started for the door.

"Just a minute," I said. "If Alta left the hotel *before* the murder was committed, it doesn't seem to me she has much to worry about."

He paused with his hand on the knob of the door. "She was seen on the street," he said, "just *after* the murder was committed."

I stood staring at the door after he'd closed it. Evidently Carter didn't know just when the murder had been committed, hadn't noticed the *exact* time that he'd seen Alta, or else was willing to dress the story up a little bit in order to give Mrs. Ashbury a trump card.

However, there was no use worrying about him. Any

time the police got the idea Alta might be mixed into it, they had a cinch. The night clerk at the hotel, the girl at the cigar counter, the man at the parking lot, the elevator boy— Oh, there were plenty of witnesses. The nice part of it was that those witnesses would have to swear that Alta had left the hotel *before* the shots were fired, but if Mrs. Ashbury thought she had a fistful of trumps, there was no reason why I shouldn't let her keep on thinking so until I saw just how she intended to play them.

I got my hat and coat, watched for an opportunity to get out when Alta couldn't see me and decided to go take a look at the joints run by the Atlee Amusement Corporation.

They had two restaurants, very swank downstairs, and I didn't have much trouble getting upstairs. The places were well fitted but small. No one seemed to pay any particular attention to me. I gambled in a small way and just about broke even on roulette. There were a few people in the place. I tried to make some excuse to get to see the manager, but it looked as though I'd have to get rough in order to do it.

Just as I was walking out of the joint, a blonde came in on the arm of a chap in evening clothes who looked like ready money.

I'd seen that hair before. It was Esther Clarde, the girl at the cigar counter of the hotel where Ringold had been bumped off.

I started kicking myself mentally. It was a chance, of course, but a chance I should have foreseen. If she'd known enough about the Atlee Amusement Corporation to answer my questions, there at the hotel, she knew enough to get a commission out of piloting suckers into the joint. I'd set my own trap, baited it, and walked right in.

She looked at me, and I saw her eyes get hard. She said casually, "Oh, hello, there. How's the luck? Any good?"

"Not so good."

She smiled at her companion and said, "Arthur, I want you to meet Mr. Smith. Mr. Smith, this is Arthur Parker."

We shook hands. I told him I was pleased to meet him.

"You're not getting ready to go, Mr. Smith?"

"As a matter of fact, I was."

"Well, you're not going to leave just as I come in. You usually bring me luck, and somehow I feel you're going to bring me lots of it tonight."

I thought I could complicate the situation by making Parker jealous. I looked at him and said, "Mr. Parker looks like a very capable mascot."

She said, "He's my escort. You're my mascot. Come on over here to the tables."

"Really, I'm a bit tired and—"

Her eyes bored steadily into mine. The light caught her hair, and it looked more than ever like that piece of hangman's hemp that I'd seen years ago. "I'm not going to let you get away," she said, laughing with her red lips, "even if I have to call the cops."

There was no laughter in her eyes.

I smiled and said, "Well, after all, that's really up to Mr. Parker. I never like to horn in."

"Oh, it's all right by him," she said. "Parker understands that you're connected with the establishment."

"Oh," Parker said, as though that explained a lot, and instantly began to smile. "Do come along, Smith, and bring us luck."

I strolled over to the roulette table with her.

She started playing with silver dollars—and losing. Parker didn't seem inclined to stake her. When she'd lost her money, she pouted a little, and he finally got five dollars in twenty-five-cent chips and let her play those.

When he had moved around nearer the foot of the table, and she had edged closer to me, she suddenly turned and again let her eyes bore into mine. "Slip me two hundred dollars under the table," she ordered.

I gave her the stony stare.

"Come on, come on," she said in a fast undertone. "Don't act dumb, and don't stall. Either come through, *or else.*"

I managed a yawn.

She could have cried she was so disappointed. She slammed the chips down on the board and lost them.

When they were gone, I slipped a dollar into her palm. "That's the extent of my donation, kid," I said, "and it's lucky. Play it on the double O."

She put it on the double O and won straight up.

"Let it ride," I said.

"You're crazy."

I shrugged my shoulders, and she raked down all but five dollars of her winnings.

I'll never know what made me say that about the double O. I was skating on thin ice, sticking my neck out. It was just a crazy hunch I had, but one of those things a man gets sometimes when he feels hot all over, as though he had clairvoyant powers. I was absolutely certain that it was going to come double O again. Don't ask me how I knew. I just knew. That was all.

The ball rattled around the wheel and finally came to rest in one of the pockets.

I heard Esther Clarde gasp, and looked over just to make certain where the ball had stopped.

It was in number seven.

"You see," she said, "you'd have made me lose."

I laughed. "You're still playing on velvet."

She said, "Well, maybe the seven will repeat," and played it for two bucks. It repeated. After that, I quit feeling lucky, and stuck around. Esther ran her roll up to about five hundred bucks, and then cashed in.

There was a brunette hanging around the tables, a slinky girl with snake hips, nice bare shoulders, and eyes that were filled with romance like a dark, warm night on a tropical beach. She and the blonde knew each other, and after Esther had cashed in I saw them swapping signals. Later they were whispering together.

Shortly afterward the brunette started making a play for Arthur Parker, and it *was* a play. She was asking his advice, getting her bare shoulder within an inch of his lips as she leaned across him to place a bet at the far end of the board, looking up at him with a smile.

I took a look at the expression on Parker's face and knew I was stuck with the blonde.

"All right," I said to Esther Clarde, "you win. Where do we go?"

"I'll sneak out to the cloakroom first," she said. "I'll be waiting. Don't try any funny stuff. In case you're interested, there isn't any back way out."

"Why should I want to get away from a good-looking girl like you?"

She laughed, and then after a moment said softly, "Well, why *should* you?"

I stuck around long enough to put a few bets on the roulette table. I couldn't lay off the double O. I never even got a smell. Parker was all wrapped up with the brunette. Once he gave a guilty start and started looking around. I heard the brunette say something about the restroom, then slip a bare arm around his shoulder and whisper in his ear.

He laughed.

I went out to the cloakroom. Esther Clarde was waiting for me. "Got a car?" she asked. "Or do we ride in taxis?"

"Taxis," I said.

"All right, let's go."

"Any particular place?"

"I think I'll go to your apartment."

"I'd rather go to yours."

She looked at me for a minute, then shrugged her shoulders and said, "Why not?"

"Your friend, Mr. Parker, won't show up, will he?"

"My friend, Mr. Parker," she said grimly, "is taken care of for the evening, thank you."

She gave the address of her apartment to the cab driver. It took about ten minutes to get there. It was her apartment, all right. Her name was on the bell marker, and she used her key and went up. Well, after all, as she'd said, why not? I knew where she worked. I could have found out all about her. The newspapers had carried her picture and an interview with her describing the man who had asked her the questions about Ringold. She had nothing to fear from me.

On the other hand, I was in it, right up to my necktie.

It wasn't a bad apartment. One look told me she didn't

keep it from the profits she made out of running the cigar stand at a second-rate hotel.

She slipped off her coat, told me to sit down, brought out cigarettes, asked me if I wanted some Scotch, and sat down on the sofa beside me. We lit cigarettes, and she sidled over to lean against me. I could see the gleam of light on her neck and shoulders, the seductive look in her blue eyes; and the hair that was like raveled hemp brushed against my cheek. "You and I," she said, "are going to be good friends."

"Yes?"

"Yes," she said, "because the girl who went up to see Jed Ringold—the one you were following—was Alta Ashbury."

And then she snuggled up against me affectionately.

"Who," I asked, with a perfectly blank face, "is Alta Ashbury?"

"The woman you were following."

I shook my head, and said, "My business was with Ringold."

She twisted around so that she could keep looking at my face. Then she said slowly, "Well, it doesn't make any difference in one way. It's information that I can't use myself—directly. I'd rather work with you than with anyone else I know," and then added with a little laugh, "because I can keep *you* straight."

"That isn't telling me who Alta Ashbury is. Was she his woman?"

I could see the blonde thinking things over, trying to decide how much to tell me.

"Was she?" I insisted.

She tried a counteroffensive. "What did *you* want with Ringold?"

"I wanted to see him on a business matter."

"What?"

"Somebody had told me that he could tell me how to beat the Blue Sky Act. I'm a promoter. I had something I wanted to promote."

"So you went in to see him?"

"Not me. I got the adjoining room."

"And bored a hole in the door?"

"Yes."

"And looked and listened?"

"Yes."

"What did you see?"

I shook my head.

She got mad then. "Listen," she said, "you're either the damnedest fool I've ever seen, or the coolest. How did you know I couldn't call the cops when you didn't slip me that two hundred under the table?"

"I didn't."

"You'd better get along with me. Do you know what'd happen if I took down that telephone receiver and called the cops? For God's sake, be your age and snap out of it."

I tried to blow a smoke ring.

She got to her feet and started toward the telephone. Her lips were clamped tightly, and her eyes were full of fire.

"Go ahead and call them," I said. "I was getting ready to call them myself."

"Yes, you were."

I said, "Of course, I was. Don't you get the sketch?"

"What do you mean?"

"I was sitting in that adjoining room with my eye glued to the hole in the door," I said. "The murderer had picked the lock about half an hour before I went in. He'd pried the molding loose, fixed the lock, gone back into the room, put the molding back into place, waited for a propitious moment, then unlocked the door, stepped into the little alcove, and went into the bathroom."

"That's what you say."

"You forget one thing, sister."

"What's that?"

"*I* saw the murderer. I'm the only one who did. I *know* who it was—Ringold had a talk with the girl. He gave her some papers. She gave him a check. He put it in his right-hand coat pocket. After she went out, he started for the bathroom. I didn't know this other person was in the bathroom, but I'd found the communicating door was unlocked on my side, and I'd locked it when I bored the hole. The murderer knew Ringold was going to come to the bathroom, and tried to slip back into four-twenty-one. The door was locked. I was in there. The person on the other side of the door was trapped."

"What did *you* do?" she asked, barely breathing.

"I was a damned fool," I said. "I should have taken up the telephone, called the lobby, and told them to block the exit, and telephone for the cops. I was rattled. I didn't think of it. I twisted the bolt on the communicating door and jerked it open. I followed the murderer out as far as the corridor. I stood in the doorway and looked up and down the corridor. Then I went over to the elevator and got off at the second floor When the squawk started, I went out."

"A sweet story," she said, and then after a moment's thought added, "By God, it *is* a sweet story—But you'll never make the cops believe it."

I smiled patronizingly at her. "You forget," I said, "that *I saw the murderer.*"

Her reaction was as fast as though someone had shot an electric current into the seat of the chair. "Who was it?" she asked.

I laughed at her and blew another smoke ring. Or tried to.

She crossed the room and sat down. She crossed her knees, held the left knee in interlaced fingers. The thing didn't make sense to her, and she didn't know what to do about it. She'd look at me, then down at the toe of her shoe. The skirt of her evening gown got in her way. She started to pull it up, then got up, walked into the bedroom, and took it off. She didn't close the bedroom door. After a minute or two she came out wearing a black velveteen housecoat. She came over again and sat down beside me. "Well," she said. "I don't know as it changes the situation a hell of a lot. I need someone to handle the Ashbury angle. You look like a good guy. I don't know what there is about you that makes me trust you—sight unseen, so to speak. Who are you, anyway? What's your name?"

I shook my head.

"Listen, you, you're not going to get out of here until you give me your name, and I mean *your name*. I'm going to see your driving license, your identification cards, take your fingerprints—or I'm going over to your apartment, find out where you live, and all about you. So get that straight."

I pointed to the door. "When I get damn good and ready, I'm going to walk right out of that door."

"I'll rat on you."

"And where will that leave you with your swell shakedown with Alta Ashurst?"

"Ashbury," she said.

"All right, have it your own way."

She said, "What's your real moniker?"

"John Smith."

"You're a liar."

I laughed.

She tried a little wheedling. "All right, John." She twisted around, drew up her knees, and slid over across my lap so she was lying on one elbow, looking alluringly up into my face.

"Listen, John, you've got sense. You and I could team up and make something out of this."

I didn't look at her eyes. The color of her hair kept fascinating me.

"Are you in or not?"

"If it's blackmail, I'm out. That's out of my line."

"Phooey," she said. "I'm going to let you in on the ground floor. Then you and I are going to make some dough."

"Just what have you got on Alta Ashbury?"

When she opened her mouth, I suddenly put my hand over it. "No, don't tell me. I don't want to know."

She stared at me. "What's eating you?"

"I'm on the other side of the fence," I said.

"What do you mean?"

"Listen, sweetheart, I can't do it. I'm not that much of a heel. You're not kidding me a damn bit. You were in on the whole play. Jed Ringold got those checks from Alta Ashbury. He turned them over to you to take up here to the Atlee Amusement Corporation. You gave the boys here a slice, had a little stick to your fingers, turned the rest of it back to Ringold, and Ringold passed it on to the higher ups—or the lower downs whichever you want to call them.

"Now, I'm going to tell-you something. You're done, finished, all washed up. Make a move against Alta Ashbury, and you'll be on the inside looking out."

She straightened up and sat looking at me. "Well, of all the damn nuts," she said.

"All right, sister, I've told you."

"You sure as hell have—you big boob."

I said, "I'll have another one of your cigarettes if you don't mind."

She gave me the cigarette case and said, "Well, strike me down. If that ain't something—I guess I'm going nuts. I see you go into a hotel, the cops start looking for you, I run into you, I ditch a date, bring you up here, and spill my guts to you without finding out who the hell you are or anything about it. I suppose you're a private dick working for Alta Ashbury— No, you'd be more apt to be hired by the old man."

I lit the cigarette.

"But what's the idea of being such a dope? Why didn't you let me go ahead turning myself inside out, pretend you were going to work with me, pump me for information, and then throw the hooks into me?"

I looked at her and said, "Kid, I'll be damned if I know," and it was the truth.

She said, "You could still be the one who bumped Jed Ringold."

"I could be."

"I could put you in a spot on that."

"Think so?"

"I know so."

I said, "There's the telephone."

Her eyes narrowed. She said, "And then you could drag

me into it, show perhaps that my motives weren't so pure, and— Oh, hell, what's the use?"

"What do we do next?" I asked.

"We have a damn good stiff drink. When I think of what you could have done to me and didn't— Dammit, I just can't figure you. You aren't dumb. You're smarter than greased chain lightning. You figured the play and called the signals, and then when I was rushing into the trap, you turned me back. Well, we live and learn. What do you want in your Scotch? Soda or water?"

"Got any Scotch?" I asked.

"Some."

I said, "I've got an expense account."

"Well now, ain't *that* something!"

"Got a dealer who can deliver this hour of the night?"

"I'll say I have."

"All right," I said, "call him. Tell him to send up half a case of Scotch."

"Listen, you aren't kidding me?"

I shook my head, opened my wallet, pulled out a fifty-dollar bill, and casually tossed it over to the table. "That's what my boss would call squandering money."

She ordered the Scotch, hung up the phone, and said, "May as well drink up mine while we're waiting for that to come."

She poured out stiff drinks. There was soda in the icebox.

She said, "Don't let me get drunk, John."

"Why not?"

"I'll get on a crying jag. It's been a long time since anyone gave me a fair break. What makes me sore is that you didn't give it to me because I'm me, but because you're you. You're just made goofy. There's something about you that can't— Kiss me."

I kissed her.

"To hell with that stuff," she said. "Really kiss me."

Fifteen minutes later, the kid came up with the half case of Scotch.

I showed up at Ashbury's place about two o'clock in

the morning. I still couldn't get that girl's hair out of my mind. I thought of that strand of the hangman's rope every time I thought of the way the light glinted along those blond tresses.

CHAPTER SEVEN

AT BREAKFAST I asked Mr. Ashbury what he knew about Amalgamated Smelters Mines and Minerals. I said I had a friend—a man by the name of Fischler who had an office in the Commons Building and had inherited a wad of dough. He wanted something to put it in and was the type that liked to gamble. I'd suggested a good mining stock.

Bob spoke up and said, "Why not keep it all in the family?"

I looked at him in surprise. "It's an idea at that."

"What's his address?"

"Six-twenty-two Commons Building."

"I'll have a salesman call on him."

"Do," I said.

Ashbury asked Bob if he'd heard anything more from the police about what they were doing on the Ringold murder. Bob said the police had checked up on Ringold, had come to the conclusion that it was a gambling kill, and were checking back on Ringold's associates, hoping to find someone who would answer the description of the man who had been seen leaving Ringold's room after the murder.

After breakfast Bob got me off to one side and asked me some more about Fischler, wanted to know about how much money he was going to inherit, and about how much I thought he wanted to invest. I told him he was getting two inheritances. He'd already received some small amount, but would get over a hundred thousand before the end of the month. I asked Bob how his company was coming along, and he said, "Fine. Things look better and better every day."

He dusted out, and Ashbury looked at me over the tops of his glasses as though he were getting ready to say something; then he checked himself, cleared his throat a couple of times, and finally said, "Donald, if you need a few thousand more for expenses, don't hesitate to ask for it."

"I won't," I said.

Alta showed up in a housecoat and made signals that she wanted to see me. I pretended not to notice and told Ashbury that I'd go out as far as the garage with him.

Once out in the garage I told him I didn't want to talk, which relieved him a lot, but did want to ride uptown with him.

He kept his eyes on the road and his mouth shut. I could see there were lots of things he wanted to ask—but he couldn't think of a single question to which he wasn't afraid to hear the answer. Twice he thought of something he wanted to say, sucked in a quick breath, hesitated with the first word trembling on his lips, exhaled, and settled down to driving the crate.

It wasn't until we were in the business district that he managed to get a question he thought was safe. He said, "Where can I drop you, Donald?"

"Oh, any place along here."

He started to say something else, changed his mind, turned to the right, went a couple of blocks out of his way, and pulled up in front of the Commons Building. "How will this do?" he asked.

"This," I said, "will be just swell," and got out.

Ashbury drove away in a hurry, and I went up to the sixth floor, and took a look at the sign on six-twenty-two. It looked all right. I opened the door and went in. Elsie Brand was hammering away on the typewriter.

I said, "For God's sake, you're just a front here. You don't need to pretend there's that much business going on."

She quit typing and looked up at me.

"The people who are coming in," I said, "think that I'm a chap who inherited money. They don't think I made it out of the business, so you don't have to spread it on that thick."

She said, "Bertha Cool gave me a lot of letters to write, told me I could take them up here, and do the work—"

"On what stationery?" I interrupted, and leaned over

her shoulder to take a look at the letter that was in the typewriter.

"On her stationery," she said. "She told me I could—"

I ripped the letter out of the typewriter, handed it to Elsie, and said, "Put it in the drawer. Keep it out of sight. Keep all of that stationery out of sight. When you go out to lunch, take the damn stuff out of the office and keep it out. Tell Bertha Cool I said so."

Elsie looked up at me with the twinkle of a smile. She said, "I can remember when you first came to work."

"What about it?"

"I figured you'd last just about forty-eight hours. I thought Bertha Cool would ride you to death. That's why all of her other detectives walked out on her. And now, you're the one who's giving orders."

"I'm going to make this order stick," I said.

"I know you are. That's what makes it so interesting. You don't stand up and argue with Bertha. You don't knuckle under to her. You just go ahead in your own sweet way, and the first thing anyone knows Bertha is muttering and grumbling, but tagging along after you and doing just what you tell her to."

"Bertha's all right when you get to understand her."

"You mean when she gets to understand you. Trying to get friendly with her is like playing tag with a steam roller—the first thing you know, you're flattened out."

"Are you," I asked, "all flattened out?"

She looked at me and said, "Yes."

"You don't seem like it."

She said, "I have one system with Bertha. I do all the work she hands me. When I've finished, I leave the office. I don't try to be friendly with her. I don't want her to be friendly with me. I'm just as much a part of this typewriter as the keyboard. I'm a machine—and I try to be a good one."

"What's all that correspondence you keep hammering away at?" I asked.

"Letters she sends out to lawyers from time to time soliciting business, and correspondence dealing with her investments."

"Many investments?"

"Lots of them. She goes to two extremes. Most of the time she's wanting something that's as safe as a government bond, but paying about twice as much interest. Then there's another side to her—the plunger. She's a great gambler."

I said, "Well, the way this office is going to be run you're not to be overburdened with work. Go down to the news-stand in the lobby, pick up a couple of motion picture magazines, and a chew of gum. Put a magazine in the top drawer of your desk. Open the drawer, and sit there chewing gum and reading the magazine. When anyone comes in, close the drawer; but not until after they've seen what you're doing."

She said, "I've always wanted a job like that. Other girls seem to get them. I've never been able to."

"This'll probably not last longer than a couple of days, but it's the sort of job you're going to have."

"Bertha will switch. She'll get you some girl from an employment office and take me back to the mill."

"I won't let her. I'll tell her that I need someone I can trust. She can get lots of girls to do typing— It might be a good idea to let her see just how hard it is to fill your place."

She looked up at me for a minute and said, "Donald, I've often wondered why it is you get people boosting for you. I guess perhaps it's because you're so darn considerate. You—" She quit talking all at once, pushed back her chair, rushed across the office and out the door as though she'd been going to a fire.

I went on into the private office, closed the door, tilted back in a swivel chair, and put my heels up on the top of a desk that had seen lots of hard usage.

After I heard Elsie Brand return to the outer office I picked up the telephone and pushed the button that connected me with her desk.

"Yes?" she asked.

"Make a note of three names, Elsie. They're Parker

Stold, Bernard Carter, and Robert Tindle. Got them?"

"Yes. What about them?"

"If any one of those people comes in, I'm busy, and I'm going to be busy all morning. I can't see them and I don't want them to wait. Understand?"

"Yes."

"If anyone else comes in, try and find out what he wants. Have him sit down and wait. Get him to give you a card if possible. Bring the card in to me."

"That all?"

"Yes."

"Okay," she said, and I heard her telephone click.

I had a lot of thinking to do, and I sat there in the chair, smoking and thinking, trying to figure things out so they made sense. I wasn't trying to solve the whole puzzle because I knew I didn't have enough facts, but I was getting facts. I felt that if I could keep my head and not make any false steps, things would open up.

About eleven I heard the door of the outer office open and close, and the sound of voices. Elsie came in with a card. The card had a man's name on it, nothing more.

I studied the card. "Gilbert Rich, eh? What does he look like?"

"High pressure," she said. "Salesman of some kind. Won't tell me what. I asked him what he wanted to see you about, and he said a sales proposition. He's forty, and he dresses for twenty-seven. He isn't exactly what *you'd* call well dressed. What *he'd* call a 'nifty dresser.' "

"Fat?"

"No, fairly slender, getting bald on each side of his forehead. Dark hair slicked back. Black eyes, no glasses. Quick, nervous, glib. His nails are well manicured and polished. He's had a fresh shoeshine this morning, and smells like a barbershop. Do you want to see him?"

"Yes."

She went out, and Gilbert Rich came in. He crossed the office with quick steps to grab my hand. His manner was nervous and magnetic. He started talking as though he'd been accustomed to try and get in as many words as possible before he got thrown out.

"Doubtless, Mr. Fischler, you'll wonder about the nature of my business. When I told your secretary it was a sales proposition, perhaps you thought that it was something I had that I wanted you to handle. As a matter of fact, it's exactly the other way around. I want to make you a lot of money, Mr. Fischler. In order to do that, I'm going to require three minutes of your time."

He jerked a watch out of his pocket and placed it on my desk in front of me.

"Kindly notice the time, Mr. Fischler. Keep your eyes right on that watch. As soon as my three minutes are up, tell me. That's all I want, three minutes of your time, and in return I'll guarantee they'll be the most profitable three minutes you've spent in the last ten years."

"Go ahead," I said. "You've got three minutes."

"Mr. Fischler, have you ever paused to think of the marvels of modern science? Don't bother to answer, because I can see that you have. You realize, Mr. Fischler, that things we regard as everyday occurrences today are things which were scientific impossibilities a few years ago.

"Now then, Mr. Fischler, in order to show you how *you* are going to make money out of modern scientific developments, it's necessary for me to turn back a page in the history of our great and glorious state. We'll turn back, not to the days of forty-nine, but to the days which followed it, days when the state was a swarming horde of gold seekers. Men were grubbing with pick and shovel, with rockers and gold pans, taking gold out of the earth, and there was a vast amount of gold taken out, Mr. Fischler. It poured back to the money centers of the East in a steady golden stream. But there was lots of gold left.

"Up in the country around Valleydale there was a rich placer deposit. The river came roaring out of the mountain carrying gold, depositing it in a vast alluvial plane over the broad agricultural valley which opened out to receive the smiling waters of a river suddenly grown placid. Men, naked to the waist, toiled through the winter rains, through the broiling summer suns, grubbing out gold, and always more gold. Then, as the richer alluvial deposits were exhausted, they moved on down, tracing the course of the river through the geological ages, finding the top soil rich for agricultural purposes, but the gold values collected on bedrock where they had settled— And then just when they were on the verge of reaping their richest harvest, they encountered the problem of surface water. They could dig down to twenty-five feet before encountering water. They got gold almost from the grass roots, but they couldn't get down to the rich deposits on bedrock. Bedrock at that point lay in a uniform bench at about forty-two feet below the surface.

"But I won't detain you with sketching the details of that picture, Mr. Fischler. Doubtless, you're familiar with it from having seen the various historical films which are masterpieces of cinematic art. We will hurry on to the edge of modern inventions. A man of vision conceived the idea of using the water, not as an enemy, but as an aid. He built a big barge, and on that he placed the machinery necessary to dredge. An endless chain of steel buckets dipped far below the surface of the water to scrape the values up from bedrock. The agricultural land was ruined, but in its place the owner received a vast royalty on the gold extracted. The entire topography of the country changed. Because of the peculiar process used in gold dredging, the silt and soil was discharged on the bottom, the rocks and boulders on the top. As a result, the rich agricultural valley became a heap of sun-bleached tailing piles.

"Years passed. The gold dredgers completed chewing up all of the profitable ground, and, as they demolished the last acre, they found themselves trapped in a rocky waste of their own fashioning. There was no further use for them. They were too bulky to dismantle and move, and, even so, there was no place for them to go. They fell into ruins as grim as the ruins of the fair land which they themselves had devastated. The barges began to leak, careened over to one side. The machinery rusted. That which could be profitably transported for junk was sold. The rest became a rusted monument to the greed of man.

"Even the dredgers had not been able to get to bedrock on all the land. In places they had been forced to leave fifteen to twenty feet of the richest pay soil on top of bedrock.

"Now then, Mr. Fischler, we come to a great dream, a golden dream, a dream which is coming true. Modern engineering has devised a means by which the land can be redredged and the boulders placed on the bottom, the silt put back on the top, so that once more the land will be fair and fertile. This has long been known. The Chamber of Commerce of Valleydale had even thought of redredging the land with modern equipment simply for the purpose of restoring it to agricultural productivity, but the process would have been too expensive. What the Chamber of Commerce didn't realize was that there was still a vast fortune of gold lying on top of bedrock waiting for the proper person to—"

"You've used up your three minutes," I said.

He looked at me, then at the watch, and said, "So I have. Well, I'm all finished, Mr. Fischler. With an ordinary man, I would have to show him the similarity between the situation which confronts the investor today and that which confronted the original operators of the gold dredge. The gold has been there for years. As engineering skill has developed, the ingenuity of man, coping with nature, has rolled over the valley in successive waves, each wave carrying on its crest a new generation of millionaires, sweeping them into power. The history of San Francisco is—"

"Your three minutes was up thirty seconds ago."

"Exactly," he said. "I was going to say that with an ordinary man, I would have to point this out, but you, Mr. Fischler, a man who is himself familiar with sales technique and therefore able to grasp business possibilities at a swift glance, can see at once the possibilities of the situation.

"The only question, Mr. Fischler, is whether this crop of new millionaires which are going to be swept into wealth and power is going to have emblazoned on its scroll the name of Charles E. Fischler."

I twisted a lead pencil between my fingers and tried to avoid his eyes. He kept moving around so that he could make me look at him, making forceful gestures, tapping the desk with his forefinger. "I won't argue with you, Mr. Fischler. You are a man of discernment. You are a man of quick, accurate judgment, otherwise you would not have made such a success with your business. You can appreciate the enormous possibilities which are offered. Not only do we make a profit from dredging the land, but when the dredging activities are finished, we have restored once more an agricultural land bathed in sunlight, covered with orchards and vineyards, ready for subdivision, while people, hungry for land which can be subdivided into acres of independence, throng eagerly to the tract offices, and lay down the purchase price.

"And in the meantime, Mr. Fischler, I have not called to your attention the most significant point of all because I know that you do not need to have that pointed out. I know that you have been watching me as I made these points and saying to yourself, 'When is he going to mention the fact that the price of gold today is virtually double that which it was when all of these fortunes were made? When is he going to mention the fact that one who has his money invested in virgin gold need have no fear of inflation? When is he going to mention the fact that gold-bearing properties are the one investment which a man can make, and then regard with equanimity a long succession of unbalanced budgets? When is he—' "

"Your three minutes are up," I said.

"I understand, Mr. Fischler. I have perhaps trespassed upon your time and your good nature, but so great is my anxiety to see that you yourself—"

"How much," I asked cautiously, "is it going to cost?"

"That is entirely up to you, Mr. Fischler. If you wish to make a hundred thousand dollars, your investment can be relatively small. If you will be content with five hundred thousand, you can make a moderate investment. If you wish to be swept on into power as a multi-millionaire, it will cost you more."

"How much," I asked, "to be a multi-millionaire?"

"Five thousand bucks," he said without batting an eye.

"How do you figure it?"

"Well, to begin with, there are these vast acres."

"Never mind going over that again," I said. "Let's get down to brass tacks."

"What do you want to know?"

"What are your shares of stock worth?"

"One hundred and fifty-seven times what we are asking for them," he said.

"Into what units is your stock divided?"

He jerked a billfold from his pocket, tapped the desk with it impressively. "Mr. Fischler, when the Foreclosed Farms Underwriters Company was established, it was an agricultural enterprise launched in the midst of a vast business depression which had for its primary object the redemption of lands which had been foreclosed in mortgage sale. Therefore, the corporation had a low capitalized stock valuation. Now that this vast new enterprise has developed, the logical thing to do would be to increase our stock capital by one thousand per cent. In other words, a share of stock which had a previous par value of one dollar should be split up into one thousand shares of stock, each of one dollar valuation. It would be readily possible to do this, but in order to accomplish it, there would be legal difficulties, a lot of red tape, incidental delays, and the making of profit for our stockholders would be delayed just that much.

"It is the policy of our directors—young vigorous men, broad-minded, aggressive, and determined—to cut away all of this red tape, to rush into production in order that our stockholders can start enjoying their profits almost immediately."

"How much would I get for five hundred dollars?"

"You would get one share of stock. The par value would be one dollar. The actual value right today would in all probability be five thousand dollars. Within sixty days, you can doubtless sell it for ten thousand five hundred dollars. At the end of a year, that stock will be worth one hundred thousand dollars."

I squinted my eyes thoughtfully. He knew then the time had come to close, and, good salesman that he was, he withdrew discreetly to the background so that I could let the details soak in.

"I haven't much money now," I said. "In about thirty days, I expect to have a lot more money."

"In thirty days," he said, "the stock will, of course, have increased in value, but it will still be a marvelous investment."

"Look here," I said, "could I buy five hundred dollars' worth of stock, and then get an option on a larger block of stock by paying another five hundred dollars?"

"I'd have to take it up with the main office," he said. "That's rather unusual. You can see what that would mean, Mr. Fischler. If you tied up a block of stock for only five hundred dollars, you could sell out within a week for a respectable profit. Inside of thirty days, you could probably realize twenty thousand dollars for your five-hundred-dollar option."

"That's the way I want to do it," I said.

"But have you considered the possibility of going to a bank, Mr. Fischler, and—"

"I've made my proposition," I said.

"I understand. But, Mr. Fischler, the situation is this. Our board of directors have to be scrupulously fair. They have other investors to consider. Many persons have bought—"

"You heard my proposition," I said. "You've used up your time allowance. I'm familiar with what you have to offer. I don't want to waste time in argument."

"How big a block of stock would you want to tie up in that option?"

"In thirty days," I said, "I'm going to have a hundred thousand dollars to invest. I'm not going to put all of my eggs in one basket. Fifty thousand dollars is the limit I'll put in your company. I'll put up five hundred dollars now to show my good faith, and I want you to tie up a block of stock which, selling at present prices, will be what I can buy for fifty thousand dollars."

"I'll see what I can do, but would it be possible for you to consider—"

"No," I interrupted, and got up out of my chair. "I'm a busy man, Mr. Rich."

"I understand, but please remember that I am here offering you a sincere service. The minutes which you have so generously given me will bear you golden dividends out of all proportion—"

"You have my proposition. The quicker you get it to your board of directors, the quicker you can give me an answer."

I walked over and held the door open.

He looked at me curiously for a minute, then shot out his hand. "Mr. Fischler," he said, "permit me to congratulate you on having made one of the most momentous decisions of your entire business career—and also upon having put across the shrewdest, most farsighted financial deal of any prospect upon whom I have called. I'll give you a ring this afternoon."

I stood in the door and watched him cross the outer office and leave through the entrance door.

Elsie Brand looked up. "Gosh, what a line," she said. "Could you hear it?"

"Not the words, but you could hear his voice pouring out through the cracks around the office door."

I said, "Get me Henry C. Ashbury on the line. You'll find him listed in the telephone book. Don't try his residence. Get his office."

I went back and sat down at the desk. Ashbury came on the phone in about thirty seconds, and I said, "Hello, Ashbury. You know who this is talking?"

"No." His voice was close-clipped and decisive as though he didn't like riddles over the telephone, and was ready to hang up.

"Your physical instructor."

"Oh, yes." His voice changed.

"Would it inconvenience you," I asked, "if your stepson

went to jail for crooked promotion?"

"If my— Good God, Donald, what are you talking about?"

"About whether it would inconvenience you if your stepson went to jail for crooked promotion."

"It would be disastrous. It would be—"

"Is it possible," I asked, "that you have watched him being promoted to the position of president, without realizing that he was simply being pushed out in front?"

"Good God!"

I hung up the telephone.

I paused in the outer office long enough to say to Elsie Brand, "I'm going over to Bertha Cool's office and tell her she'll have to get another secretary."

She smiled. "Bertha will have kittens."

"That's fine. In about an hour Mr. Rich will call to tell me that he's managed to get my proposition through for immediate action, but that he can't hold it open longer than two or three o'clock this afternoon, that I'll have to get the money and have it ready in the office, and he'll be here with contracts to sign. Make an appointment for whatever time he says, and call me at Bertha Cool's office to let me know."

"Anything else?" she asked.

"If a Mr. Ashbury should call or come in, tell him Mr. Fischler is busy and you don't know just when he'll be back."

CHAPTER EIGHT

I'D BECOME SO ACCUSTOMED to hearing the rapid fire of Elsie Brand's typewriter when I opened the door of the agency office that the ragged tempo of *click—clack-clack—clack—click—clack-clack* sounded strange to me as I walked down the corridor, and made me pause to convince myself that I had the right office.

I pushed open the door.

A rather good-looking girl sat over at Elsie Brand's desk with her arms wrapped around the typewriter, digging away at the paper with a circular rubber eraser.

She looked up with a perfectly blank face.

I jerked my thumb toward the inner office. "Anybody in there?"

"Yes." She reached for the telephone.

I said, "Never mind. I'll wait."

"Won't you give me your name?"

"It isn't necessary."

I walked over to the corner, sat down, and picked up a newspaper. I turned to the sporting section and lit a cigarette as I settled down to reading.

The girl finished her erasure and started at the keyboard again. From time to time she'd look at me. I didn't look up to meet her eyes, but didn't need to. She had a habit of stopping the typing whenever she looked across at me.

I could hear voices in Bertha Cool's office, just a few stray bits of conversation without being able to distinguish words.

After a while the door opened, and a man came out. I had the paper up in front of my face at the time, but I could look under the edges of the paper and see his legs from the knees down, and his feet.

There's an old exploded theory that detectives wear big square-toed shoes. At one time they may have done it, but the good detectives quit it long before the public ever knew anything about it.

This man had lightweight tan shoes and well-creased trousers, but there was something about the way he handled his feet that made me keep the paper up. He started to walk out, then suddenly paused, turned around, and said something to Bertha Cool. The toes of his shoes were pointing directly at me. I held the paper up, and he kept on standing there.

I put down the paper, looked up with a blank look, and said, "Mrs. Cool?"

She took a quick breath.

The man was about forty-five, tall, and fairly broad across the shoulders. He seemed a quiet, reserved chap, but there was something in his eyes I didn't like, although I didn't look at them.

Bertha said, "What do *you* want? Don't tell me you're selling anything. I've subscribed to all the magazines and made all the donations I'm going to."

I smiled and said, "Whenever you're at liberty," and returned to my paper.

The man said, "Good morning, Mrs. Cool," and walked across the office. Bertha Cool stood there until the outer office had clicked shut, then she jerked her thumb, motioning me into the office.

I followed her in and closed the door. She lit a cigarette. Her hand was trembling. "My God, Donald," she said, "how did you know?"

"What?"

"That he was a detective looking for you?"

"Something in the way his shoes were pointed toward me," I said. "He acted like a bird dog."

"Well, God knows it was a lucky hunch," she said, "but it isn't going to do you any good."

"What does he want me for?"

"You should know."

"What did he say?"

"Said that he was making a routine checkup on some people he wanted to interview in connection with that murder. He wanted to know if I had a man working for me named Lam, and asked if he was doing some work for a Mr. Ashbury."

"What did you tell him?"

"I told him that I wasn't at liberty to make any statements about what my employees were doing. That was up to Mr. Ashbury."

"They're wise," I said. "They're after Alta on another matter, and they've found out I'm out at the place."

She said, "They've found out you answer the description of the man they want in connection with that Ringold murder."

"Probably."

"Well, what are we going to do?"

I said, "I'm going to duck out for a while."

"Are you making any headway on the case?"

"Some."

She said, "Donald, you get me into more damn trouble. During the time you've been with me I've got in hot water on every case I've tackled."

"You're making ten times as much money, too," I pointed out.

"Well, what of it? You're too wild. You take too many chances. Money isn't any good in jail."

"Is it my fault that a man chooses the particular moment I'm working on a case to bump someone off?"

She couldn't think of any answer to that so didn't make any. She looked at me with hard, glittering eyes and said, "I telephoned Elsie to find out how the work was getting on, and she said you'd told her to stop it."

"That's right."

Her face flushed. "I'm running this office."

"And I'm running Fischler's office. What's the use of going to all the trouble making a plant if a man comes in the door and sees a secretary writing letters on the stationery of B. Cool—Confidential Investigations?"

"Well, I can't have her sitting over there twiddling her thumbs, doing nothing. I'm paying her a salary. I have work that has to go out."

"Get another girl," I said, "and charge it to expenses."

"Expenses nothing. I'm going to trade with you. You take *this* girl over there, and I'll have Elsie come back here."

"Okay, if you say so."

"Well, I say so."

"You're the boss."

She waited for me to argue, and I didn't argue.

"Well, what's wrong with it?" she demanded.

"Nothing, if you want it done that way. Of course, the way things are shaping up now, it might make it a little involved if this girl should go home and talk to her mother, or her boy friend about how she'd been switched."

"I'll fire her and get another. This one's no good anyway."

I said, "All right, be sure you get one who doesn't have a sweetheart or a family."

"Why?"

"Because girls talk when they go home. That office over there in the Commons Building— Well, you know how it is. I can't turn out any work. It's just a plant. A girl with any sense would know it's a plant."

Bertha took a deep drag at her cigarette. "Well, things can't go on this way."

"That's right."

"Donald, they're going to get you. They'll drag you over to that hotel. The people will identify you, and you'll be in jail— And don't think your salary goes on while you're in jail."

I said, "I'm going to spend a thousand dollars of expense money this afternoon."

"A *thousand* dollars!"

"That's right."

Bertha Cool tried the cash drawer to make sure it was locked. It was. "Well, you've got another think coming," she snapped.

I said, "I've spent it already."

"You've done what?"

"Spent it already."

She blinked her eyelids once, then stared steadily.

"Where'd you get it?"

"Ashbury."

"So you went to him direct after getting all that money from me."

"No. He came to me."

"How much did you get?"

I waved a hand in an airy gesture. "There's no limit. He told me whenever I needed a few thousand to call on him."

She said, "*I'm* making the business arrangements for this agency."

"Go ahead and make them, only see that my style isn't cramped."

She leaned over and toward me, getting as close to her desk as her figure would permit. "Donald," she said, "you take in too damn much territory. *I'm* running this business."

"No question about that."

"Well, when I—"

There were hurried steps across the office. I could hear the bleat of the new substitute secretary as she tried to stem the human avalanche which dashed across the office and wrestled with the doorknob. The door jerked open, and Henry Ashbury came puffing in. "There you are," he said to me. "What were you trying to do, give me heart failure?"

"Simply telling you the truth," I said.

"Well, you and I are going to talk things over. Come on. Let's get out of here."

Bertha Cool said with dignity, "In the future, Mr. Ashbury, you'll get reports from me. Donald is going to submit regular typewritten reports. I'll get the information and pass it on to you. This agency has been getting too damned irregular."

Ashbury turned to her and said, "What are you talking about?"

"Your arrangements are with me. In the future kindly make *all* arrangements through me. I'll give you the information."

He looked at her over the top of his glasses. His voice was low, well modulated, and exceedingly polite. "I take it," he said, "that I've been getting a little out of hand."

"Donald has."

"About the expense money perhaps?"

"That's part of it."

Ashbury said, "Come with me, Donald. You and I are going to have a talk."

Bertha Cool said acidly, "Don't mind me. I'm just his employer."

Ashbury looked at her. He said quietly, "My principal concern is for myself, and I happen to be the one who's paying *all* the bills."

That had Bertha falling all over herself. She said, "Why certainly, Mr. Ashbury. We're representing your interests. The thing we want the most is to do what you want."

Ashbury took my arm. "All right," he said. "Come on."

"Where are we going?"

"Downstairs in my car."

"It might be a good plan to travel," Bertha Cool said to me.

"I've thought of that. Where's the agency car?"

"In the garage."

"See you later," I said.

"When can I have Elsie back?"

"I don't know."

Bertha Cool struggled with her temper, and Ashbury took my arm, led me across the office, and down to a parking station where he'd left his big sedan. "All right," he said, "we talk here."

He slid in behind the steering wheel. I sat beside him. "What's all this about Bob?"

I said, "Use your head."

"I am. I should have done it a long time ago, but that possibility never occurred to me."

"What other reason could there have been?"

"I thought it was a frame-up to get my money in the business. I thought Bernard Carter was the real brains behind the thing and was making all the money. I thought

Mrs. Ashbury wanted to get him in on some easy pickings, and they decided the best approach would be through Bob."

I said, "Well, it's a racket. They're pushing Bob out in front. I don't think Bernard Carter has much to do with it."

"Well, he's mixed up in it."

"A shrewder mind than Carter's is back of it, and if Carter's in it, he's probably being played for a sucker—From all I can gather, Carter wouldn't exactly want to have Mrs. Ashbury's son get into trouble on his account."

Ashbury gave a low whistle. "What's the racket?" he asked.

I said, "They bought up some valueless tailings up by Valleydale, and are spreading a line of hooey that they're rich in gold."

"Are they?"

"I don't think so. The dredging company didn't dredge much where they couldn't get down to bedrock."

"That's the idea back of it?"

"That's it."

"What are they doing?"

"Selling stock of a par value of one dollar in a defunct corporation at the modest price of five hundred dollars a share."

"Good God, how can they do that?"

"Shrewd salesmanship, high-pressure, once-over, glib-talking men who work the rush act and dangle a golden bait in front of a man's eyes. They set themselves a limited time for their talk. They stick a watch in front of the sucker. The sucker is always so imbued with the idea of being a busy executive that when it comes time for him to ask questions, he taps his fingers on the dial of the watch and sternly reminds the salesman that he's taken up his allotted share of time."

"That's the way they work the rush act?"

"Yes. The customer really rushes himself."

"It's a swell idea," Ashbury said. "Damned good psychology, when you stop to figure it."

"It seems to be working."

"So the prospect doesn't ask any questions?"

"No. Every time he does, the salesman starts in talking as though he was finishing up the sales argument which the prospect interrupted because he'd run over his appointed time. That makes the prospect mad, and he shuts him off."

"By gosh," Ashbury said, "if Bob thought of that, he's a lot cleverer than I gave him credit for."

"He didn't."

"Who did?"

"I don't know—probably an attorney by the name of Crumweather, who also worked out a scheme for beating the Blue Sky Act."

"Is the scheme legal?"

"Probably not, the way they're working it. That's why Bob's president."

"There's nothing wrong with that method of salesmanship?"

"No. It's damn clever."

Ashbury drew a handkerchief across his forehead. "And to think that I was so damn dumb—so eager to keep out of the boob's business confidences—I didn't see what was happening."

I didn't say anything.

After a while he said, "What are you planning to do, Lam?"

"How badly do you want to keep Bob out of jail?"

"No matter what happens," he said, "we can't have anything like that."

"I thought I'd run up to Valleydale for a day or two."

"Why?"

"That's where they're operating."

"What do you expect to find up there?"

"I might find the records of the old dredging company dealing with a survey of the land they dredged."

"Then what?"

"If I could get them," I said, "and they show what I think they'll show, I'll make a deal with the lawyer—but

I don't think I can get them."

"Why not?"

"The brain that thought up that sales canvass and beating the Blue Sky Act has probably taken care of all that."

"What else will you do?"

"Look the ground over and try and find the crooked part of the scheme."

"And while you're gone, how about—er—this other matter?"

"This other matter," I said, "is getting hot, too hot for me to handle right now without getting my fingers burned. I thought I'd stay away for a day or so and let it cool off."

"I'm not certain I like that. Alta telephoned a little while after you'd left. She said that she thought you were coming back, that you'd just gone to the garage with me. She wants to see you. She's worried— She's— Dammit, Donald, we're all getting so we depend on you."

"That's what I'm hired for."

"I know, but this is different. Alta would be lost if you left."

"Alta has to leave, too."

"What?"

"You heard me."

"You mean go with you?"

"No. Go some place. Visit someone. Spend a few days with some out-of-town friend— And don't let anyone know where she's going."

"Why?"

"Because I don't want anyone asking her questions until I know a few more answers."

"Then why are you going away?"

I said, "Detectives are on my trail right now. They're checking up— Do you want me to tell you what they're after?"

"No."

"All right, then. I'll tell you what I'm going to do, and what you can do."

He thought for a minute, took a cigar from his pocket, clipped the end off, and struck a match. "When are you going?" he asked.

"Now."

"Where can I get in touch with you?"

"It's better that you don't. If anything comes up, get in touch with Bertha Cool."

"But you're going up to Valleydale?"

"Yes."

"You don't know how long you'll be gone?"

"No."

"You'll be going out to the house to pack up some things and—"

"I won't be going anywhere to pack up anything. I'm going over to the garage, get the agency car, and get started. I'll buy what clothes I need."

"You're leaving right away?"

"Just one thing I have to attend to."

"What's that?"

"Winding up Mr. Fischler's business transaction."

"I can drive you up to the Commons Building."

"Let's telephone first," I said. "Wait here. I'll be back."

There was a public phone in the gas station at the parking lot. I called up the number Elsie Brand had given me. She answered the phone. "Hear anything?" I asked.

She said, "You must have thought they didn't want your money."

"Why?"

"You said they'd tell you you had until about two o'clock this afternoon."

"What did they say?"

She said, "The salesman's been here twice. He's coming back in ten minutes. He said to tell you that he could put it across, but the time expired at one."

I said, "Stick around. I'm going to draw up the option agreement."

"He has one with him."

"I don't think I'll like it."

"Do you want me to tell him?"

"No. Just stick around. I'm coming right up."

I walked back to the car and said to Ashbury, "Okay,

drive me up to the Commons Building if you will—or I can take a taxi."

"No. I want to keep my finger on the pulse of things."

Ashbury waited outside while I went up to the office. Rich was waiting for me when I came in. He pumped my hand up and down, and said, "Congratulations, Mr. Fischler! The shrewdest buying brain I've contacted in fifteen years of salesmanship. You win!"

He took my arm and piloted me into the private office as though he owned the joint. He whipped a stock certificate out of his pocket and said, "There you are. One share. Here you are. An option agreement duly signed by the president and secretary of the company."

"You work fast," I said.

"I had to, to put a deal like that across. They hit the ceiling, but I explained to them that your money wasn't available right at the moment, that you were a hundred-per-cent sold, that you'd make us a good stockholder, that you—"

He kept on talking, but I quit listening. I was reading the option agreement. To my surprise, it was exactly what I had instructed him to have. I signed an okay on the duplicate option agreement, gave him one thousand dollars, and put the share of stock and original option agreement in my pocket. The option was signed by Robert Tindle as president and E. E. Matts, secretary. I shook hands with Rich, told him I had an appointment, and eased him out of the office. I said to Elsie, "Remember, you're to keep the office open until I get back."

"Where are you going?"

"I'm out of town on a business trip."

"You explained to Bertha about the work?"

"Yes."

"What did she say?"

"It's all right."

"Then I'm to sit here and just read magazines?"

"That's right. Do a little sewing if you want to. Smoke cigarettes during office hours, and chew gum. That's the sort of business this is, one of those happy-go-lucky affairs."

She laughed. "I'll feel like a kept woman."

"That's what I want you to look like," I said. "Get the idea?"

Her eyes flashed me a smile. She said, "Good luck, Donald."

"Keep your fingers crossed," I said, and went out to tell Ashbury I was all ready to go. He insisted on driving me over to the garage where Bertha Cool kept the office jalopy. His eyes were wistful as I pulled away into traffic.

CHAPTER NINE

VALLEYDALE HAD AT ONE TIME BEEN something about which a Chamber of Commerce could wax eloquent. The mountains, covered with digger pine, chaparral, manzanita, and, lower down, with big live oaks, broke into peaceful rolling hills, then into what had once been a fertile agricultural valley.

Now, it was a mass of rocks, piled in serrated ridges where the conveyor belts of the gold dredgers had dumped them. They were rounded rocks that had been worn by ancient glaciers and rivers. They were the bones of what had at one time been huge boulders, and now they glistened in the sunlight like bleached bones in the desert. Here and there an attempt had been made to level off the ground and plant orchards. On the rolling hillsides which the dredgers hadn't touched, the massive oaks cast dark pools of inviting shadow. The slopes were broken here and there with bits of vineyard and, in places, with the green of orchards. They gave a clue to what the country must have been at one time.

A river, flowing down from the mountains, broke through a cut near the town of Valleydale, spread out into smooth placid waters, and then ran through the ugly piles of rock tailings.

I found an auto court and registered, giving the license of the agency car and the name of Donald Lam. Later on, when it would be necessary to account for every minute of my time to the police, I didn't want to have it appear that I'd taken an alias, or resorted to flight.

I went right to work.

The people who were left in the town hated gold-dredging with a bitter hatred. The ones who had owned the land originally had made their clean-up, taken the cash, and gone to the bigger cities. The dredgers had pumped prosperity into the town through payrolls, machine shops, and offices, then they had worked out the ground. The machine shops had been moved. The offices stood deserted. There was an air of funereal despair about the town. Those who were left went dejectedly about their business, moving with the listless lassitude of persons who have lost their chance at winning big stakes and are plugging away simply because they can't figure out how to quit.

No one knew what had happened to the records of the dredging company. The head offices had always been somewhere else. The books were gone, the machinery was gone, and the employees were gone.

I made inquiries to find whether some of the old employees were still in the country. A man who kept a drygoods store told me he thought an old hermit bachelor named Pete Something-or-Other had worked on the original dredgers and on the drills when the ground was prospected. He didn't know Pete's last name, and didn't know exactly where he lived, but he had a shack about a mile down the river. There was a little strip of land the dredgers hadn't got. Pete lived on it. He came into town once in a while for supplies. He paid cash and wasn't sociable. No one seemed to know exactly how he lived.

I learned that a new company was planning to use some sort of a new invention to put the rocks underneath and bring the soil back on top. Old-timers said that even if the soil were put back on top, it would be years before it could grow anything. Others were of the opinion that scientific fertilization would have it producing crops in no time. None of them tried to marshal facts and reach an intelligent, impartial opinion from those facts. They advanced an opinion first, then selected illustrations, gossip, and garbled rumor to support that opinion. Anything which didn't support it was ignored entirely. I figured there wasn't much chance finding out anything from them.

It was getting dark when I found Pete's shack. It had at one time been the operating house on a gold dredger, with windows all around it. About half of the windows were covered with tin which Pete had flattened out from old five-gallon coal-oil cans and nailed over the openings.

Pete was somewhere in the late sixties. He was big-boned and didn't carry much flesh. There was no sag to him anywhere. His last name was Digger.

"What do you want?" he asked, indicating a homemade bench by a dilapidated stove which had been salvaged from a junk pile. There was a fire going in the stove, and a pot of beans simmering.

"I'm trying to get some of the old history of the place," I said.

"What you want it for?"

"I'm a writer."

"What you writing?"

"A history of gold-dredging."

Pete took the pipestem from his mouth and jerked it over his shoulder in the general direction of Valleydale. "They can tell you all about it."

"They seem rather prejudiced," I said.

Pete chuckled. It was a dry chuckle that was packed with philosophic amusement. "Helluva bunch," he admitted.

I looked around the cabin. "This is a mighty cozy little place."

"Suits me all right."

"How did it happen the dredgers didn't chew it up?"

"They had to leave it to keep the river out of the ground they were working. They intended to swing around and build a levee with tailings so they could come back to it later on. It didn't work out that way."

"How big a strip is it?"

"Oh, maybe half a mile long by a couple of hundred yards wide."

"It's nice-looking country. Was it all like this before the dredgers came?"

"Nope. This was wasteland. It had been worked by hand. The old tailing piles left by the Chinese are still here. They weren't big piles, just four or five feet—There was some pretty good land here before the dredgers started —farther up the valley."

"This strip looks nice to me."

"Uh huh."

"I saw some rabbits on it as I drove in."

"Quite a few rabbits. I get a meal from 'em once in a while." He jerked his head to indicate a rusted twenty-two-caliber rifle which hung on the wall. "She don't look like much outside, but she's smooth as a mirror inside."

"Who owns the land?"

His eyes glittered. "I do."

"Makes it nice," I said. "It's better living this way than in town."

"It is for a fact. The town's dead. This place is all right. How'd you happen to find it?"

"Someone in town told me you were down here and could tell me something about the gold-dredging."

"What do you want to know?"

"Oh, just general facts."

Pete jerked his pipe stem in the general direction of Valleydale again. "Those folks make me sick. I've seen the whole damned business from the start. The land around here was pretty good. In the old horse-and-buggy days it was just a jerkwater country town—then someone started promotin' gold-dredgin'. Most of the inhabitants thought it wouldn't work. They hung crape all over the idea, then when they found it would work, they went hog-wild. Real estate started goin' up, an' kept on goin' up. No one would sell because they thought it was goin' even higher. The Chamber of Commerce got busy. They kowtowed to the dredgin' outfit, turned the whole town over to them. Everybody in town that wanted to work had a job, then the company started importin' men, lots of 'em. The town started boomin'. The merchants jacked prices up for all the traffic would bear. Every once in a while somebody would raise the question about what was goin' to be left when the dredgin' companies got done, and they'd all but tar an' feather him an' ride him out of town on a rail.

"Well, after a while things sort of leveled off. Then the birds that held the real estate thought it would be a good time to unload. The purchasers didn't think so. Dredgers started cutting down on payrolls. There were homes for sale. Even then the Chamber of Commerce didn't face the facts. They tried whistlin' to keep their courage up. They thought a railroad was comin' through. The town would be a big railroad center. They were goin' to put in rock crushers. There was a lot of hooey. Then things started goin' downhill fast. Now, it's like you see it today. Everybody's cussin' the dredgin' company."

"You worked for the dredging company?"

"Uh huh."

"When did you start working?"

"Just about the time they started dredging. I prospected this country."

The fire blazed up a bit. The beans started bubbling until the steam raised the cover on the pot. Pete got up and shoved the beans a few inches to one side.

I said, "I'm very much interested in this."

"A writer you say?"

"Yes. If you wanted to make a few dollars, I could spend an evening with you, picking up some local color, and make it worth your while."

"How much?"

"Five dollars."

"Give me the dough."

I gave him a five-dollar bill.

"Stay for supper?"

"I'd like to."

"Nothin' but beans, hot cakes, and sirup."

"It sounds good to me."

"You ain't a game warden?"

"No."

"Okay, I've got a couple of cold quail. Let's get the eatin' over with an' we can talk later."

"Can I help?"

"Nope. You sit still. Keep out of the way over in that corner."

I watched him get supper and found myself envying him. The place was crude, but it was clean. Everything was shipshape, a place for everything, and nothing hanging around where it shouldn't be. Cupboards had been made out of wooden cases which had originally held two five-gallon oil cans. These boxes had been placed one on top of the other and nailed in strips. Pete found two agate-ware plates, knives, and forks. The sirup, he explained, was homemade, half white sugar and half brown, with a little maple flavor. The hot cakes were big flapjacks cooked in a huge skillet and turned by the simple process of flopping them over. There was no butter. The beans had lots of garlic. The gravy was thick. The quail had been broiled, Pete explained, over wood coals. He said that he killed game, when it was out of season, away from the camp, picked it, cleaned it, buried the skins, entrails, legs, and heads, built a little fire, broiled the game, and carried it in already cooked. He kept it in a place where "no damn snooping game warden would find it."

"Bothered much with them?" I asked.

"There's a guy in town that got himself appointed a deputy," Pete said. "He comes out once in a while and looks the place over." He gave his characteristic chuckle again, and said, "He don't find nothin'."

It was a nice dinner. I wanted Pete to let me help with the dishes, but he had them washed and dried while I was still arguing about it. Everything went back to its place in the boxes. Pete put the coal-oil lamp on the center of the homemade table.

"Like cigarettes?" I asked.

"Nope. Stay with my pipe. It's cheaper. I like it. More satisfaction in it."

I lit a cigarette. Pete lit his pipe. It was a big hod, so thoroughly soaked with nicotine that it filled the place with a heavy odor I could all but taste. It smelled good.

"What do you want to know?" he asked.

"You did prospecting?"

"Yep."

"How did you prospect? I shouldn't think it would be possible, since the values were all under water."

"In those days," he said, "we had a Keystone Drill. It's simple to prospect. You punch down a casing right through to bedrock. You lift the stuff out with a sand pump. Everything that comes out of the sand pump goes into a tub, and you pan that out and save the colors of gold."

"Colors?" I asked.

"Yep. It's gold that's been ground down by the action of rivers and glaciers until it's in little fine flakes about as big around as a pinhead and thin as a piece of paper. Sometimes it'll take a lot of 'em to make even a cent's worth of gold."

"Then you must get pretty much out of each hole you drill."

"Nope. You don't. Those big dredgers could work ground at a profit when there was a value of only ten cents a cubic yard. That's more than a man could have handled in a day by old methods."

"But how could they get an accurate idea of values from that sort of prospecting?"

"Cinch," he said. "The engineers knew down to a cubic inch how much dirt had been inside the casing by the time it was punched down to bedrock. They got the gold from each hole. They weighed it out carefully, and punched down holes every so many feet."

"And they didn't get a great deal of gold from any one hole?"

"Nope, just colors."

I waited a while, then said, as though thinking out loud, "It would seem easy to doctor the results on that kind of a prospect."

He took the pipe from his mouth, looked at me a minute, clamped his lips together in a firm, straight line, and said nothing.

"This the only place you prospected?" I asked.

"Nope. After I got to know the game," he said, "they took me all over the country. I prospected up in the Klondike where the ground was frozen so solid you had to thaw it out with steam pipes before you could get a hole down. I was down in South America prospectin'. I went all over the country—then I came back and worked on dredgers."

"Saved your money?" I asked.

"Not a damn cent."

"But you're not working now?"

"Nope. I get by."

I was silent for a while, and then Pete said, "Don't cost me hardly anything to live. I get most of my stuff from rustling around the country. Get a sack of beans once in a while, and I got a little vegetable patch out here. Buy my smokin' tobacco, a little sugar, an' flour in town. Buy a little bacon an' save the grease for cookin'. You'd be surprised how little it takes for a man to live."

I did a little more thinking and said, "I didn't realize I was going to have an evening in such a comfortable place. There's only one thing lacking."

"What's that?" he asked.

"A good shot of hooch. Suppose we take a run into town and pick up a bottle?"

He didn't say anything for a long time, just kept looking at me. "What kinda hooch do you drink?" he asked.

"Anything, just so it's good."

"How much you generally pay for it?"

"Around four dollars a quart."

He said, "Stick around here a minute. I'll be back."

He got up and walked outside. I could hear his steps as he walked out about twenty feet from the door. Then he stood perfectly still. After that, his steps moved again. It was moonlight outside. Through the windows which weren't covered with tin, I could see the moon casting black shadows beneath the digger pines and oaks. In the background the white piles of tailings caught and reflected the moonlight in a cold glitter that reminded me of the desert.

After a while Pete came back in and sat down. I looked at him for a minute, then took out my wallet, and took out four one-dollar bills.

He handed me back two of the dollar bills. "I only brought a pint," he explained.

He took a bottle from his hip pocket and put it on the table while he got glasses. He poured some in each glass, then put the bottle back in his pocket.

It had a deep-amber color. I tasted it. It wasn't at all bad.

"Good stuff," I said.

"Thanks," Pete said, modestly.

We sat there and drank and smoked. Pete told me stories of old mining camps, of lost mines in the desert, of claim-jumping, of feuds, and interspersed his conversation with comments about the old gold-dredging days.

Over the second glass, with my head feeling a little woozy, I said, "There's some talk about a new dredging company coming in."

Pete chuckled.

"Didn't they miss a lot of bedrock around here?" I asked.

Pete said, "The company I was working for was run by old man Darniell. Anything he missed you could put in your eye."

"But there were some places where they couldn't get down to bedrock?"

"Yep."

"Quite a lot of them?"

"Yep."

"Then why can't they redredge this country?"

"They can."

"And make money?"

Pete pursed his lips. "Maybe."

"And they can turn it back into agricultural land?"

"That's what they claim."

"Why wouldn't it be a good thing?"

"Maybe it would."

"I suppose they've got the old records of the prospecting that you did, know just how deep the old dredgers could go, and know just where to go after the stuff they want."

Pete leaned forward. "Damnedest crudest bunch of salting I ever saw in my life."

"What do you mean?"

"The drilling they're doing."

"They're doing drilling?" I asked.

"Sure. Down here about a mile and a half. My God, but they're crude!"

"What do you mean?"

"Mean!" he said. "Hell, they just dump the gold in the

121

drill pipe and then pan it back out. Every once in a while they come up with a bunch of suckers. The suckers stand gawking over the gold pan. What they don't notice is that the drill man has to keep a hand on the rope in order to steady the bit when it's going up and down. You watch that hand, and every so often you'll see him dip into his pocket with one hand and take the other hand out of his pocket to steady the drill rope. Watch closer than that, and you can see little colors of gold dribbling down every time he does it— Mind you, he's pretty slick at it. He doesn't do it so it shows up too big. He's got it all figured out, and they don't bring up any gold at all until they get below the place where the old dredger worked. But, brother, you take it from me, when they hit bedrock they put it in plenty rich. You can take the figures they're getting from their holes and figure the acreage they've got lined up, and the mint would have to go out of business. They'd have to dig up the whole darn state of Kentucky to find a place to store the gold."

"That must take quite a bit of gold."

"What? To salt the hole?"

"Yes."

He shook his head. "It don't take much. They're damn fools. They're goin' to get caught."

"How many holes have they put down?"

"Three. They're on the fourth. They're just started."

"Know who's back of it?"

"Nope. Some crowd from the southern part of the state. They're sellin' most of their stock around there."

"How does the town feel about it?"

"Oh, they're divided. You'll find croakers and boosters. The minute it begins to look as if they're goin' to start puttin' up a dredger though, you'll see the Chamber of Commerce standing on its head and wiggling its toes— Only they ain't goin' to put in no dredger."

"Why not?"

"Because it would show up their prospects too much. The minute a dredger works that country, it'd show that the ground had been salted. I don't think they intend to spend no money to put up a dredger. They're doin' a lot of talkin', pourin' gold into the ground, and gettin' it back so they can pour it into the next hole. How about fillin' your glass again?"

I said, "No thanks. That stuff has authority."

"It packs a wallop. That's what I made it for."

"Go ahead," I said. "I've got to drive the car back."

"I don't hit it very hard, but I like it when I'm sittin' around talkin' with a friend. You're a good guy—a writer, eh?"

"Uh huh."

"What do you write?"

"Oh, articles about different things."

"You don't know much about mining, huh?"

"Not a damn thing."

"How'd you happen to pick this to write about?"

"I thought it would go over swell—not in a mining journal, but in an agricultural journal."

He looked at me for a while without saying anything, then he tamped the tobacco down into his pipe, and relaxed to the comfort of smoking.

After a while I told him I'd be on my way, that I'd come back later on perhaps and get some more information. I told him I'd pay him five dollars an evening. He said that was fair enough, and shook hands. "Any time you want to come back and visit," he said, "it ain't goin' to cost you no five bucks. I like you. You fit in. It ain't everybody I let sit down and visit. And it ain't one person in a hundred that ever gets to sample any of this stuff." He jerked his head in the direction of the glass on the table.

"I can understand that," I said. "Well, so long."

"So long."

I drove back to the auto court. A big shiny sport coupé was parked in front of the cabin I'd rented. I took my key out of my pocket and opened the door. I heard the sound of motion in an adjoining cabin, and closed my door quickly. Then I heard feet on the graveled walk, light steps on the porch, and a knock on my door.

Well, this was it. I'd done the best I could.

I opened the door.

Alta Ashbury was standing on the threshold. "Hello," she said.

I held the door open for her. "This," I said, "isn't a good place for you to be."

"Why not?"

"Lots of reasons. For one thing, the detectives are looking for me."

"Dad told me."

"For another thing, if they should find us here, the newspapers could make a nice story of it."

"You mean love nest?"

"That's right."

"How thrilling," she said, and then added after a moment, "It'll be all right, in case you're worried."

"I am worried."

"What about, your good name?"

"No, about yours."

She said, "Dad's coming up. He'll reach here about midnight."

"How's he coming?"

"Plane."

"How did you know I was in this court?"

"I covered them all until I found you. There are only four, you know. I hit this second."

"Why is your dad coming up?"

"Oh, things are getting hot."

"What are the new developments?"

"Mr. Crumweather called me on the telephone and asked me to meet him at his office tomorrow afternoon at two o'clock."

"Don't go."

"Why not?"

"I think he has the missing letters. I think he's getting ready to twist the screws."

"You mean that he had them all?"

"Yes."

"You don't believe this about the detectives selling out the district attorney?"

I shook my head and said, "Take a load off your feet. You're here now, so you may as well enjoy yourself."

"Donald, you've been drinking."

"And how!"

"What's the idea of the celebration?"

"I was having a session with a bootlegger."

"I didn't know they had them any more."

"They've always had them. They always will."

"Was he a nice bootlegger?"

"Uh huh."

"Was it good stuff?"

"Pretty fair."

"Didn't you bring any with you?"

"Just what I carried away inside of me."

"It smells as though that had been a lot." She came closer and sniffed. "Garlic, too."

"Bother you?"

"Lord, no. I'm sore that you didn't take me with you. I could have had a lot of fun calling on bootleggers and eating garlic. What was the garlic in?"

"Beans."

She sat down in one of the creaking auto court chairs. "Got a cigarette, Donald? I got excited when I heard you drive up, and dashed off without my purse."

"Where is it?"

"Over in the other cabin."

I handed her a cigarette. "Got any money in it?"

"Some."

"How much?"

"Six or seven hundred. I don't know exactly."

"Better get it," I said.

"Oh, it's all right. Tell me, Donald, why did you come up here?"

"I'm trying to get some stuff on Crumweather."

"Why?"

"So when he puts the screws on you, I can put the screws on him."

"Think you can do it?"

"I don't know. He's pretty sharp."

"This is where Bob's company had its land, isn't it?"

"Do you know anything about that?"

"Only a little that Bob's told me."

I looked at her. "I'm going to ask you a question and you may not want to answer."

"Don't do it, Donald. We're getting along nicely. I hate to be questioned."

"Why?"

"I don't know. I like to be independent and live my own life. When people start asking me too many questions and make me answer, it makes me feel I have no privacy. I'll answer them if I like the person who asks them, but I resent it afterward. I've always been that way."

"I'm going to ask it just the same."

"What is it?"

"Have you given your stepbrother any money?"

She narrowed her eyes.

"I suppose Dad wants to know."

"*I* want to know."

"Yes," she said.

"Much?"

"No."

"Money to put in his company?"

"No, not a cent. Just to keep him going and give him a chance to get started when Dad shut down on him."

"How much?"

"Do I have to answer that?"

"Yes."

"I don't want to."

"I want you to."

"I will if you make me, but I won't like it afterward."

"How much?"

"About fifteen hundred dollars."

"Over how long a time?"

"About two months."

"When did you quit?"

"When he started working."

"You haven't given him any since?"

"No."

"He wanted more after you shut down on him, didn't he?"

"Yes. That made me mad. Understand, Donald, I don't care too much for him. I think he's an awful pill, but, after all, he's been dragged into the family, and I have to make the most of him or else go out and live by myself."

"Why don't you do that?"

"Because of the awful mess of things Dad made."

"You mean his second marriage?"

"Yes."

"How did he get roped into that?"

"I'm darned if I know, Donald— Oh, it's a hell of a thing to talk about."

"Go ahead. You've started now."

"Well, it was my fault."

"How?"

"I went to the South Seas, and then down into Mexico, and then on a yachting trip."

"Well?"

"Dad was alone. He's a peculiar combination. He's crusty and hard-boiled, and down underneath he's a rank sentimentalist.

"He'd been very happy with Mother, and Dad and I always got along like nobody's business. His home life had been very happy, and it meant a lot to him. After Mother's death—she had an independent fortune you know —her will left it divided between Dad and me. I was— Oh, I suppose I've got to tell you. I was mixed up in a love affair that had given me a lot of heartbreak. I'm over it now, but for a while I didn't think I'd *ever* get over it, and Dad told me to go ahead. I packed up and skipped out. When I came back, he was married."

"How did it happen?" I asked.

"How do those things always happen?" she said bitterly. "Look at her! I don't want to talk about her, but I don't have to. You've seen her. How could a ball and chain like that get anyone to fasten herself onto? There's only one way."

I stared at her. "You mean a sort of blackmail. Do you

mean—"

"Of course not," she said. "Figure it out for yourself. The woman is a consummate actress. Didn't you ever wonder, Donald, why it is that so many women who have strong individual characters and are just dandy good fellows never get married, while some nagging, whining piece of feminine humanity usually gets a pretty good husband?"

"Are you going to let your back hair down and tell me secrets of sex?" I asked.

"Yes, if you have to be told," she said with a half-smile. "You're old enough now to know the facts of life, Donald."

"All right, tell me."

"The people with individualities," she said, "are just the same all the time. They won't resort to all the little sneaky tricks of character-changing.that the hypocrites will. Women of that type simply show themselves. They show themselves as they are. A man can either like them well enough to marry them or not.

"Then there's the other type. They don't have any personalities of their own except disagreeable personalities, and they know enough to keep those defects of character covered up. Well, Dad's present wife found out that he was lonely, that he wanted a home, that his daughter was out traveling around the world and would probably get married. She invited him out to her home for dinners.

"Bob was swell, gave the picture of man-to-man good-fellowship, and she was nothing like the way you see her now. Dad never heard about her blood pressure until after he married her. She was just a sweet, home-loving thing who didn't care about going out, who wanted to make a home for someone, who would stroke Dad's forehead when he was tired and play chess with him— Oh, she just *adored* chess—" Alta's eyes glittered. "She hasn't played a single game of chess with him since they were married." She raised her voice so that it mimicked her stepmother. " 'Oh, I'd lo-o-ove to, Henry. I miss those games so-o-o-o much, but my *poor* head! It's my blood pressure, you know. The doctor says I must have things very quiet and easy.' "

Suddenly she stopped and said, "There you go. You got me started. I suppose you've been waiting for this opportunity, figuring that sometime you'd get me when I was mad enough to tell you the whole damn thing."

"On the contrary," I said, "I don't care a great deal about it. I wanted to know about what financial arrangements you'd had with your brother."

"That's gratitude for you," she said with a little laugh. "I bare my soul, and you say you didn't want to hear it."

I grinned at her. "Had anything to eat?"

"No, and I'm ravenous. I kept waiting around, thinking perhaps you'd come in."

"I think they roll the sidewalks up in this town about eight-thirty, but we might find an all-night place on the highway somewhere."

"Know something, Donald?"

"What?"

"That garlic breath of yours—"

"Offensive?" I asked.

She laughed and said, "You're a nice boy, Donald, but you do drive the damnedest heaps. Here, take the keys to my car and let's go out in search of adventure."

"When'll your dad be here?"

"Not until midnight. You certainly have made a hit with him."

She opened the car door and jumped inside.

I fitted the ignition key to the lock and switched on the motor. There was a smooth rush of purring power that ran as silently as a sewing machine and had as much power as a skyrocket. I put it in low and stepped on the throttle and nearly jerked our heads off. Alta laughed, and said, "This isn't that old heap of yours, is it, Donald? You start this thing in second gear—unless you're on a steep grade or stuck in the mud or something."

"So I've found out," I said.

We found a little Spanish place, and she ate her way down the menu. "Let's drive around for a while in the moonlight," she suggested when we got out.

I figured there'd be a road that would come out on the

flat lands above the river. I finally found it, and we left the pavement when we were about a thousand feet above the valley, to drive out on the dirt road that led to a spur where we could look down over the country below. From that height, the tailing piles didn't seem hard and glittering. The moonlight was soft, and the whole panorama of the valley was a part of the night, of the stars, and of those mysterious rustling noises that emanated from wild life.

I switched off the motor and the lights. She snuggled over to me. A cottontail hopped across a patch of moonlight directly in front of the car. An owl swooped down on a mouse. The shadows were dark blotches in the canyons. The ridges were splashed with vivid moonlight, and the valley below bathed in tranquil brilliance. I could feel her body close against mine, could hear the even sound of her regular breathing. I looked down at her once, thinking she was asleep, but her eyes were wide open, drinking in the scenery.

Her hand came over and took possession of mine. Her pointed fingernails traced little designs along the edges of my fingers. Once she sighed, a tremulous sigh of deep content, then suddenly she looked up and asked, "Donald, do you like this?"

By way of answer, I leaned over and brushed my lips gently against the side of her forehead.

For a moment I thought she was going to put up her lips to be kissed, but instead she snuggled closer and sat perfectly still.

After a while I said, "We'd better go, and be there in the camp when your father arrives."

"I suppose so."

We had driven down the curving ribbon of concrete to the outskirts of Valleydale before she said anything. Then she said simply, "Donald, I could love you forever for that."

"What?"

"Just everything about it."

I laughed. "I didn't make the view," I said.

"No," she said, "and there's a lot of other things you didn't try to make— Gosh, Donald, you're a nice kid."

"What," I asked, "is all this leading up to?"

"Nothing. I just wanted you to know. It wouldn't have been the same with anyone else. Other men I know would have talked too much, or pawed too much, or made me fight. I just relaxed with you and felt that you were a part of the scenery, and it was all a part of me."

"In other words, I'm something of a noncombatant. Is that it?"

"Donald, stop it! You know better than that."

"I understand a man is supposed to consider it a dubious compliment when a girl says she feels perfectly safe with him."

Her laugh was nervous. "If you knew how utterly unsafe I felt with you, it would surprise you. What I meant was that it just all fitted in— Oh, why did I try to explain it? I'm no good at that stuff anyway. Can't you drive with one hand, Donald?"

"Yes."

She took my right hand off the steering wheel, slipped it around her shoulders, and cuddled over. I drove slowly through the deserted streets of the little city, a city of ghosts, of memories, with houses that needed paint, with shade trees catching the moonlight on polished green leaves and shimmering it back into the night, while the dark blotches of shadow below seemed to be pools of India ink which had been splotched on the ground with some big brush.

Henry Ashbury was waiting for us at the auto court. He'd chartered a plane and then hired a car to take him the rest of the way.

"Beat your schedule, Dad, didn't you?" Alta asked.

He nodded and looked us over with thoughtful eyes. He shook hands with me, kissed Alta, and then turned to look at me again. He didn't say anything.

"Well, don't be so serious about it," Alta said. "I hope you've got some whisky in that bag of yours because this town is closed up tight. There are some pans in here, and

I could make a nice little toddy as a nightcap."

We all went into the double cabin where Alta had registered for herself and her father. We sat down, and Alta made some hot whisky drinks, poured them in cups, and came in and joined us.

"What have you found out?" Ashbury asked me.

"Not very much," I said, "but enough."

"What's happening?"

"They're prospecting. It seems they prospect dredging land with a drill. Because a dredge can operate at a profit in ground where there are low values per cubic yard, it doesn't require a great deal of gold to make a good job of salting a claim— And they can use the same gold over and over."

"How much?"

"I don't know, just a few dollars, I should judge."

"How heavy are they salting it?"

"Apparently pretty heavy."

"Then what's going to happen?"

"The promoters will milk the company dry and skip out. They'd never dare to put a dredge on it. If they did, there would be such a discrepancy in values that it would show conclusively the ground had been salted."

He bit the end off a cigar and smoked for a while in silence. Twice, I caught him looking over the tops of his glasses at Alta.

"Well?" I asked.

"What do you mean?"

"The next move," I said, "is up to you."

"How do you figure that?"

"It all depends on what you want to do."

"I'm going to leave things entirely in your hands. I'm satisfied you can take care of *us*."

I said, "You forget that tomorrow at this time I'll probably be in a cell somewhere charged with murder."

Alta Ashbury gave a quick little involuntary gasp.

Her father swiveled his eyes around to look at her for a moment, then back to me.

"What do you suggest?" he asked.

"How important is it that you keep Bob out of trouble?"

"Damned important. I'm engaged in some promotional work myself with three associates. To have something come up now that would rock the boat would put me in a most embarrassing position—not financially, but— Dammit, it would make people look down their noses at me. There'd be a wagging of heads every time I walked into the club. Whispered conferences would stop abruptly when I came walking into a room. The whole damn petty mechanics of character assassination carried on right under my nose where I'd have to pretend I didn't know anything about it."

I said, "There's only one way you could handle the thing."

"How's that?"

I said thoughtfully, "We might kill two birds with one stone."

"What's the other bird?"

I said, "Oh, just an incidental development."

Alta pushed her cup and saucer to one side, and leaned across the table. "Dad, look at me."

He looked at her.

"You're worried because you think I've fallen in love with Donald, aren't you?"

He met her eyes squarely. "Yes."

"I don't think I have. I'm trying not to. He's helping me, and he's a gentleman."

"I gathered," Ashbury said acidly, "that you'd taken *him* into your confidence. You didn't take me."

"I know I didn't, Dad. I should have. I'm going to tell you now."

"Not now," he said. "Later. Donald, what's your idea?"

I said hotly, "I'm not trying to horn in on the Ashbury millions or thousands or hundreds or whatever the hell they are. I've tried to give you a square deal, a—"

His hand came over to rest on my arm. The fingers tightened until I could feel the full strength of the man's grip. "I'm not kicking about you, Donald," he said. "It's Alta. Usually, men flock around her, and she makes them jump through hoops. It makes me sore the way she treats them, not sore at her, but sore at my sex for standing all that damn bossing around—" Abruptly, he turned to face Alta, and said, "And you may feel relieved to know that before I left, I told Mrs. Ashbury she could see her lawyer, arrange a settlement, go to Reno, and get a quiet divorce, and take her son with her. Now then, Donald, what's the idea?"

I said, "The brains back of this whole business is a lawyer by the name of Crumweather. I thought I could head things off and put the screws on him. I can on one end of it. I can't on the other. There's been too much stock sold."

"How much?"

"I don't know. Quite a smear. There's going to be an awful squawk go up."

"How about the Commissioner of Corporations?"

"Crumweather's found a hole in the Blue Sky Act, or thinks he has."

"Can't we put him on the spot?"

"Not because of that. He's too slick. He's sitting back in the clear with a ten-per-cent rake-off. The officials of the company will get the jolt."

"Well, what *can* we do?"

"The only thing to do," I said, "is to find the stockholders and get them to sell their stock."

He said, "Donald, that's the first time I've known you to make an utterly asinine suggestion."

Alta rushed to my defense. "Dad, it sounds perfectly feasible to me. Can't you see it's the only way?"

"Bunk," he said, slouching down in his chair and chewing at his cigar. "The people who bought stock in that company bought it as a gamble, not as an investment. They're looking forward to a hundred-to-one, or five-hundred-to-one, or five-thousand-to-one profit. Try to buy that stock at what they paid for it, and they'd laugh at you. Offer them ten times what they paid for it, and they'd think there'd been a strike, and you had inside information."

I said, "I don't think you understand what I'm driving at."

"What is it?" he asked.

"There's only one person who could buy it back, and that's Crumweather."

"How could he buy it back?"

"He could suddenly discover that all of the sales had been illegal transactions, have the salesmen go around and tell the prospects that the idea wasn't feasible, and that the Commissioner of Corporations had ordered them to return the money received from stock sales."

"How much would it cost you to do that?" he asked dryly. "I'd say about half a million dollars."

"I think we could do it for five hundred dollars."

"What was that figure?" he asked.

"Five hundred dollars."

He said, "Either you're crazy, or I am."

"Is it worth five hundred to you?"

"It'd be worth a cool fifty thousand."

I said, "Alta's car's outside. Let's go for a ride."

"Can I come?" Alta asked.

"I don't think so. We're going to call on a bachelor who's already retired."

"I like bachelors."

"Come on," I said.

We sat three in the front seat, and I drove over the rough road through the tailings until the headlights, dancing along ahead, showed the outlines of Pete Digger's old shack.

"You sit here," I said. "I'll get out and see if he's ready to receive visitors."

I slid out of the car and started toward the house. A cracked voice from the shadows said, "Hoist 'em brother, and hoist 'em high!"

I swung around and shot my hands up in the air. The illumination of the headlights showed my features, and Pete Digger said savagely, "Might have known you was a god-darn stool pigeon— All right, go ahead and try to find it, you cheap, tin-star, two-faced hypocrite. A writer, huh? That car looks like you was a writer. If you ain't got a warrant, get the hell out of here. If you have, serve it."

I said, "You've got me wrong, Pete. I want some more information, only this time I'm going to pay more money for it."

The answer was under his breath and reflected on my parentage.

Suddenly the door of the car swung open. Alta got out and walked straight toward the shadows. She said, "Honestly, it's all right. Donald brought my dad and me down to talk a little business with you."

"Who are you?"

"My name's Alta."

"Get over there in the light where I can get a look at you."

She moved over beside me in the light.

Henry Ashbury said cheerfully, "I guess I'm next." He got out and came shambling over to stand beside us.

"Who the hell are you?" Pete Digger asked.

I said, "You damn fool, he's Santa Claus," and put my hands down.

CHAPTER TEN

PETE DIGGER HAD PULLED ON a pair of pants and pushed his feet into boots when he had heard the car coming. He was a bit embarrassed about coming out and meeting people, but after I persuaded him it was all right, he seemed sheepish about the gun act. It was Alta who saved the day. She acted interested and perfectly natural.

Pete wanted to make up the bed before he had us come in, but Alta said, "Nothing doing," and we all filed in. The windows were open, and the stove was cold, but I found a pile of twigs and dried bark and started the fire while Pete was apologetically getting into a shirt and coat. That seemed to make a hit with him.

There was one thing about the little shack. It heated up quickly, and the stove roared into a businesslike job. Pete came over and sat down, looked longingly at the fragrant Perfecto handed him by Ashbury, and said, "Nope. That's rich man's fodder. I'm a poor guy. My pipe is my friend, and I don't go back on my friends. See?"

Alta and I had cigarettes. After we were all blowing smoke into a blue cloud which hung heavy over the table and the roaring fire made the place seem even warmer and more cozy than the thermometer would indicate, Pete said, "Okay. What you got on your mind?"

"Pete," I said, "I'm going to give you a chance to make five hundred dollars."

"Make what?"

"Five hundred dollars."

"What's the catch?" he asked.

I said, "You've got to salt a claim."

"What for?"

"Can I trust you?"

"Damned if I know," Pete said with a grin. "I don't double-cross my friends, but I raise hell with my enemies. Pay your money and take your choice."

I leaned over across the table. "I was stringing you when I told you that I was a writer looking for local color," I said.

Pete Digger threw his head back and roared. "That's the funniest thing I've heard in forty years," he said.

"What is?" Ashbury asked.

"This young chap thinkin' I didn't know he was lyin' when he told me he was a writer. He's up here snoopin' around. I figure he's a young lawyer tryin' to get somethin' on that dredgin' company. That's what he was after. Writer, *he?* Haw haw haw!"

I grinned and said, "Well, we've got that over with. Now then, Pete, I'm stuck on that stock proposition."

"*You* are?"

"Uh huh. I got soft and bought some stock in there," I said.

Pete's face darkened. "The damn bunch of crooks," he said. "We'd oughta go down there an' dynamite their drill rig, give 'em a coat of tar and feathers, and dump 'em in the river to cool 'em off."

"No," I said. "There's a better way."

"What's that?"

"Do you think they know how much gold they're putting in those holes?"

"Sure, they do. The way a proposition like that figures, the ground has to test uniform. If you get one hole that runs way up, an' another hole that runs down, capital gets suspicious. A river don't deposit gold that way. That gold's been droppin' down in that channel for millions of years. Get the idea?"

"All right, that's the way I hoped it would be. Now, then, they're keeping track of the gold they take *out*, aren't they?"

"Sure."

"Pete," I said, "you mentioned that you could salt a claim artistically. What do you mean by it?"

Pete looked at us and said, "You said I could make five hundred bucks. What did you mean by *it?*"

Ashbury, who was a good judge of character, and had

138

been studying Pete over the tops of his glasses, wordlessly took a wallet from his pocket, and counted out five one-hundred-dollar bills. "That's what he meant," he said, and shoved them across to Pete.

Pete picked the bills up, looked at them, twisted them in his fingers, then dropped them and let them lie in the center of the table.

"Don't want them?" Ashbury asked.

"Not until you say the word," Pete said.

"I'm saying it."

"Wait until you hear what I got to say."

"Go ahead," I told him.

"Well," Pete said, "I know a couple of pretty smooth ways of salting a gold-dredger claim so that the devil himself can't figure it out."

"What are they?"

"Well, now," Pete said, "in order to really get the sketch, I got to tell you a couple of stories. This goes back to the Klondike when a big company was figurin' on comin' in there. A guy had a bunch of ground he wanted to sell, and the company didn't think it was any good, but the bird told such a story they decided to drill it.

"Well, the minute they started drillin' it, they knew they'd struck a bonanza. Values were there just the way they should be. They started low at the top, and were heavy down on bedrock. They punched hole after hole, and every hole gave 'em the same results. The ground was absolutely uniform. They bought the place, but just before they started dredgin' somebody got a bright idea and punched down a couple more test holes— The values were so thin you couldn't see 'em with a magnifying glass."

"What had happened?" I asked. "Was the claim salted?"

"Sure it was salted."

"But weren't they looking out for that?"

"Of course they were watching out for it, and the guy salted it right under their noses. Here, I'll show you how. Ever see gold panned?"

I shook my head.

Pete picked up a gold pan with its typical sloping sides,

and curled rim. He squatted down on his heels and held
the gold pan balanced in between his knees. "This is the
way a guy pans gold, see?" He twisted the pan back and
forth, shaking it with his wrists. "You keep the stuff under
water. The idea is to get all the gold mixed up with the
water so it settles to the bottom of the pan."

I nodded.

"Well," Pete said, "a man pans like this. He's smokin'.
See? He's always got a right to smoke. He takes a sack of
tobacco outa his pocket an' rolls his own, or, if he's a little
different type, he has a package of tailor-made cigarettes
in his pocket. Me, I use my own, because the minute I
started smokin' tailor-made cigarettes, anybody that knew
me would get suspicious."

"Go on," I said.

"Well," Pete said, "that's all there is to it."

"I don't get you," Ashbury said.

"Don't you see? The tobacco is just about a quarter gold
dust. I put just as much tobacco as I want into the cigarette, and I determine the values in each pan by the length
of time it takes me to pan it out. While I'm smoking, the
ashes from the cigarette are droppin' down into the gold
pan. Nobody thinks anything of that."

Ashbury gave a low whistle.

"And then there's another way," Pete went on. "You
climb up on a drill rig, an' you take a marlinspike an'
spread the strands of the rope apart, then you put in a
bunch of gold dust. You do that all the way down the
whole length of the rope, then in the mornin' when they
start drillin', the jar of the bit on the ground dislodges
little particles of gold dust which drop down the casing
into the hole."

I said, "All right, Pete, what we want is to have those
holes show so much more gold coming *out* than they're
putting *in*, that they'll come to the conclusion they *really*
have a bonanza. But it'll have to be done so all the values
show up after they get below the old level of work."

"Shucks," Pete said. "They don't know where the old
level of work was. That bunch don't know anything.

They're just goin' through motions. I watched 'em. They're so damn clumsy, I swear to God I almost started over and said to the driller, 'Look here, buddy, I don't want to tell a man his business, but if you can't make a better job of salting a claim than that, for God's sake, stand to one side and let a guy that really knows how give you a few pointers.' "

Ashbury chuckled. Alta laughed out loud. I pushed the five one-hundred-dollar bills across the table toward Pete Digger. "It's all yours," I said.

Pete picked up the bills, folded them, and put them in his pocket.

"When can you start?" Ashbury asked.

"You're in a hurry?"

"Yes."

"I got a little dust in there," Pete said, jerking his head toward a cupboard. "Stuff I've picked up here and there in the pockets, pay dirt that had dropped out of some of the old cleanups. It's enough for what we'll want."

"How can you get on the property?" I asked him.

"That's a cinch. They've been trying to get me to work ever since they started. They don't know too much about handling the job."

"You don't dare to have values start running up just after you go to work. It would be too much of a coincidence," I warned.

"Leave that to me, brother. I'm going down there to-night in the moonlight an' take a marlinspike, an' salt a bunch of gold in that drill rope. Their values'll start pickin' up tomorrow. I think that drill rope's all I'm goin' to need."

I said, "Keep it up until I tell you to stop."

"How'll you tell me?"

"When you get a postal card signed 'D.L.' saying, 'Having a wonderful time. Wish you were here,' you'll know it's time to quit."

"Okay," he said. "I'll get started in about half an hour."

We shook hands all around, and as we climbed in the car Ashbury said, "That's a fine piece of work, Donald."

CHAPTER ELEVEN

No ONE TALKED MUCH as I drove the car to the main highway, turned into the automobile court, and switched off
the lights and motor. I got out and started to open the
door on the other side, then saw a car I hadn't seen before,
and got a glimpse at an E embedded in a diamond on the
license plate.

I didn't say a word to the others, but walked directly
toward my own cabin.

Two men stepped out of the shadows. One of them said,
"Your name Lam?"

I said, "Yes."

"Donald Lam?"

"Yes."

"Come on in. We want to talk with you. We have tele-
graphic instructions to pick you up."

I was hoping that Ashbury and Alta would have sense
enough to keep out of it. They got out of the car and stood
by the door. Alta's face was white in the moonlight.

"Who are these folks?" the officer asked, indicating Ashbury and his daughter with a jerk of his head.

"They picked me up down the road a piece and asked
me if I wanted a ride."

One of the officers wore the uniform of the state highway patrol, and the other, I gathered, was a local officer.

"What do you want?"

"Didn't you leave rather suddenly?"

"I'm working."

"On what?"

"I'd prefer not to make any statements."

"Did you know a man named Ringold?"

"I read in the paper about his murder."

"Know anything about it?"

"No, of course not. Why?"

"Weren't you in the hotel the night he was killed?

Didn't you talk with a blonde at the cigar stand, and again with a clerk, trying to pump them about Ringold?"

"Gosh, no!" I said, backing away a step or two and staring at them as though I thought they were mad. "Say, wait a minute. Who *are* you birds, anyway? Are you officers?"

"Of course we're officers."

"Got a warrant?"

"Now listen, buddy. Don't go getting hard, see? And don't start playing wise guy. Right now we're asking questions. That's all."

"What do you want to know?"

"According to the D.A., you could have had an interest in Ringold."

"How do you figure?"

"Well, buddy, it's this way. Jed Ringold was working for the Foreclosed Farms Underwriters Company, see? And that company has a bunch of land up here near Valleydale. Now the president of the Foreclosed Farms Underwriters Company— Cripes, it tangles my tongue to say the damn thing. What did they want to get a name like that for? Well, anyway, the president is a guy named Tindle, and you've been out living with him and taking orders from him."

I said, "You're nuts. I've been visiting out at Ashbury's house. Tindle is Henry Ashbury's stepson."

"You ain't been workin' for him?"

"Hell, no. I've been taking some fat off Ashbury. I'm giving him jujitsu lessons."

"That's what *you* say. Tindle's got interests up here. Ringold is working for Tindle. Somebody goes into the hotel and bumps Ringold off. This guy has a description that's a helluva lot like yours, and—"

I moved forward to stare at him. "Is *that* what's eating you?" I asked.

"That's right."

"All right, when I get back, I'll go call the cops and tell them how crazy they are. There were a couple of people who saw the guy that went into the hotel, weren't there? Seems to me, I remember reading about it in the papers."

"That's right, buddy."

"All right, I'll be back in a couple of days, and we'll clean it up."

"Well, now, suppose you ain't the guy that was in the hotel?"

"I'm not."

"You'd like to get it cleaned up, wouldn't you?"

"Not particularly. It's so absurd I'm not even bothering about it."

"But suppose you *are* the guy? Then something might happen, and you just wouldn't remember about going back."

"Well, you're not going to take me back just because I happen to know the president of this corporation, are you?"

"No; but the D.A.'s office got hold of a photo of you, Lam, and showed it to the clerk at the hotel, and the hotel clerk says, 'That's the guy you want.' So *now* what?"

Ashbury and his daughter had taken the hint. Instead of going on into their cabin, they'd got back into the car and turned it around. Ashbury rolled down the window on the driver's side, leaned out, and asked, "Is there anything I can do for you, my friend? Are you in any trouble?"

"Nothing," I said, "just a private matter. Good night, and thanks for the lift."

"You're entirely welcome," Ashbury said and slid the car into gear and whisked out of the auto court.

"Well?" the officer who had been doing the talking asked.

I said, "There's only one answer to that. We're going back. I'll make that damn clerk get down on his knees and eat those words—every one of 'em. The guy's just plain nuts."

"Now that's the sensible way to look at it. You know we could *take* you back, but we'd have a lot of notoriety which wouldn't do anybody any good. If it's a mistake, the less said about it the better. You know how it is, buddy. It's kind of hard to identify people from a photograph. We drag you back and get a lot of newspaper publicity that the clerk's positively identified you as the guy. Then he takes a look at your mug and says he ain't so certain. Then a while later the real bird turns up. He looks something like you, but not too much, and the clerk says, 'Sure. That's the guy.' But you know what some shyster lawyer would do? He'd make that clerk look like two bits on the witness stand because he'd identified somebody else first."

"Sure," I said. "The fool clerk makes a false identification and puts me to a lot of trouble, but it's the shyster lawyer for the defendant that's to blame."

The cop looked at me for a minute. "Say, buddy, you ain't trying to kid me, are you?"

"How do we go?" I asked.

"We drive you down the road about a hundred miles. There's an airport there and a special officer that telephoned us to go pick you up. He's waiting with a plane. If it's all a mistake, he'll bring you back, and you can take a stage from the airport right back here."

"And I won't be out anything except stage fare and a day's time," I said sarcastically.

They didn't say anything.

I did a little thinking. "Well, I won't travel on a plane at night for anyone. I'll drive down with you. I'll go to a hotel with the officer. I won't leave until tomorrow morning. I've got some irons in the fire I can't shove to one side—"

"Kinda independent, ain't you, buddy?"

I looked him in the eyes and said, "You're damn right. If you want me to go voluntarily, that's the way I'll go. If you want to advertise it in the newspapers that the clerk has made a bum identification, you can take me."

"Okay," the man said. "Get in. We're taking you."

The special investigator for the district attorney's office who was waiting at the airport wasn't entirely easy in his mind. My attitude made him a lot less easy, but he was good and sore at the idea that I was going to stay overnight in a hotel and wouldn't travel by plane at night. He kept trying to argue with me. I told him simply that I was afraid to travel by air at night.

The officer couldn't figure it out. "Now, listen, Lam, if you want to get back on the job, this is the way to do it. I've got this plane here, and it's chartered. I can put you under arrest and take you back if I have to and—"

"You can if you put a charge against me."

"I don't want to put a charge against you."

"All right, then, we leave in the morning."

After a while he said to the officers who had brought me down, "Keep an eye on him. I'm going to put through a telephone call."

He went into a booth and put through a long-distance call. It took him about twenty minutes. The highway patrol and I sat in the lobby of the hotel. They tried to sell me on the idea of going back and getting it over with.

The special investigator came back from the telephone booth and said, "All right, buddy. You asked for it. We're going back."

"Going to charge me?"

"I'm going to arrest you on suspicion."

"Got a warrant?"

"No."

"I'm going to call a lawyer."

"That won't do you any good."

"The hell it won't. I'm going to call a lawyer."

"We haven't time to wait for a telephone right now. The aviator is ready to take off."

I said, "I have a right to call a lawyer," and started for the telephone booth.

They stopped me so fast my head jerked. One of them grabbed one shoulder. The other grabbed the other shoulder. The clerk in the lobby looked at me curiously. A couple of loungers got up and moved away. The investigator from the D.A.'s office said, "Okay, boys, let's go."

They gave me the bum's rush out to the automobile, cut loose with the siren, and got out to the airport in nothing flat. A cabin plane was there with the motors all warmed, and they pushed me inside. The man from the D.A.'s office said, "Since you're asking for it the hard way, buddy, I'll just see that you don't get any funny ideas

while the plane's up in the air and try to start anything."
He slipped a handcuff around my wrist and handcuffed
the other loop to the arm of the chair.

"Fasten your seat belts," the pilot said.

The deputy fastened my seat belt. "It would have been
a lot better if you'd done it the easy way," he said.

I didn't say anything.

"Now, when we get down there, you're not going to
make a kick about going to the hotel where this clerk
can take a look at you, are you?"

I said, "Brother, *you're* the one that's doing it the hard
way. I told you I'd go down tomorrow morning, walk into
the hotel or any place you wanted, and let the fellow take
a look at me. You got hard—I'm not going to any hotel.
If you take me down, you put me in jail, and I tell my
story to the newspaper boys. If you want anybody to
identify me, you put me in a line-up, and have the identification made that way."

"Oh, it's like that, is it?"

"It's like that."

"Now, I'm damn sure you're the one who went in the
hotel."

"You're just knocking your case higher than a kite," I
said. "The newspapers are going to play it up that you
charged me with murder, that the hotel clerk made an
identification from a photograph—"

"A tentative identification," the officer corrected.

"Call it whatever you want to," I said. "When he tries to
identify the real man, there's going to be hell to pay—
And you're going to catch it."

He got sore then, and I thought he was going to paste
me one, but he changed his mind, went over, and sat down.
The pilot looked back, made certain our seat belts were
fastened, gunned the motors, took the plane down the
field, turned, came up into the wind, and took off.

It was smooth flying. I leaned back against the cushions.
Occasional air beacons leered up at me with red eyes that
blinked ominously. At intervals, clustered lights marked
the location of little towns. I'd look down and think how

people, snuggled in warm beds, would hear the roaring beat of the motor echoing back from the roof, roll over sleepily, and say, "There goes the mail," without realizing it was a plane taking a man on a death gamble, with the cards stacked against him.

The pilot turned around and made signs to us when we started over the mountains. I gathered he meant it was going to be rough. He did. We went way up to try and get over it, but instead of going over it, we went through it. I felt like a wet dishrag when we came slanting down to the airport.

The pilot landed at the far end. The D.A.'s man got up, came over, and unfastened one end of the handcuffs. He said ominously, "Now, listen, Lam, you're going to get into a car, and you're going to that hotel. There isn't going to be any fuss about it, and no publicity."

"You can't do that," I said. "If you're arresting me, go ahead and book me."

"I'm not arresting you."

"Then you had no right to bring me down here."

He grinned, and said, "You're here, ain't you?"

The plane turned and taxied up to the hangars. I heard the sound of a siren, and a car came up. A red spotlight blazed its beam to a focus right on the door of the plane.

The man from the D.A.'s office jabbed me in the small of the back. "Don't act rough now," he said. "It would be a shame to have an argument. You've been a nice little man so far. Just keep on going."

They turned the spotlight into my eyes so it would blind me. The deputy pushed me out. Hands grabbed me, and shoved me forward, then I heard Bertha Cool's voice saying, "What are you doing with this man?"

Somebody said, "Beat it, lady. This guy's under arrest."

"What's he charged with?"

"None of your damn business."

Bertha Cool said, "All right," to somebody who was just a shadowy figure in the darkness, and the man stepped forward and said, "I'll make it my business. I'm an attorney. I'm representing this man."

"Beat it," the officer told him, "before something happens to your face."

"All right, I'll beat it, but first let me give you this nice little folded paper. That's a writ of habeas corpus issued by a superior judge ordering you to produce this man in court. This other paper is a written demand that you take him immediately and forthwith before the nearest and most accessible magistrate for the purpose of fixing bail. In case you're interested, the nearest and most accessible magistrate happens to be a justice of the peace in this township. He's sitting in his office right now, with the lights on and his court open waiting to fix the bail."

"We don't have to take him to no magistrate," the man said.

"Where are you going to take him?"

"To jail."

"I wouldn't advise you to go anywhere without stopping to see the nearest and most accessible magistrate," the lawyer said.

Bertha Cool said, "Now listen, you, this man's working for me. I'm running a respectable detective agency. He was working. You yanked him off the job and chased him down here. Don't think for a minute you're going to pull this stuff and get away with it."

The man from the district attorney's office said, "Just a minute, boys. Stick around." He said to the lawyer Bertha Cool had, "Let's talk things over a minute."

Bertha Cool horned in on the conference. Her diamonds caught the rays from the spotlight, and made blood-red scintillations as she moved her hands. "I'm in on this, too," she said.

"Now listen," the D.A.'s man said, obviously worried and pretty much on the defensive, "we don't want to put any charges against this boy. For all we know, he's just a nice kid that hasn't done a thing in the world, but we're trying to find out whether he's the man who went into Jed Ringold's room the night he was murdered. If he isn't, that's all there is to it. If he is, we're going to charge him with murder."

"So what?" Bertha Cool asked truculently.

The D.A. man looked at her and tried to outstare her. Bertha Cool pushed her face toward him, and, with her eyes glittering belligerently, demanded again and in a louder voice, "So what? You heard me, you worm. Go ahead and answer."

The D.A.'s officer turned to the lawyer. "There isn't any need for a habeas corpus, and there isn't any need to take him before a magistrate because we don't want to charge him."

"How did you get him down here if he wasn't arrested?" Bertha asked.

He tried ignoring her question, and said to the lawyer, "Now the clerk at the hotel takes a look at this guy's picture and says he *thinks* this is the bird. All we want to do is to take him into the hotel. The clerk takes a look at him. Now that's reasonable enough, ain't it?"

For a fraction of a second, the lawyer hesitated. Bertha Cool reached out with an arm and shoved him to one side as easily as though he'd been just an empty bag of clothes. She pushed her face up in front of the deputy from the D.A.'s office and said, "Well, it isn't all right, not by a damn sight."

A little group had gathered. Passengers from one of the airliners that had come in, a few of the ground crew, and a couple of aviators. The red spotlight was out of my eyes now, and I could look around and see their faces grinning. They were getting a great kick out of Bertha Cool.

Bertha said, "We know our rights. You can't identify a man that way. If you're going to charge him with murder, you lock him up. You put him in a line-up, and you be goddam certain there are two or three other men in that line-up who have the same build and physical characteristics as the man you're looking for. *Then* you bring the clerk in and let him look at the line up. If he picks Donald, that's an identification. If he picks somebody else, that's different."

The D.A.'s man was bothered.

The lawyer said, "As a matter of law, officer, you know

that's absolutely correct."

"But we don't want to cause this bird a lot of trouble. It may be just a flash in the pan. If he isn't guilty, what's he making such a squawk for?"

I said, "Because I don't like the way you did this. I told you I'd come down with you voluntarily tomorrow morning, go into the hotel, and talk with anyone you wanted; that I couldn't leave tonight, that if you brought me down in that plane tonight, you'd have to put me under arrest."

"Aw, nuts," one of the officers said.

"What did you do?" I demanded, raising my voice. "You and two highway police grabbed me and gave me the bum's rush out to a car. You threw me in and dragged me down here without any charge being made against me. That's kidnaping. I'll have the federal men on your neck. I'm not going to be pushed around, that's all. Wait until tomorrow morning, and I'll go to your damned hotel."

There was a moment of silence.

I turned to Bertha and said, "You know where this plane came from, and you know a lawyer up there who has pull with the sheriff. Get him on the phone, have him get the sheriff out of bed, and get a warrant for kidnaping issued against this officer."

"Listen, punk," one of the officers said, "it isn't kidnaping when you arrest a man for murder."

"What do you do with him when you arrest him for murder?"

"We take him down to jail and throw the book at him, and if he acts rusty, we throw something else at him."

"Swell," I said. "Take me to a magistrate, and if he says so, you take me to jail, but don't detour me to any hotels. The minute you do that, that's kidnaping— Get the point, Bertha?"

The lawyer grabbed at it. "That's right," he said. "The minute they try taking you any place except in accordance with the statutes in such cases made and provided, it's kidnaping."

Bertha whirled to face the officers. "All right, you," she said. "You've heard what the lawyer says."

"Aw, dry up," one of the officers said. I could see the district attorney's investigator was getting little beads of perspiration on his forehead.

Bertha said, "And don't think you're going to strong-arm your way out of it simply because you're in your own county. The kidnaping took place in another county, and if you knew how some of these other counties hate the guts of you men from this part of the state, you'd know what's going to happen."

That was the bombshell that did the work. I could see the D.A.'s man cave just as though his knees had buckled. He said, "Now, listen, there's no use losing our tempers and yelling at each other. Let's be reasonable. If this man's innocent, he should be as anxious to prove it as anyone."

I said, "That's better. What do you want?"

"We want to find out whether you were the man who had the adjoining room in that hotel on the night of the murder."

"All right, let's find out."

"Cripes, brother, that's all we were trying to do."

I said, "Let's find out in a fair way."

"What do you think's a fair way?" one of the officers asked.

I said, "I'll go down to the jail. You get five or six other people that are generally of my build and complexion, and have them dressed just about the same. While we're doing it, let's do it right. How many people saw this man who went to the hotel?"

"Three."

"Who were they?"

"The night clerk, a girl who runs a cigar counter, and some woman who saw him standing in the door."

"All right, get those people, put them side by side in three chairs, and tell them not to make any comments until after the whole line-up has filed past. Then ask them separately if anybody in the line-up was the man they saw there the night of the murder."

The D.A.'s man lowered his voice. "Now, listen," he said, "you sound like a good egg. Let me give you the low-down. The old gal that was in the upper corridor saw this man standing in the doorway. She had her glasses off. She could see him all right but—well, you know how it is, brother. She wears glasses during the daytime, and she didn't have them on. A slick lawyer could crucify her on that. The minute we run you into the hoosegow, the newspaper men are going to be on the job. They'll take flashlight photographs of you, and there'll be big headlines. 'Police Arrest Private Detective on Suspicion of Murder.' Then in case the identification falls down, we're sunk. Now, if you are guilty, go ahead and rely on all your constitutional rights. More power to you. We'll send you to the gas chamber just as sure as hell. If you aren't guilty, for God's sake, have a heart and co-operate."

I said, "I'm not guilty, but you know what's going to happen. That pinheaded clerk has identified a photograph of Donald Lam as being the man who came in and got the room. You tell him you're going to get Donald Lam and bring him in. You come through the door dragging me in, and that clerk's going to say, 'That's the guy,' before he even gets his eyes focused."

The D.A.'s man hesitated.

"Of course he is," Bertha Cool said indignantly. "I saw his picture in the paper. He looks like just that sort of a nitwit, a long, thin drink of water, all mouth and Adam's apple. What the hell can you expect of a goof like that?"

Somebody in the outskirts of the crowd gave a belly laugh. One of the cops turned around and said, "Beat it, you guys. Go on. Get out of here."

No one paid any attention to him.

I said, "Wait a minute. There's one other possibility."

"What's that?" the D.A.'s man asked.

"Is there anyone who saw this man who went into the hotel who doesn't know that you've picked on me, who hasn't seen my picture?"

"That girl at the cigar counter," the D.A.'s man said.

"All right. We go up to her apartment. You call her out. Ask her if she's ever seen me before. If she says I'm the guy, we go to jail, and you book me. If she says I'm not, you turn me loose, the newspapers don't blow the works, and we forget the kidnaping charge."

He hesitated, and I went on quickly. "Or you can take the woman who stood in the doorway. You can—"

"Nix on her," the D.A.'s man said hastily. "She didn't have her glasses on."

I said, "Suit yourself."

The investigator reached his decision. "Okay, boys," he said. "Has anybody got the name and address of that girl?"

"Yeah," one of the men said. "Her name's Clarde. I was talkin' with her right after the shootin'. She gave me a description of the man. It fits this guy to a T."

I yawned.

My lawyer said hurriedly, "Look here, Lam, that's rather an unfair test you're giving yourself. The officers drag you up there. She looks at you, and you alone. She knows you're suspected—"

"It's okay," I said wearily. "I was never in the damn joint in my life. Let 'em get it out of their system."

"And you'll co-operate so we can keep it absolutely on the QT?" the D.A.'s man asked.

"I don't give a damn what you do. I want to go to bed and get some sleep. Let's get it over with."

Bertha Cool said, "Now listen, Donald, I think that other way was the best. You go down to the jail and—"

"My God!" I shouted at her. "You act as though *you* thought I was guilty, both of you."

That quieted them. Bertha looked at me in a dazed sort of a way. The lawyer was a good guy in his place, but he'd shot his broadside. When he made his demand and passed over the papers, he didn't have anything for a follow-up.

"And just so there won't be any mistake about it," I said, "Mrs. Cool and my lawyer are going to ride right in the same car with us."

"Okay," the D.A.'s man said. "Let's get started."

While we were screaming through the streets, making time behind the siren and red lights, the D.A.'s man did a lot more thinking. He said, "Now, listen, Lam, you know

154

the position we're in. We don't want a false identification any more than you do."

"Personally," I said wearily, "I don't give a damn. If she identifies me, I can spring an iron-clad alibi for the whole damn night. It's just the principle of the thing, that's all. If you'd played fair with me, I'd have come down and gone to the hotel with you in the morning. I didn't like that bum's rush, that's all."

"Well, you're sure rusty when you get rusty. How the hell did you get that woman and the lawyer tipped off so they were waiting at the airport?"

I yawned.

"Any leak out of your place, Bill?" the investigator asked one of the officers.

The officer shook his head. "It looks fishy to me," ne said.

The D.A.'s investigator stared at me. "Say, listen, suppose you tell me about your alibi first. Maybe we could check on that, and we wouldn't have to bother getting this girl up out of bed. Why didn't you tell me about that sooner? I could have used a telephone and maybe saved you a trip down."

"To tell you the truth, I didn't think of it. The way you folks gave me the rush act—and you know how it is. Try thinking where you were every minute of the time two or three nights ago, and—"

"Well, where were you? What's the alibi?"

I shook my head. "We're down here now," I said, "and it'll be easier to get this girl out of bed than to get all of my witnesses out of bed."

"How many are there?"

"Three."

He leaned over and whispered something to one of the officers. The officer shook his head dubiously.

Bertha Cool looked at me with her forehead puckered in lines of worry. The lawyer looked smugly down his nose as though he'd actually done something.

We hit the city, and went screaming through the streets. The intersections whizzed past. The distances of city blocks dissolved under the wheels of the speeding automobile. That siren certainly flattened out traffic. In no time at all we were at the door of the apartment house where Esther Clarde lived.

I said to Bertha Cool, "Come on. I want a witness."

One of the officers stayed with the car. The other one came along with us. The lawyer also got in on the party. We sounded like an army on the march pounding up the stairs. It was a walk-up, and the D.A.'s investigator, putting me in the lead, kept prodding me from behind. I think he thought he was going to leave Bertha Cool behind, but he reckoned without Bertha. She hoisted her two hundred and fifty-odd pounds up those stairs, keeping her place in the procession.

We got up to the third floor. One of the officers pounded on Esther Clarde's door. I heard her voice saying, "Who is it?" And the D.A.'s man said, "The law. Open up."

There was silence for four or five seconds. I could hear Bertha's breathing. Then Esther Clarde called out, "Well, what do you want?"

"We want in."

"Why?"

"We want you to look at a man."

"Why?"

"We want to see if you know him."

"What does the law have to do with that?"

"Nuts. Open up. Let us in."

"All right. Wait a minute. I'll let you in."

We waited. I lit a cigarette. Bertha Cool looked at me with a puzzled expression in her eyes. The lawyer looked as important as a rooster in a hen yard. The officers fidgeted, exchanged looks.

Esther Clarde opened the door. She had on that black velveteen housecoat with the zipper up the side that she'd worn the night before. Her eyes looked a little sleepy. She said, "Well, I guess it's all right. Come on in and—" She saw me and jerked the door shut. She yawned and said, "Okay, what is it?"

The investigator from the D.A.'s office jerked his thumb

156

at me. "Ever see this guy before?" he asked.

The lawyer corrected meticulously, "Any of these men before. After all, you should be fair—"

Esther Clarde shifted her expressionless eyes over my face, looked at the lawyer, pointed her finger at him, and said, "You mean this guy? Is he the one?"

The district attorney's man took my shoulder and pushed me forward. "No, *this* guy. Is he the one who was in the hotel the night of the murder?"

I looked at Esther Clarde and didn't move a muscle in my face. She looked at me, frowned a minute, and said, "Say, he *does* look something like the same guy."

She squinted her eyes and looked me over, then she slowly shook her head. "Say," she said to the officer, "don't let anybody kid you. There's a resemblance, all right."

"Well, are you certain it isn't the same one?"

"Listen," she said, "I've never seen this guy in my life before, but, no fooling, he looks like the man who *was* in there. If you want to get a good description, you can take this man to work on. That fellow was just exactly the same height, and *almost* the same weight. He was a little bit broader-shouldered than this guy. His eyes weren't quite the same color, and there's a difference about his mouth, and the shape of the ears is a lot different. I notice people's ears. It's a hobby of mine. This man that was in the hotel, I remember now, didn't have any lobes on his ears at all."

"That's a valuable point," the officer said. "Why didn't you tell us that before?"

"Never thought of it," she said, "until I got to looking this man over. Say," she asked me, "what's your name?"

"Lam," I said. "Donald Lam."

"Well," she said, "you sure do look a lot like the man who was in the hotel. Taken from a distance, a person might make a mistake."

"But you're sure?" the officer asked.

"Of course I'm sure. My gosh, I talked with the guy that was in there. He leaned up against the cigar counter and asked me questions. This man's ears are different, and his mouth is different. He isn't quite as heavy. I think he's just about the same height— Where do you work, Lam?"

"I'm a private detective. This is Bertha Cool. I work for her. It's B. Cool—Confidential Investigations."

"Well, say," she said, "you'd better keep out of the way of that old biddy who looked out of the room door on the fourth floor. She told me afterward that without her glasses all she could see was a blur, but she knew it was a young man, and—"

"Never mind that," the officer interrupted.

Esther Clarde said casually, "Walter—that's Walter Markham, the night clerk—didn't get such a good look at him either. He was asking me only this morning about some things, trying to make sure about the color of the man's eyes and hair. I guess I'm the only one that *did* get a good look at him."

The D.A.'s investigator said, "Okay, that's all."

"How do I get back to where I was picked up?" I asked.

He shrugged his shoulders. "Take a bus."

"Who pays the fare?"

"You do."

I said, "That's not right."

Esther Clarde said, "Well, I guess I've lost enough of *my* beauty sleep." She took keys from her pocket, unlocked the spring latch on her door, and went in. We heard the bolt turning on the inside.

The whole procession trooped down the stairs. Bertha Cool was in the rear. Out on the sidewalk, I said, "Now listen, I was picked up several hundred miles from here. It cost me money to get there and—"

The officers opened the door of the police car. The district attorney's investigator piled in. The door slammed. The car shot smoothly away from the curb and left us standing there.

Bertha Cool looked at me with eyes that were bugged out in astonishment, said softly under her breath, "I'll be a dirty name!"

CHAPTER TWELVE

WE WENT DOWN to Bertha Cool's office. Bertha Cool got rid of the lawyer, and we went into the private office and sat down. Bertha brought out a bottle of whisky from the lower drawer of her desk. "God, Donald," she said, "that was a close squeak."

I nodded.

"That damn lawyer wasn't worth his salt. Served a couple of papers, and then didn't know what to do next—like a bum card player who plays all of his aces, and then crawls under the table."

"How did you happen to get him?" I asked.

"*I* didn't get him. For Christ's sake give me credit for *some* sense! I'd never get a boob like that."

"Ashbury?" I asked.

She poured out two slugs of whisky, then corked the bottle, started to put it away, and said, "Hell, I'm twice as big as you. I need twice as much to keep me going." She added another two fingers to her glass. "Well," she said, "here's how."

I nodded and we drank.

"That Ashbury is a good guy," she said. "He rang me up as soon as the officers loaded you in the car. He figured there was a plane waiting. He told me to get hold of this lawyer, explain what was happening, and go out to the airport armed with the necessary papers so we could be on the job."

"How did you know which airport?" I asked.

"Jesus, lover, do I look as dumb as all that? I found out what charter planes were out, what field this flyer had taken off from, and put through a telephone call to the field up north to be notified as soon as he left there; then I rounded up the lawyer, and we all went down— So you got that little blonde in your pocket, too? My God, Donald, how they fall for you is—"

"Be your age, Bertha," I said. "She didn't fall for me."

"Any time you think she didn't. I'm a woman. I can tell when I see that look in a woman's eyes."

I jerked my thumb toward the telephone. "What do you think I'm doing here?"

"Drinking whisky and relaxing," she said.

"I'm waiting for that phone to ring," I told her. "The blonde won't do it until she's certain no one's on her trail."

"You mean it's business with her?"

"Of course."

"How much will she want?"

"Probably not money. Something else."

"I don't care what she asks for," Bertha insisted, eyeing her empty whisky glass in thoughtful contemplation. "She's fallen for you, *hard*."

I lit a cigarette and settled back to the cushioned comfort of the chair.

The telephone rang sharply just as Bertha Cool was getting ready to say something. Bertha grabbed the telephone, jerked the receiver off the hook, put it to her ear, said, "Hello," then, "Who is this calling? . . . All right. He's sitting here waiting for you."

She handed me the telephone. I said, "Hello," and Esther Clarde's voice said, "You know who this is?"

"Uh huh."

"I have to see you."

"I figured you'd want to."

"Are you free to leave?"

"Yes."

"Can I come to your apartment?"

"Better not."

"You hadn't better come to mine. Perhaps I can meet you somewhere."

"Name the place."

"I'll be at the corner of Tenth and Central in fifteen minutes. How'll that be?"

"Okay. Now listen, if I'm being tailed when I leave here, I'll try and ditch the shadow. If I can't do it, I'll take him for a run-around and be back in half an hour. If I don't meet you at Tenth and Central in fifteen minutes, you ring me here in exactly thirty minutes. Got that?"

"Got it," she said, and hung up.

I nodded to Bertha Cool.

Bertha said, "Watch your step, lover. You're in the clear now. After what she said, she can't ever back up on her testimony, and it wouldn't do them much good to have the clerk identify you now. The woman who was standing in the door couldn't see straight up without her glasses. I'll bet she couldn't identify me twenty feet away."

"What are you getting at?"

"Tell that blonde to go jump in the lake. If she's sucker enough to put all the cards in your hands, go ahead and play them."

"That's not the way I play, Bertha."

"I know it isn't. You're too damn soft and sentimental— I don't mean you should give her the go-by entirely. Get Ashbury to slip her a little piece of change, but don't go sticking your neck out."

I got up and put on my hat and coat. "I'm going to take your coupé. You can go home in a taxi. I'll be seeing you in the morning."

"Not until then?"

"No."

"Donald, I'm worried about this. How about coming by my apartment later on?"

"I will," I said, "if anything turns up."

She reached in the desk drawer. I could tell from the slope of her shoulder and the rigid angle of her arm that she had her fingers clasped around the neck of the whisky bottle all ready to lift it out as soon as I'd left the office.

"Good night, lover," she said.

I walked out.

I made a figure eight around a couple of blocks, found out I wasn't being followed, and started down to Tenth and Central. I spotted Esther Clarde walking along on Central, midway between Eighth and Ninth, but didn't give her a tumble. I ran around the block twice to make certain she wasn't being followed. When she got to Tenth and Central, I picked her up.

"Everything all clear?" she asked.

"Yes."

"Was that you in the car that went by a couple of times just now?"

"Yes."

"I thought it was. I didn't want to seem interested. No one on *my* tail, is there?"

"No."

"What kind of a job did I do for you tonight?"

"Swell."

"Grateful?"

"Uh huh."

"*How* grateful?"

"What do you want?"

"I thought perhaps you could do something for me."

"Perhaps I can."

She said, "I want to get out of here."

"Out of where?"

"Out of the city. Out of the country. Away."

"From what?"

"From everything."

"Why?"

"I'm in a jam."

"How come?"

"You know, the police. They'll get after me. Honestly, Donald, I don't know what made me do what I did tonight. I guess it was because you were so decent with me— I just couldn't rat on you to the bulls."

"All right," I said. "Go home and forget it."

"No, I can't. They'll check up on me."

"How?"

"With Walter."

"The night clerk?"

"Yes."

"What about him?"

"He'll identify you."

"Not if you tell him not to."

"What makes you say that?"

162

I had been driving aimlessly. Now I pulled in to the curb, and stopped where I could look at her face while I was talking. "He's pretty sweet on you."

"He's frightfully jealous."

"You don't need to tell him the truth. Just tell him that I'm not the man."

"No, that won't work. He'd be suspicious—think I had a crush on you or something. It would make him all the worse."

"How much," I asked, "do you want?"

"It isn't a question of money. I want to get out of here. I want to take a plane for South America. I can take care of myself after I get there, but I need some getaway money, and I need somebody to engineer it who's smart, someone who knows the ropes. You can do it."

I said, "Try again, Esther."

Her eyes rose to mine. For a moment there was glittering hatred in them. "You mean that after all I've done for you, you won't do it?"

"No. It isn't that. Try again telling me why you want to leave."

"It's just as I told you."

"No, it isn't."

She was silent for a while, then she said, "It's not safe for me here."

"Why?"

"They'll— I'll— The same thing that happened to Jed will happen to me."

"You mean they'll kill you?"

"Yes."

"Who?"

"I'm not mentioning any names."

I said, "I'm not going into it blind."

"I went into it blind for you."

"Is it Crumweather?" I asked.

She gave a quick start when I mentioned his name, then shifted her eyes and didn't look at me for five or ten seconds. She was staring down at the illuminated dials on the dashboard of the car. "All right," she said after a while.

"Let's say it's Crumweather."

"What about him?"

She said, "That business with Alta Ashbury was all planted. They intended to sell her two-thirds of the letters. The other one-third that had all the damaging things in them was to go to Crumweather."

"What was *he* going to do with them?"

"He was going to make Alta Ashbury kick through with everything he needed to get Lasster acquitted."

"You know about him?"

"Of course."

"And about Alta Ashbury?"

She nodded.

"Go ahead."

"Crumweather was going to make the last shakedown. The first two payments went to someone else."

"And Jed Ringold gave her the third batch of letters," I asked, "and double-crossed everyone?"

"No. That's the funny part of it. He didn't. He only gave her an envelope with some hotel stationery in it."

"Did you know he was going to do that?"

"No. No one knew it. It was a racket Jed thought up for himself. He thought he could pocket the money and get out, but—things just didn't work that way."

"Where's that batch of those letters now?"

"I don't know. No one knows. Jed played along all right for a while, and then he got ideas of his own. I told him it was dangerous."

"You were Jed's woman?"

"What do you mean?"

"You know what I mean."

"Why, the idea of saying things like that to me!"

"You were, weren't you?"

She met my eyes, then glanced away and didn't say anything.

"You were, weren't you?"

She waited a moment, then said, "Yes," in a voice that was almost a whisper.

"All right, let's go on from there. When the officers

came up to your apartment tonight and pounded on the door and told you they were officers, and told you to open up, you were frightened stiff, weren't you?"

"Of course I was. Anyone would have been under those circumstances."

"You were in bed?"

She hesitated again, then said, "Yes. I'd just got to sleep."

"You opened the door and came out into the corridor, and closed the door behind you?"

"Yes."

"You had your keys with you?"

"Yes, in the pocket of my housecoat."

I said, "The reason you were so frightened when you heard the police, the reason you didn't let them go into your apartment and talk there, was because someone was in the apartment. Who was it?"

"No, no! I swear it wasn't! I'm telling you the honest truth. It wasn't the law. It was—something else."

"When do you want to leave?"

"Right now."

I lit a cigarette and didn't say anything for quite a while. She was watching me anxiously. "Well?" she asked.

I said, "Okay, sister. I'll have to get some money. I don't have it with me."

"But you can get it?"

"Of course."

"From Ashbury?"

"Yes."

"When can you have it?"

"As soon as Ashbury gets back. He's up north on a mining deal."

"He was up with you?"

"Yes."

"When will he be back?"

"He should be back almost any time. I don't know whether he'll drive back or take a plane."

"Listen, Donald, as soon as he comes back, you arrange to get some money so I can leave. Will you do that for me?"

"I'll take care of you."

"But what am I going to do in the meantime?"

I said, "Let's go to a hotel somewhere and register under an assumed name."

"How about my clothes?"

"Leave them where they are. Just disappear."

She thought for a while, and said, "I haven't a cent with me."

"I have some money. Enough to cover hotel bills, incidental expenses, and getting some new clothes."

"Donald, will you do that for me?"

"Yes."

"Where do we go?"

I said, "I know a little hotel that's quiet."

"You'll take me there? Go there with me?"

"Yes."

"You know how it is, Donald. A woman alone at this hour of the night without any baggage— Well, you come and register with me."

"As husband and wife?"

"Do you want to?"

I said, "I'll tell them you're my secretary, that you had to do a lot of work tonight, and have got to start early in the morning, and I want to get you a room in the hotel. It'll be all right."

"They won't let you stay there with me?"

"Of course not. I'll take you up to your room, and then come back down. Here's a hundred. It will take care of you for the time being."

She took the hundred, thought things over for quite a little while, and then said, "I guess perhaps that's the best way. Thanks, kid. You're white. I like you."

I started the car and drove to the hotel I had in mind—a little place on a side street where a night clerk and an elevator operator ran the whole place after midnight.

Just before we went into the hotel she said, "Donald, if I could get hold of the rest of those letters, I'd be sitting pretty."

"How do you figure?"

"Crumweather wants them, Alta Ashbury wants them, and the D.A. would pay money to get them so he could build up a case against Lasster."

"The D.A. can't pay anything."

"He could make a bargain."

"On what?" I asked. "Immunity?"

"Yes, if you want to put it that way."

"With whom?"

She didn't say anything.

"Where do *you* think the letters are?" I asked.

"Honest, Donald," she said, "I don't know. Jed walked up to the hotel with me. He was a little afraid that something might happen, and he'd get pinched in a blackmail racket. He had been tipped off that Ashbury was going to get a detective to find out what his daughter had been doing with her money."

"Where did that tip come from?"

"I don't know, but Jed knew it. I suppose it came from Crumweather. Anyway, Jed didn't want to have the letters in his possession until the last minute. He walked up to the hotel with me, and I was carrying the letters under my coat. I handed them to him just before I went in behind the cigar counter. I know he had them when he went up in the elevator and— Well, he never came down, that's all. The murderer must have got them."

I'd walked around to open the car door and help her out. Now I stood there, thinking. "Jed Ringold wasn't his real name?"

"No."

"How long had he been going under that name?"

"Two or three months."

"What was the name before that?"

"Jack Waterbury."

"Get this," I said, "because it's important. What was the name on his driving license?"

"Jack Waterbury."

"One other thing. When I came in and asked you about gamblers, why did you tell me about Ringold?"

She said, "Honestly, Donald, you had me fooled. You

certainly took me in on that one. You didn't look like a
detective. You looked like a—well, a sucker— You know
what I mean. Occasionally a man comes in and gets in
touch with either Jed or Tom Highland. They'll have a
poker game running."

"Who's Tom Highland?"

"He's a gambler."

"Connected with the Atlee outfit?"

"Yes."

"And he's in the same hotel?"

"Yes, room seven-twenty."

"Why not look him up? If the papers went upstairs with
Ringold and didn't come down, and Highland is in the
hotel, why doesn't that add up to make an answer?"

"Because it doesn't. Highland hasn't them."

"How do you know?"

"Because Highland wouldn't dare to hold out. There
was a poker game going on in Highland's room at the
time, and they all say Highland never left it."

"In a killing of that sort, the one who has the most
perfect alibi is usually the one who did it."

"I know, but these weren't the sort of people who would
lie. One of them was a businessman. He'd have a fit if he
thought he was being dragged into it as a witness. You
were following Alta to the hotel, weren't you?"

"Yes."

"She'd asked you to do it?"

"No. Her dad."

"How much does he know?"

"Nothing."

"Well," she said, "let's not stand here and talk. Do you
want to come up for a while?"

"No. I'll get you your room and then go raise some
money."

She put her hand in mine to steady herself as she came
out of the car. Her hand was cold. I walked into the hotel
with her, and said to the night clerk, "This is Evelyn
Claxon. She's my secretary. We've been doing some work
late at the office. She has no baggage, so I'll register and

pay in advance."

The clerk gave me a fishy eye.

I said to Esther for his benefit, "You go on up and get to bed, Evelyn. Get a good night's rest. You won't need to come to the office in the morning until I telephone you. I'll make it as late as possible. Perhaps not before nine or nine-thirty."

The clerk handed me a fountain pen and a registration card. "Three dollars with bath," he said, and then added, "*single.*"

I registered for her and gave him three one-dollar bills. He called the bellboy over and handed him a key. I gave the bellboy a dime, raised my hat, and walked out.

I went as far as the car, stood there for a minute, and then came back. The clerk's lips tightened when he saw me. I said, "I want to ask you some questions about rates by the month."

"Yes?"

I said, "It isn't very satisfactory to me, having my secretary live way out in the sticks where it's a nuisance getting back and forth. She has a sister who's working here in town, and the two of them have been talking some of getting a place in town where they could be together. How about a monthly rate?"

"Just the two girls?" he asked.

"Just the two girls."

"We have something very attractive—some nice rooms we could give them on a permanent basis."

"A corner room?"

"Well, no, not a corner room. It'd be an inside court room."

"Sunlight?"

"Yes, sir. Sunlight. Not a great deal— Of course they wouldn't be here during the day except on Sundays and holidays if they're working."

"That's right."

The bellboy came back down in the elevator.

"Whenever they get ready to move in, I'll be glad to talk rates with them," the clerk said.

"Do you happen to have a floor plan of the hotel so I can look at the rooms and figure on prices? I might have to make some salary adjustment. You see the girls are living at home now."

He reached under the counter, took out a floor plan of the hotel, and started pointing out rooms. The switchboard buzzed. He moved over to it, and I picked up the floor plan, walked over, and started talking to him while he was taking the call. "How about this suite of rooms on the corner in front? Would that—"

He frowned at me and said, "What was that number again, please?"

He was holding a pencil over a pad. I shifted around so as to get a better light on the floor plan and be where I could watch his pencil as he wrote the number down. I didn't need to. He repeated it. "Orange nine-six-four-three-two. Just a moment, please."

He dialed the number on an outside extension, then when he had it on the line, plugged in the line and moved over to me. "What was it you wanted to know?"

"About that suite."

"That's rather expensive."

"Well, you might give me prices on these three." I checked three rooms. He went over to the desk, looked over a schedule, and wrote the prices on a slip of paper with the room numbers opposite. I folded the paper and put it in my pocket.

"You understand," he said, "that includes everything— light, heat, maid service, and a complete change of linen once a week, fresh towels every day if desired."

I thanked him, said good night, and went out. Two blocks down the street, I found a restaurant with a public phone. I went in and looked in the directory under the C's, found Crumweather, C. Layton, attorney, office Fidelity Building. Down below that was the number of a residence telephone. It was Orange nine-six-four-three-two.

That was all I wanted to know.

CHAPTER THIRTEEN

BERTHA COOL, clad in gaudy striped silk pajamas and a robe, was sprawled out in a big easy chair, listening to the radio. She said, "For Christ's sake, Donald, why don't you go to bed and get some sleep? And let me get some."

I said, "I think I've found out something."

"What?"

"I want you to get dressed and come with me."

She looked at me in contemplative appraisal. "What is it this time?"

I said, "I'm going to put on a show. I may get into an argument with a woman. You know the way women work me. I won't be tough enough. I want you along for moral support."

Bertha heaved a tremulous sigh that I could see rippling all the way up from her diaphragm. "At last," she said, "you're getting some sense. That's about the only excuse you could have made that would have dragged me up and out after I've got ready for bed. What is it, that blonde?"

"I'll tell you about it after we get started."

She heaved herself up out of the huge reclining chair and said acidly, "If you're going to keep on giving the orders, you'd better raise my salary."

"Let me have the income, and I will."

She walked past me into the bedroom, the floor boards creaking under her weight as she walked. She flung back over her shoulder, "You're getting delusions of grandeur," and slammed the bedroom door.

I switched off the radio, dropped into a chair, stretched my feet out, and tried to relax. I knew there was a tough job ahead.

Bertha's sitting-room was a clutter of odds and ends, tables, bric-a-brac, books, ash trays, bottles, dirty glasses, matches, magazines, and an assortment of odds and ends piled around in such confusion that I didn't see how it was ever possible to get things dusted. There was only one clear place in the whole room, and that was where Bertha had her big chair stretched out, a magazine rack on one side, a smoking stand on the other. The radio was within easy reaching distance, and the doors of a little cabinet were open, showing an assortment of bottles.

When Bertha made herself comfortable, she settled down to make a good job of it, and thoroughly relaxed. She didn't believe in halfway measures in anything that affected her personal comfort and convenience.

Bertha was out in about ten minutes. She crossed over to the humidor, filled up her case with cigarettes, looked at me suspiciously, and slammed closed the doors on the liquor cupboard. "Let's go," she said.

We got in her coupé.

"Where are we going?" she asked.

"Out to Ashbury's."

"Who's the woman?"

"Alta Ashbury."

"What's going to happen?"

"I don't know. I'm going to get rough. Alta may try to interfere. Mrs. Ashbury's having perpetual hysterics. Her husband's announced that he's through. He's told her she can go to Reno. She'll be running a blood pressure, with a doctor at her bedside and a couple of trained nurses in attendance. She figures her husband will probably show up sooner or later to pack some of his things and move out. She's getting all ready for him when he comes."

"Nice party you're getting me into," Bertha Cool said.

"Isn't it?"

"What am I supposed to do?"

"If the women keep out of things, it's all right," I said, "but if they start horning in on the party, I want you to horn 'em out. Alta may try to work a sympathy gag. Mrs. Ashbury may get tough."

Bertha lit a cigarette. "It isn't such a good idea quarreling with a customer's wife."

"They're going to get a divorce."

"You mean he wants one."

"Yes."

"That's a hell of a long way from getting one," Bertha said, and then added significantly, "when a man has the dough *he's* got."

"He can always buy his way out."

"Through the nose," Bertha said, and relaxed to enjoy her smoking.

Halfway out there, Bertha ground out her cigarette and looked at me. "Don't think you're getting away with all this stuff, Donald. I'd ask you some questions if I weren't so damned afraid of the answers." Then she lit another cigarette, and settled back to dogged silence.

We pulled up in front of Ashbury's residence. There were three cars parked at the curb. Lights were on all over the house. Ashbury had given me a key, but because of Bertha, I rang the bell and waited for the butler to let us in. He was up, all right. He looked at me with mild disapproval, and at Bertha with curiosity.

"Has Mr. Ashbury returned yet?"

"No, sir. Mr. Ashbury is not here."

"Nor Miss Alta?"

"No, sir."

"Robert?"

"Yes, sir. Robert is nere. Mrs. Ashbury is very ill. The doctor and two nurses are in attendance. Robert is at her bedside. Her condition is critical." He looked at Bertha and said, "And if you'll pardon the suggestion, sir, there are no visitors."

I said, "That's all right. We're waiting for Mr. Ashbury," and we walked on in.

"Mrs. Cool will wait in my room," I said. "When Mr. Ashbury comes, tell him that I'm up, and that Mrs. Cool is with me."

"Mrs. Cool?"

"That's right," Bertha said, turning to stick a bulldog jaw out at him. "The name's Bertha Cool. Which way do we go, Donald?"

I led the way up to my room.

Bertha looked it over and said, "You seem to rate."

173

"I do."

"A nice place, Donald. He must have some dough tied up here."

"I suppose he has."

"It must be hell to be rich—not that I wouldn't mind taking a fling at it. That reminds me, I've got some letters to write in connection with a couple of stocks. When's Elsie coming back?"

"Two or three days," I said.

"I've got two girls up there now," Bertha said, "and neither one of them is worth a damn."

"What's the matter? Can't they take shorthand?"

"Sure, they can, and they can type, too, but it takes the two of them to do the same amount of work in a day that Elsie did."

"They're pretty good girls, then," I said.

She glowered at me. "Donald, don't tell me you're going to start falling for Elsie. My God, but you're susceptible to women! All a woman has to do is to put her head down on your shoulder and cry, and you start oozing sympathy. I suppose she's been beefing about what a tough job she has."

"She hasn't said anything. I'm the one who did the talking."

"What did you say?"

"Told her to take it easy up in that new office, and have a rest."

Bertha made a sound of indignation. It was half sniff and half snort. "Paying a girl," she said, "to sit around on her fanny and look at her fingernails while I'm slaving my fingers to the bone trying to make both ends meet." The humor of her remark struck her as soon as she made it, and she added, with a half-smile, "Well, perhaps not clean to the bone—Donald, what the hell did we come here for?"

"Sit tight," I said. "We're getting ready to go into action."

"What do you want me to do?"

"Wait here."

"You're going some place?"

"Yes, down the hall to look in on Mrs. Ashbury. If you hear her voice raised in an argument, come on down. Otherwise, stay here until the party gets rough."

"How will I know it's her voice?"

"You can't miss it," I said, and slipped out of the room to tiptoe down the corridor. I tapped gently on the door of Mrs. Ashbury's room, and opened it a crack.

Mrs. Ashbury was in bed with a wet towel over her forehead. She was breathing heavily, and her eyes were closed, but they popped open when she heard the door. She was expecting Henry Ashbury, and was all ready to put on an act. When she saw who it was, she snapped her lids back down again and made up for any false impression I might have had because of her interest in the door by groaning audibly.

Dr. Parkerdale sat at the bedside, wearing his most professional manner, one hand on her pulse, his face grave. A white-clad nurse stood at the foot of the bed. There were bottles and glasses and medicinal gadgets scattered all over a bedside table. The lights were low. Robert was sitting over by a window. He looked up as I came in, frowned, and raised a finger to his lips.

There was a hush in the room—an air of subdued silence which is usually associated with funerals and deathbeds.

I tiptoed over to Bob. "What's happened?" I asked.

The doctor glanced sharply at me, then back at his patient.

"Her whole nervous system's been thrown out of coordination," Bob said.

As though the whisper carried to the patient on the bed, she started twitching, making little spasmodic motions with her arms and legs, twisting her facial muscles.

The doctor said, "There, there," in a soothing voice and nodded to the nurse. The nurse glided around the bed, took the cover from a glass, dipped in a spoon, and held a small towel beneath Mrs. Ashbury's chins while she tilted the spoon.

Mrs. Ashbury blew out bubbles and sputtered drops of liquid up in the air like a miniature fountain, then swallowed, coughed, choked, caught her breath, and lay still.

Bob said to me, "Where's Henry? Have you seen him? She keeps calling for him. Bernard Carter telephoned he'd tried every one of the clubs and hadn't found him."

I said, "Step in my room a minute where we can talk."

"I don't know whether I dare to leave her," he said, glancing solicitously over toward the bed, but getting up at the same time he started speaking.

We tiptoed out of the room. I looked back over my shoulder, and saw Mrs. Ashbury open her eyes at the sound of the clicking doorknob.

I piloted Bob down the hallway to my room. He looked surprised when he saw Bertha Cool. I introduced him.

"Mrs. Cool," he said, as though searching his memory. "Haven't I heard the name somewhere—" He broke off to look at me.

I said, "B. Cool—Confidential Investigations. This is Bertha Cool herself. I'm Donald Lam, a detective."

"A detective!" he exclaimed. "I thought you were a jujitsu expert."

"He is," Bertha said.

"But what are you doing here?"

"Killing two birds with one stone," I said. "Training Mr. Ashbury and making an investigation."

"What's the investigation?"

I said, "Sit down, Bob."

He hesitated a moment, then dropped into a chair.

"I just missed meeting you earlier this evening," I remarked casually.

He raised his eyebrows in surprise. "I'm afraid I don't understand."

"How long's your mother been sick?"

"Ever since Ashbury said the things he did to her. By God, I'd like to get my hands on him. Of all the dirty cads, of all the—"

"You didn't know it until you got home?"

"No."

"That hasn't been very long, has it?"

"No. About an hour or so. Why? What made you ask?"

"Because, as I said, I just missed meeting you earlier this evening."

He raised his eyebrows in a somewhat exaggerated gesture of surprise. "I'm afraid I don't get you."

"Up at Esther Clarde's apartment. It must have given you quite a start when you heard knuckles hammering on the door, and someone said it was the police."

For a second or two he remained rigidly motionless. There wasn't so much as the trace of an expression on his face. Even his eyes didn't move. Then he looked up at me and said, "I don't know what the hell you're talking about."

I dropped into a chair, and put my feet up on another chair.

"You were in with Esther Clarde, the blond girl who works at the cigar counter," I said, "the one who was Jed Ringold's mistress."

His lips came together. He looked me straight in the eyes and said, "You're a liar."

Bertha Cool stifled a yawn and said casually, "Well, for Christ's sake, let's get down to brass tacks."

I slowly got up from my chair, intending to point my finger at him as I made my direct accusation. He misunderstood what I had in mind. I could see the sudden flash of fear in his eyes as he remembered my reputation as a jujitsu expert. "Now wait a minute, Lam," he said hastily. "Don't get hotheaded about this thing. I lost my temper. That was rather a direct statement you made. I won't say you're a liar. I'll just say the statement is untrue. You're mistaken. Somebody's been lying to you."

I followed up my advantage. I let my eyes close to narrowed slits. I said, "I suppose you know I could lift you out of that chair, tie you up like a pretzel, throw you into the garbage, and you wouldn't get untangled until they lifted you out to put you in the incinerator."

"Now, take it easy, Lam, take it easy. I didn't mean it that way."

Bertha Cool gave a choking cough which sounded almost like Mrs. Ashbury's reaction to the medicine.

I kept my finger pointed at him. "You," I said, "were up at Esther Clarde's apartment tonight. You were there when the cops came up."

His eyes shifted.

I said, "That business of *three* detectives getting letters out of Alta's room is the bunk. The homicide squad might have had three detectives, but the D.A.'s office never had three investigators it could put on a job like that, and the thing had already been dumped in the D.A.'s lap by the police. It was up to the D.A. to uncover his own evidence."

Bob looked at me and swallowed twice before he said anything. "Now listen, Lam," he said, "you're getting me wrong. I was up there. I went up to get those letters back. I knew what it meant to the kid. Nobody thinks I'm worth a damn around here except Mother, but I'm a pretty decent guy just the same."

"How did you know about the letters?" I asked.

He twisted in his chair, and didn't say anything.

I heard a commotion in the hallway, voices raised in protest, someone saying, "You can't do that," and then the sound of a scuffle. Mrs. Ashbury, attired in a filmy nightgown and nothing else, jerked the door open. The nurse grabbed at her, and Mrs. Ashbury pushed her away. The doctor trotted along at her side mouthing futile protests. He took hold of her arm and kept saying, "Now, Mrs. Ashbury—now, Mrs. Ashbury—now, Mrs. Ashbury."

The nurse came back for another hold. The doctor glared at her, and said, "No force, nurse. She mustn't struggle, and she mustn't get excited."

Mrs. Ashbury stared at me. "What," she demanded, "is the meaning of this?"

Bertha Cool answered the question. "Sit down, dearie, take a load off of your feet, and keep your trap shut."

Mrs. Ashbury turned to stare at Bertha Cool. "Madam, do you know whose house this is?"

"I haven't looked up the record title," Bertha said, "but I know damn well who's throwing this party."

I said to Bob, "Crumweather hired you to get those letters out of the way. Instead of giving them to him, you arranged with Esther Clarde to use some of them to raise a little dough. You—"

There were quick steps in the corridor. Henry Ashbury came striding in through the open door, and stared at the party over the tops of his glasses.

Mrs. Ashbury looked at me, then at Bob, then at her husband. "Oh, Henreeeeee! Where *have* you been? Poor Bernard's spent the whole night looking for you. Henry, this is the most awful thing—the most hideous thing! Henry, dear, I'm going to faint."

She closed her eyes and swayed around on her feet. The nurse and the doctor closed in. The doctor muttered soothingly, "Now, Mrs. Ashbury, you simply *can't* excite yourself."

"If you'll just go to bed quietly," the nurse said.

Mrs. Ashbury let her eyelids flutter down until the eyes were almost closed. She gurgled in her throat, and tilted her head back so she could watch what was going on through the slits at the bottoms of her eyelids.

"Henry, darling."

Ashbury didn't pay any attention to her. He looked at me.

I said, "I'm just pinning something on Bob. I think he's responsible for the thing you wanted investigated."

Bob said, "I'm not. I swear you've got me wrong. I—"

"Stole some of Alta's letters," I finished.

He was up on his feet. "You look here, Lam. I don't care if you can lick Joe Louis with one hand tied behind you. You're not going to—"

Mrs. Ashbury saw that her husband had swiveled his eyes around to glare at Bob. His face had colored and set in hard lines. She decided fainting wasn't going to do any good. She planted her feet on the floor, swept the doctor and the nurse to one side, and said, "So *that's* it. You've been hiring a detective to come in here and frame horrible crimes on my son. I want you people to be witnesses to the things that have been said in this room. Henry, you're going to pay for this, and pay dearly. Robert, darling, you come with Mother. We won't waste time talking to these people. I'll see my lawyer in the morning. Things which I hadn't understood before are perfectly plain to me now. Henry's trying to frame something on you so as to make me leave him."

Bob moved to his mother's side. She put an arm around his shoulder, and sighed.

Bertha Cool got up, slowly and majestically. Her manner was that of a master workman getting ready to tackle a difficult chore in a businesslike manner.

Henry Ashbury raised his eyebrows, looked over the top of his glasses at Bertha Cool, held up his hand, and said, "Don't."

There was a second or two of silence. Bertha Cool looked to me for instructions.

Ashbury shook his head at me. "Let it go, Lam," he said. "I think I'm getting somewhere."

"You just *think* you're getting somewhere. If you were, I'd let you go, but the cards are stacked against you."

Mrs. Ashbury said, "The doctor will testify that I'm in no condition to answer questions."

"I most certainly will," Dr. Parkerdale said. "This whole procedure is outrageous."

Bob was glad of the opportunity to get out. "Come, Mother, I'll get you back to bed."

"Yes," she said, in a voice that was a little above a whisper. "Things are going around and around."

Bertha Cool pushed a chair to one side, strode over to the door, and kicked it shut.

Ashbury looked at her and said, "No."

Bertha heaved a sigh. She was itching to pitch in and handle the situation, but a hundred dollars a day was a hundred dollars a day and instructions were instructions.

The nurse came toward the door. Bertha moved to one side. The nurse opened the door, and the doctor and Bob led Mrs. Ashbury down the corridor and into her bedroom. The door slammed. I heard the turn of a key in the lock.

Bertha Cool said, "Nuts."

Ashbury said, "We can't risk it, Donald. It's all right if we stood a chance, but that doctor knows which side of the bread has the butter. This will look like hell in a divorce court."

"You're the boss," I said. "Personally, I think you've scrambled the eggs."

A door down the corridor was opened, slammed, then locked. Dr. Parkerdale came striding indignantly into the room. "You have all but killed her," he said.

"No one invited her to this party," I said. "Send Bob back here. We want to question him."

"He can't leave his mother's bedside. I won't be responsible for consequences if—"

"No one wants you to be responsible for anything," Bertha Cool said. "You couldn't kill that woman with a sledge hammer, and you know it. She's putting on an act."

Dr. Parkerdale said, "Madam, like all laymen, you're prone to judge from external appearances. I'm telling you, her blood pressure has reached a dangerous point."

"Let it come to a boil," Bertha said. "It'll do her good."

Ashbury said to the doctor, "You think she's in a dangerous physical condition?"

"Very critical," the doctor said.

"Yes," Bertha Cool snorted. "So critical that he leaves his patient to strut down the hall and try and make evidence for a divorce court."

The significance of that remark soaked into Dr. Parkerdale's mind. He turned wordlessly and walked back down the corridor to Mrs. Ashbury's room. He knocked. The door was unlocked, opened, and locked again.

Bertha Cool kicked my door closed.

Ashbury said, "I'm sorry, Donald, but they've ganged up on us. The nurse won't contradict the doctor."

I reached for my hat. "It's your funeral," I said. "I had a winning hand until you trumped my ace."

"I'm sorry."

"You don't need to be. If you want to do a good day's job, start getting worried about your wife."

"That would be playing right into their hands."

"So worried," I went on, "that you insist on a consultation. Get a doctor of some real standing in the profession, get him out here right away, and *take her blood pressure.*"

He looked at me for a minute, then his eyes softened into a twinkle. He started for the telephone.

I said, "Come on, Bertha."

CHAPTER FOURTEEN

Tokamura Hashita sat on the edge of the bed, blinked his eyes against the light, and listened to my proposition. I said, "These experts say the stuff's no good, Hashita. They claim it only works with rubber knives and unloaded guns. They claim they'll put on a test and tie you in a bow-knot like a shoelace. They offer to bet fifty bucks. I tried to show them what you'd taught me, and they jammed me into a garbage can and told me they could do the same with you."

His eyes reflected back the lights as though they'd been burnished with black lacquer. "Excuse please," he said. "Plant acorn. After a while is very big oak tree, but cannot make lumber from green sapling. Must allow time for growth."

I said, "Well, if you think it'll work, I'm willing to be shown, but the way things stand right now, I think it's just a stunt. I've got fifty bucks to cover their bets."

He got up and pushed his feet into straw sandals, slippety-slopped across to a closet, opened a door, peeled off his pajamas, and pulled on clothes. When he turned to me, there were reddish lights in his eyes. He didn't say a word.

I led the way out of the door. He put on a coat and hat, and went down to where the taxicab was waiting at the curb, the meter clicking merrily away. He didn't say a word as we got in, and he didn't say a word all the way to the gambling club.

When he was dressed up, he wasn't a bad-looking chap, a bit heavy in the waist. But it was just thick body muscles, not fat, that gave him that chunky appearance.

I walked over to the roulette table and started gambling. He stood a couple of paces behind me, looking at me scornfully.

The brunette who had taken over Esther Clarde's date looked up, saw me, and hastily averted her eyes. A moment later she slid quietly out of the room and through a door marked *Private*. I pushed some chips in the Jap's hand and said, "Put those on the board." I quit playing. The brunette came back, said something to the man at the wheel, and looked right through me as though she'd never seen me before in her life.

The Jap put a chip on number thirty-six, and the ball, whirring and jumping around the track of the wheel, popped into pocket thirty-six.

The croupier raked in all the chips.

I said, "My friend had a chip on thirty-six."

The croupier looked at me and shook his head. "Sorry. Your mistake."

"The hell it is," I said, and turned to Hashita. "Where did you put that chip, Hashita?"

He placed a thick, capable forefinger on the thirty-six.

The croupier said, "You'll have to take this up with the manager."

A man appeared as by magic at my elbow. "This way," he said.

It was done that simply. None of that movie stuff of having a couple of tight-lipped men move up on each side —just a matter of putting the customer in a position where he had to beef, telling him to take the beef to the manager, and marching him through that door marked *Private*.

"Come on, Hashita," I said.

The man who escorted us into the office didn't bother to come in. He pulled the door shut. A lock clicked—probably an electric bolt which could be released by pressing a button somewhere on the manager's desk.

The manager was a thin-mouthed chap with high cheekbones, gray eyes, and restless hands. The long, slim fingers seemed delicately fragile. The hands were those of a poet, a musician—or a gambler.

He looked up at me and said, "Sit down, Lam," and then looked questioningly at the Jap.

I said, "This chap put a chip on the thirty-six. The thirty-six turned up, and the croupier raked in all the chips."

"Dollar chips?" the manager asked.

I nodded.

He opened a drawer, took out a stack of silver dollars, and shoved them across to the Jap. "All right," he said, "that disposes of *you*."

He looked at me and said, "Now that you're here, Lam, you can sit over there at that desk and write out a statement that you were in room four-twenty-one when Jed Ringold was killed, that you went through his pockets, and took out a check for ten thousand dollars payable to cash."

I said, "You can go to hell."

He opened the humidor on the desk. There was a peculiar click as the cover swung back, but all that was inside was a row of cigarettes. He took one out and closed the cover. The humidor didn't move by so much as a hair's breadth. It might have been a part of the desk itself. The signal wires ran through it, of course, down through the desk and under the carpet.

A door opened. Two men came in.

The man behind the desk said, "Frisk them."

I said to Hashita, "Stand perfectly still."

The men came over and rammed their hands along our bodies, then stepped back. "They're clean, Sig," one of the men said.

The manager indicated the desk. "Go ahead and write, Lam," he said.

"What do you want me to do, stick my head in a noose?"

"Just tell the truth," he said. "No one's going to hurt you."

"I know damn well no one's going to hurt me."

"Unless you act rusty," he went on.

"I guess you don't know the news. The cops picked me up and tried to pin that hotel room on me. I guess you framed that. Well, it didn't work. The witnesses won't identify me."

He acted very bored. He said to the Jap, "You got your money all right."

The Jap looked at me.

I said, "He's taken care of."

"All right, show him out."

The two men moved toward the Jap, who stood his ground quietly, his muscles seemingly completely relaxed, but there was something solid about the way he stood.

When the men were close to him, I said, "All right, Hashita, let's win that bet."

One of the men grabbed him by the shoulders and started to push him around.

I couldn't see exactly what happened. The air got full of arms and legs. The Jap didn't seem to exactly throw them. He juggled them, as though they'd been tenpins, and he was putting on a vaudeville exhibition in stage juggling.

The manager opened a drawer in his desk and reached inside.

One of the men sailed through the air with his head down and his feet up. He hit a picture on the wall in that position. The glass broke, and the man, the picture, and the frame hit the floor at the same time.

I made a grab for the manager's arm.

The other man jerked a gun out of his pocket. From the corner of my eye, I saw what happened. Hashita grabbed his wrist, twisted his arm, swung his own body around, smacked his shoulder up under the other man's armpit, jerked down on the guy's arm—and threw him at the manager.

The guy hit the top of the desk and the manager and the manager's gun all at the same time. The swivel chair gave way with a crash under the impact. The drawer splintered, and the men sprawled on the floor.

Hashita didn't look at them. He looked at me. There was still that burning red light in his eyes.

I said, "All right, Hashita, you win."

He didn't smile. He kept looking at me with ominous intensity.

One of the men scrambled up from behind the desk. He lunged forward. I saw blued-steel in his hand. The Jap leaned across the desk and chopped down on the guy's forearm with the edge of his open hand.

The man yelled with pain. His arm and the gun hit the desk together. The gun bounced. The arm lay there on the desk. The man couldn't get enough strength in his muscles to move it.

Hashita walked around the desk with quick, business-like steps.

I went to work. I went through that desk with as much attention to detail as the circumstances and time element permitted. The manager on the floor looked up at me with the dazed expression of a punch-drunk fighter.

I said, "Tell me where those Ashbury letters are hidden."

He didn't answer me. He may not even have heard me. If he did, the words probably didn't make sense.

I went through the desk. I found an agreement which showed that C. Layton Crumweather owned a controlling interest in the Atlee Amusement Corporation. I found a statement of net profits, of gross income, a recapitulation of operating expense—I didn't find any letters to Alta Ashbury. I was so disappointed I could have chewed up a bag of tenpenny nails.

The side door opened. A man stuck his head in, stared incredulously, and jumped back.

I said to the Jap, "All right, Hashita, that's all."

There was another side door. It led into a private toilet and washroom. Another door from there opened into an office which would have made a bank president turn green with envy. It didn't look as though it had been used for some time. There was dust on the desk and on the chairs. I figured that would be Crumweather's office. A door led to a corridor, and then there were back stairs. The Jap and I went down.

I shook hands with the Jap and gave him fifty dollars of my expense money. He didn't want to take it. I could see the red glints still in his eyes. I said, "The pupil begs the pardon of Honorable Master. The pupil was wrong."

He bowed, a stiffnecked bow of cold courtesy. "It is master," he said, "who is very dumb. Good night please. Do not call again—ever."

He got in the taxi and went home.

I turned around to look for another cab.

One was pulling in toward the curb. I flagged it, and motioned to the driver I'd pick him up as soon as he dropped his passenger. He nodded, brought the car to a stop, hopped out, and opened the door.

The man who got out of the taxi was C. Layton Crumweather.

He looked at me, and his bony face wreathed into a cordial smile. "Well, well," he said, "it's Mr. Lam, the man with the oil-land proposition. Tell me, Mr. Lam, how are things coming?"

"Very well," I said.

He reached out with his hand, and I took it. He kept shaking my hand, hanging on to my right, pumping it up and down and smiling at me. "I see you completed your business in the Atlee Amusement Corporation."

I said, "I presume that brunette girl telephoned you as soon as she tipped off the manager."

"My *dear* young man," he said, "I haven't the faintest idea what you're talking about. It just happens that I eat here in the restaurant occasionally."

"And have an interest in the gambling upstairs," I supplemented.

"*Gambling!*" he exclaimed. "What gambling? What are you talking about?"

I laughed.

"You astound me, Mr. Lam. Do you mean to say there's gambling going on in the restaurant?"

"Save it," I said.

He kept holding my right hand. "Let's drop into the restaurant for a bite to eat."

"Thanks, but I don't like their coffee. Let's go across the street to that restaurant."

"*Their* coffee is perfectly atrocious."

Crumweather kept holding my right hand. He looked back over his shoulder toward the door of the restaurant as though expecting something to happen. Nothing did.

Reluctantly, he let me withdraw my hand from his. "You haven't told me about the oil."

"Going fine," I said.

"By the way, I find we have some mutual friends."

"Yes?"

"Yes. Miss Ashbury. Miss Alta Ashbury. I have taken the liberty of asking her to be at my office tomorrow afternoon. I know she's a very popular young woman and can't arrange her time to suit the convenience of a crusty old lawyer, but you might impress upon her, Mr. Lam, that it would be very much to her advantage to be there."

"I'll tell her if I see her."

"Well, come and join me in a cup of coffee."

I shook my head. "No, thanks."

"You were in there?" he asked, jerking his head toward the building.

"Oh, yes."

He looked me over as though trying to find signs of violence.

"My business in there," I said, "was concluded very satisfactorily to all concerned."

"Ah, yes." His face wrinkled into a smile that reached his ears. "You did the wise thing, Lam, my boy. No one will make any trouble for you as long as you show a spirit of co-operation. I am very glad you saw things our way. We can use you." He groped out for my hand again. I pretended not to see the gesture.

"Well," I said, "I must be going."

"I think now that we understand each other, we'll get along much better," Crumweather said. "Kindly remember that I want Miss Ashbury at my office tomorrow afternoon without fail."

"Good night," I said, and stepped in the cab.

He was still standing on the curb, looking beamingly after me as I gave the cab driver Alta Ashbury's address.

CHAPTER FIFTEEN

IT WAS EIGHT-FORTY when I strode into the hotel where I'd left Esther Clarde. A young woman telephone operator was on duty at the switchboard. I told her to ring Miss Claxon's room, and tell her that Mr. Lam was waiting in the lobby.

She said, "Miss Claxon has checked out."

"How long ago?" I asked.

"Sometime last night."

"Can you find out exactly when?"

She said, "You'd better ask the room clerk."

I walked over to the registration desk and asked the room clerk. He moved down to the window marked *Cashier* and said, "She paid in advance."

"I know she paid in advance. What I want to know is when she left."

He shook his head, started to push back the drawer of cards, then some notation caught his eye. He turned it over to the corner and looked at the pencil note. "She went out about two o'clock this morning," he said.

I thanked him and asked if there were any messages for me. He looked through a stack of envelopes and said there were none.

I called up Bertha Cool from a booth in a restaurant a couple of doors down the street. No one answered at either the office or her apartment.

I had breakfast and smoked cigarettes over two cups of coffee. I got a newspaper, glanced through the headlines, and read the sporting news. I called Bertha Cool's office again, and she was in.

"Anything new?" I asked.

"Where are you, Donald?"

"At a pay station."

Her voice was cautious. "I understand the police are making headway in the Ringold murder."

190

"Yes?"

"Yes. There are some recent developments they can't figure out."

"Such as what?"

"Someone got into the hotel room, apparently early this morning, and ripped it all to pieces. The upholstery was cut open, curtains were pulled down, carpets torn up, pictures taken out of the frames— A hell of a mess."

"Any clues?"

"Apparently none. The police aren't exactly communicative. I had to get information that was bootlegged out."

"Nice going," I said.

"What are you going to do, lover?"

"Just keep circulating."

"Mr. Crumweather's office called up. It seems that Mr. Crumweather is very anxious to see you."

"Say what he wanted?"

"No. He just wanted to talk with you."

"Sociable old buzzard, isn't he?"

"Uh huh. Donald, watch your step."

"I'm watching it."

"Bertha couldn't use you, you know, if you were sleeping in a room that had iron bars all over it."

I pretended to be surprised and hurt. "You mean you'd stop my salary if I had to go to jail over trying to solve a company case?"

Bertha fell for it, hook, line, and sinker. She said, "You're goddam right I'd stop your salary, you impudent little squirt," and slammed up the telephone so hard it sounded as though she'd pulled the receiver hook out by the roots.

I went back and had another cup of coffee on the strength of that, then went over to Crumweather's office.

Miss Sykes gave me one look, said, "Just a minute," and dove into Crumweather's private office. It was a good minute before she came out. I figured she'd had fifty seconds worth of instructions.

"Go on in, Mr. Lam."

I went into the private office. Crumweather beamed all

over his face. He pushed out a bony hand at me, and was as effusively cordial as an applicant for a loan greeting a bank appraiser who's called to go over the physical assets.

"Well, well, Lam, my boy," he said, "you certainly *are* an active little chap—damnably active! You certainly do get around. Yes, sir, you certainly do."

I sat down.

Crumweather pushed his bushy eyebrows together in level speculation, pushed his glasses up on his nose, and looked me over with cold, hard appraisal. He tried to soften the severity of his eyes by freezing his lips into a smile.

"What have you been doing since I saw you last, Lam?"

"Thinking."

"That was clever, that idea of yours about the oil company— Now tell me, Lam, just what made you use *that* approach."

"I thought it would be a good one."

"It was a good one, very good indeed! Too good. Now, I want to know who put you up to it."

"No one."

"There's been a leak somewhere. Someone has been talking about me. A man in my position can't afford to have his professional reputation questioned."

"I understand that."

"Rumors have a way of traveling, getting garbled, distorted out of all sense of proportion."

"They do for a fact."

"If you've heard anything about any of my legal activities and came to me because it had been rumored I could beat the Blue Sky Act— Well, I want to know about it. I'd be willing to be generous— You know, grateful."

"I didn't hear anything."

His eyes narrowed. "I take it," he said sarcastically, "the idea just popped into your head. You said to yourself, 'Now, I want to approach Crumweather and get him to talk. What's the best way to get him to open up? Ah, I have it. Tell him I want to beat the Blue Sky Act.' "

"That's right."

"Bunk!"

I puffed at my cigarette.

He studied me for a while, and then said, "You know, Donald—I'm going to call you Donald because you seem like a boy to me, not that I'm commenting on your immaturity, but simply because I'm a much older man, and I've taken a fatherly interest in you."

"Have you?"

"I have indeed. You know you have a very shrewd mind. There's something about you that appeals to me. I've investigated your past a bit— You'll understand my interest in you?"

"I understand."

He beamed, then the beam expanded into a chuckle. "You do, at that," he said.

We were silent for a minute, then Crumweather went on. "I find that you've had a legal education. Most interesting. I consider a legal education a wonderful foundation for success in almost any field of endeavor."

"Primarily in the law business," I said.

He threw back his head and laughed. "A dry sense of humor, my boy, very dry, very interesting. You know, a man with your keenness of perception could make a great deal of money in the law business—*if he had the proper connections*. It's very difficult for a young lawyer to open an office, finance the purchase of books and office furniture, and then wait for clients to come in."

"So I understand."

"But persons who have a well-established law practice are sometimes willing to consider offering junior partnerships to men with the right amount of ability."

I didn't say anything.

He said, "I find, Donald, that you had an argument with the grievance committee in regard to legal ethics. You told a client how to commit a murder and avoid all legal responsibility."

"I didn't tell him anything of the sort. I was discussing abstract law."

"The committee didn't so understand it. The committee

also said that you were in error."

"I know they did, but it worked out. It actually held water."

He rocked back and forth in his swivel chair, chuckling. "It did for a fact," he admitted. "I happen to know one of the members of the grievance committee. I called the matter to his attention. He found it an embarrassing subject."

"You cover a lot of territory yourself," I observed.

"At times I do—not physically, but mentally. I find that a person keeps his mind keyed to a higher pitch if he conserves his physical energy as much as possible."

I said, "All right, let's quit beating around the bush. Where's Esther Clarde?"

He stroked the long angle of his bony jaw with gnarled fingers. "I'm glad you've brought that up. I was wondering just how to broach the subject. I—"

The secretary popped her head in the door. "A long distance call," she said, "from—"

The smile left Crumweather's face as though he'd ripped off a mask. His lips were ugly and snarling, his eyes hard and intolerant. "I told you I wasn't to be interrupted. I told you what to do. Get out there and do it, and don't—"

"It's a long-distance call from Valleydale. The man says it's terribly important."

Crumweather thought that over for a minute. "All right, I'll take the call."

He picked up the telephone on his desk. His face was without expression. Only his eyes gave evidence of extreme mental concentration. After a while I heard a click and Crumweather said, "Hello. . . . Yes, this is Crumweather. What do you want?"

I couldn't hear anything coming in over the wire, but I could watch his face. I saw him frown, then the eyebrows rise just a bit. The mouth tightened. He glanced at me as though afraid that, through some psychic eavesdropping, I might be hearing what was reaching his left ear through the receiver. My expression reassured him, but the tendency to furtive secrecy was strong in the man. He cupped the palm of his right hand over the mouthpiece as though that would bottle up the telephone.

After a few seconds Crumweather moved his hand from the mouthpiece long enough to say, "You have to be absolutely certain you aren't making any mistake about this," and then slid his hand back quickly.

Again he listened, and slowly nodded. "All right. Keep me posted."

He listened a little while longer, then said, "All right, good-by," and hung up. He looked at me speculatively, doubled his left fist, wrapped the fingers of his right hand around the knuckles, and squeezed until the knuckles popped. He picked up the telephone, and said to his secretary, "Let me have an outside line." He dialed a number, taking pains to see that I couldn't watch what number he was calling. He said, "Hello, this is Crumweather. . . . All right. Now listen, get this straight. I want the operations reversed . . . Where you've been selling, you'll have to buy . . . *Quit selling immediately and buy back what you've sold.* . . . That's right. . . . I can't explain . . . not right now. Do what I say. . . . Well, suppose there was more of a foundation of fact than you'd thought . . . Everything was just the way you . . . Well, let's look at it this way. Suppose a man was making a three-minute talk, and suppose everything he said in that three minutes happened to be not only true but true on a bigger scale than he'd even dared to dream. . . . That's right . . . You haven't any time to waste. This thing is going to leak out. Call in all the men and get busy."

He hung up the telephone and turned to me. It took him a minute to pick up the thread of the conversation.

"Esther Clarde," I reminded him.

"Oh, yes," he said, and his face once more settled into that fixed, frozen smile. "You know you made a most remarkable impression on that young woman, Donald."

"Did I?"

"You did. I mean you *really* did."

"I'm glad to hear it."

"You should be. It was most advantageous for you, but you see, I'm an older man and a wiser man, and, if I may say so, an older friend. Before she'd take any drastic steps, she'd consult me."

"You've known her for some time?"

"Oh, yes, a very nice young woman. A *very* nice young woman."

"That makes it nice," I said.

"I can appreciate her generosity," Crumweather said, "in trying to protect you, Donald, but I can't condone it."

"No?"

"No, not for a moment. Of course, Donald, a desperate man will do almost anything, but, even so, I can't appreciate how any man could so far forget himself as to let a woman put herself in the position of being an accessory after the fact, an accomplice to the crime of murder."

"Indeed."

"And I have so advised Esther Clarde. It may interest you to know, Donald, that I talked with her early this morning. I have an appointment with her at ten-thirty. I've persuaded her that the only thing to do is to call in the officers and confess frankly that she tried to protect you."

"You mean reverse her statement?"

"That's it exactly."

"Her identification won't amount to much if she goes on the stand now and swears I was the one who went into the hotel."

He was positively beaming. "That's right, Donald, that's right. You do have a very clear legal mind, *but* if she said that you had *bribed* her not to identify you, that it was because of this bribe she lied to the officers, but that after-ward she had competent legal advice and realized that that made her an accessory after the fact— Well, Donald, that legal mind of yours won't have any difficulty in putting two and two together."

"It doesn't," I said.

"I didn't think it would."

"Very clever," I told him.

"Thank you," he said, flashing his teeth in a grin. "I thought it was pretty good myself."

"All right, what do you want?"

The grin left his face. He looked at me steadily. He said, "I want that last bunch of letters that Jed Ringold was supposed to have delivered in that envelope."

"Why?"

"As a lawyer, Donald, you don't need to ask that question."

"But I am asking it."

He said, "My client is going to be tried for murder. It's one of those cases where a jury will act on prejudice rather than evidence. Those letters could build up a prejudice against my client, and the results would be disastrous."

"Why didn't you destroy them when you got your hands on them, then?"

He blinked his eyes at me. "I don't think I understand, Donald."

I said, "You got those letters. You wanted them destroyed so the D.A. could never use them. But you were too smart to burn them up yourself. You decided you'd let Alta burn them up and pay thirty thousand dollars for the privilege. That would get the letters out of the way just as effectively as though you'd struck the match yourself, and you'd be thirty grand to the good."

He turned the idea over in his mind for a moment, and then nodded his head slowly. "That would have been a *splendid* idea, Donald, a splendid idea. As I told you, Donald, two heads are always better than one. A young man, particularly if he's ingenious, thinks of things an older man might well overlook. You really must consider that partnership proposition. It would mean a career for you, my boy."

Suddenly his eyes hardened. "But, in the meantime, Donald, don't forget I want those letters. I'm not a man to be easily put aside or trifled with. Much as I respect your ingenuity and intelligence, *I want those letters.*"

"How long have I got?" I asked.

He looked at his watch. "Thirty minutes."

I walked out. He wanted to shake hands, but I managed not to see his paw.

I went down to the agency office. Bertha had rented another typewriter and desk and moved them in. The girls were getting more familiar with the work. Both of them were clacking merrily away at typewriters. I walked on across to the private office and opened the door.

Bertha Cool, reading the newspaper and holding a cigarette in a long, carved ivory holder between the fingers of her jeweled left hand, said, "God, Donald, you certainly do keep things stirred up."

"What's the matter now?"

"Telephone calls," she said. "Lots of them. They won't leave their names. People want to know when you're coming in."

"What did you tell them?"

"That I didn't know."

"Men or women?"

"Women," she said, "young women, from the sound of their voices. God, lover, I don't know what it is you do to them. I could understand it if you were one of these indifferent heartbreakers, but you certainly aren't a matinée idol. And you fall for them just as hard as they do for you—not in the same way. You're not on the make, Donald. You put women up on a pedestal and worship them. You think just because they have skirts wrapped around their waists they're something different, noble, and exalted. Christ, Donald, you'll never make a good detective until you learn that woman is nothing more or less than the female of the species."

"Anything else?" I asked.

She glared at me and said, "None of your impudence, Donald. After all, you're working for me."

"And making a hundred bucks a day for you."

That registered. "Sit down, lover," she invited. "Don't mind Bertha. Bertha's cross this morning because she didn't get much sleep last night."

I sat down in the client's chair.

The telephone rang.

Bertha said, "This is another one of those women calling for you."

198

"Find out who it is," I said. "If it's Esther Clarde or Alta Ashbury, I'm in. If it's anyone else, I'm out."

"Those two women," Bertha said, "falling for them both at the same time! That Clarde woman is just a common little strumpet, and Alta Ashbury is a rich girl who considers you a new toy. She'll play with you until she breaks you, and then she'll throw you on the junk heap without so much as—"

The phone had kept on ringing. I said, "You'd better answer it."

Bertha picked up the telephone and barked savagely, "Yes. Hello."

She was handling her own calls now that Elsie Brand wasn't there on the switchboard, and it griped her.

Bertha listened for a moment, and I saw the expression on her face change. Her eyes got hard. She said, "How much?" and then listened again. She glanced across at me and said, "But I don't see why . . . Well, if you didn't have any authority . . . Well, when can . . . Goddammit, don't keep interrupting me whenever I try to say anything. Now listen, if you didn't have any authority to complete that deal, how did you . . . I see. How much? . . . I'll ring you back sometime this afternoon and let you know. . . . No, this afternoon. . . . No, not by one o'clock. Later. . . . Well, by three o'clock. . . . All right, by two, then."

She hung up the telephone and looked at me with a puzzled expression.

"Something about the case?" I asked.

"No, another thing. A man came in here the other day and said he wanted to talk for three minutes. I agreed to give him exactly three minutes of my time. When he ran over it, I called him. He thought he'd have me so interested I wouldn't say anything, but I certainly *did* give him a jolt— Donald Lam, what the hell are you smiling at?"

"Nothing," I said, and then after a moment asked, "How much do they want to pay?"

"Who?"

"The people who sold you the stock."

"How do you know that was the people who sold me the

stock. How do you know I bought any stock? What the hell have you been doing? Snooping around in my affairs? Getting into my desk? Have you—"

"Forget it," I said. "I read you like a book."

"Yes, you do!"

"And so does everyone else," I said. "That's an old racket in the sucker game."

'What is?"

"Telling a person you want three minutes and guaranteeing to complete what you have to say in that three minutes. You tell them everything you want to, then keep right on talking. The sucker is so anxious to show you that he can't be bluffed, he keeps calling the time limit, and doesn't ask the questions he otherwise would. It's a nice high-pressure method of selling stock."

Bertha looked at me, gulped twice, picked up the telephone, dialed a number, and said, "This is Bertha Cool. I've thought it over. I'll take it. . . . All right, have the money here . . . I said the *money*. I don't want any goddam checks. I want cash."

She slammed the receiver back on the hook.

"How much did they offer?" I asked.

"None of your business. What have you been doing?"

"Stalling around."

"What the hell do you mean by stalling? You're hired to solve a murder and—"

"Get it out of your head," I interrupted, "that we're hired to solve a murder. We were hired to get Alta Ashbury out of a jam."

"Well, she's in it worse than ever."

"We're still hired."

"Well, get busy and go to work."

"We're getting paid by the day, aren't we?"

"Yes."

I lit a cigarette.

She glowered at me and said, "Sometimes, Donald, you make me so damn mad I could tear you apart. What the hell did you do to Tokamura Hashita?"

"Nothing. Why?"

200

"He rang me up and said there wouldn't be any more lessons."

I said, "I guess I hurt his feelings."

"How?"

"I told him that that stuff of his would work all right in a gymnasium, but I knew a couple of men who said that it had been exposed two or three times as not being any good at all in the conditions which confront a man in real life. I told him they said they could draw empty guns if he didn't know *when* they were going to do it and make him look like a monkey. I offered to give him fifty dollars—"

"Fifty dollars!" she interrupted with a half-scream. "*Whose* fifty dollars?"

"Ashbury's."

She settled back, somewhat mollified. "What did he do?"

"He took the dough."

"Then what happened?"

"He was right."

"Then you'd better continue with the lessons."

"I think Hashita figures someone slipped something over on him."

"Donald, how did you know that three-minute gag was a high-pressure stock-selling stunt? I'd never heard of it."

"How much did they stick you for?"

"They didn't stick me. I'm going to get twice what I paid—"

"Thanks," I said.

She just sat there glaring at me. After a while, she said, "Some day I'm going to fire you."

"You may not have to. Crumweather wants me to go in partnership."

"*Who* does?"

"Crumweather, the lawyer."

Bertha Cool leaned across the desk. "Now listen, lover, you don't want to get back in that law business. You know what would happen. It would be the same thing all over again. You'd build up a good practice, and something you'd do would irritate those long-haired scissor-bills at the bar association, and you'd be out pounding the pavements again looking for work. You have a nice berth here, and there's a chance to work up. You can make—"

"About a tenth what I could practicing law."

"But there's a future to it, lover, and you couldn't leave Bertha. You've got Bertha so she depends on you."

I heard voices raised in excited comment in the outer office, then quick steps. The door of the private office jerked open, and Esther Clarde stood in the doorway. One of the secretaries was peering over her shoulder, tugging at her arm in a halfhearted way.

I said, "Come on in, Esther."

Bertha Cool said, "Indeed she *won't* come in. That's a hell of a way to try to crash my office. She'll go back and sit down and be announced and—"

"Sit right here," I said, getting up and indicating the client's chair.

Esther Clarde came in. Bertha Cool said, "I don't give a damn *who* she is, Donald. No one's going to—"

I closed the door in the new secretary's face, and said, "What is it, Esther?"

She said, "That lawyer's trying to get me to double-cross you, and I wanted you to know I won't do it."

"Did you tell him you would?"

She shifted her eyes for a moment, said, "Yes," and then added by way of explanation, "I had to."

Bertha Cool said, "Now you look here, Donald. You can't step in and start running things. You can't invite people in this office—"

"She wants you to go out," I said to Esther Clarde.

Esther Clarde got up. Her eyes were swollen. I could see she'd been crying. "I just wanted you to know, Donald."

"You called him last night?"

"Who?"

"Crumweather."

"Yes."

"Why?"

"He's been my friend— Oh, it hasn't been an unselfish friendship, but he's—"

Bertha Cool interrupted. "Donald, you look at me. We're going to have this thing out right here and now. It isn't a question of whether we're going to talk with this girl. It's a question of who the hell is running this office. Now you—"

I said to Esther, "She wants us to get out of here. Perhaps we'd better go," and started for the door.

It took a moment for that to soak in, then Bertha pushed her hands down on the arms of the swivel chair and tried to lift herself out of the chair quickly. "You come back here," she yelled at me. "I want to know what's going on in this case. You can't leave me batting around in the dark. What's Crumweather trying to do? What's the double-cross he—"

I opened the door, escorted Esther Clarde through.

"Donald, you little runt, you heard me! You come back here an—"

The closing door cut off the rest of it. I walked across the outer office with Esther, while the two secretaries stared openmouthed. The door of Bertha Cool's private office jerked open just as I opened the door to the corridor. She knew better than to try to catch up with us. Her big beam and avoirdupois were too much handicap. As we went out, she was still standing in the door of the office.

In the corridor, I said, "Listen, Esther, there's one thing I have to know. Don't lie to me. Who gave you those letters?"

"I never saw the letters," she said, "until after Jed Ringold had them, and I haven't any idea who gave them to him."

"Bob Tindle?" I asked.

"I suppose so but I don't know."

I stood in front of the elevator shaft and pressed the button. "Did Ringold have any home other than that hotel?"

"No."

"No other place where he lived?"

"Except with me," she said.

The door of the agency opened. Bertha Cool came barging out. An elevator showed a red light just as an ascending elevator came to a stop. The door opened. Two men got out. One of them started toward the agency office. The other turned to check up on us. He stopped abruptly and said, "Okay, Bill. Here he is."

The men came walking over. One of them flashed a badge. "Okay, buddy," he said, "you're going for a little ride."

"Who with?" I asked.

"Me."

"What's the idea?"

"The D.A. wants to talk with you."

"I don't want to talk with anyone. I'm busy."

The descending elevator came to a halt. The two detectives pushed us on in. Bertha Cool screamed, "Hold that elevator. I want down."

She came along the corridor, walking as rapidly as she could. The operator held the cage. One of the passengers snickered.

The cage jiggled as Bertha Cool's weight was added to that of the other passengers. The attendant slid the door shut. Bertha Cool turned around and faced the door. She casually pushed the rest of us back in the cage. She didn't say a word to me.

We shot straight down to the ground floor. There was a long passageway past the building directories and a cigar stand near the street entrance. Bertha Cool was first out. She started walking down the passageway. I stood to one side for Esther Clarde to get out. The detective on my right said, "Hold the jane there, Bill," and pushed me out into the passageway. Three other men were standing there. They all closed in. We started walking. I said to the detective, "Wait a minute. What's the idea?"

He didn't say anything. A man was sitting on the shoe-shining stand, getting his shoes shined. I didn't pay any particular attention to him until I heard his voice shrill out in an excited shout. "There he is! That's the one!"

The whole outfit stopped. I looked up. The man who was getting his shoes shined was the night clerk at the hotel where the murder had been committed. He was pointing his finger directly at me.

The detective grinned and said, "Okay, buddy, there's your line-up, and that's your identification." He turned back toward the elevator and said, "Okay, Bill, bring along the skirt."

Lots of things happened all at once. The grinning detective said to the three men who had been walking along with me, "You boys can leave now. Remember to be available when we call on you." The other detective brought Esther Clarde out from the elevator. Bertha Cool, without looking back, walked to the telephone booth at the end of the hallway. She squeezed herself in, but wasn't able to get the door closed. I saw her drop a coin and dial a number. She put her lips up close to the transmitter so people outside couldn't hear what was being said. The hotel night clerk came hopping down off the shoe-shining stand. One shoe was shined. The other wasn't. His pants cuffs had been doubled back. He was dancing with excitement. He kept pointing his finger at me and saying, "That's the one. That's the fellow. I'd recognize him anywhere."

He saw Esther and ran toward her. "Look, Esther, there's the guy. That's the one. That's—"

Esther said, "You're crazy, Walter, that isn't the man. He looks something like it, but it isn't the man."

He looked at her in astonished surprise. "Why, it is too. You can't mistake him. He's—"

"He has the same build," Esther said, "and about the same complexion, but the man who came in the hotel was a little broader, a little heavier, and I think a year or two older."

The clerk hesitated dubiously, staring at me.

The detective said, "Be your age, guy. She's been playing around with him and is trying to protect him."

The clerk's face went white as a sheet. He said, "That's not so! Esther, you know that isn't so! Tell him it's a lie."

"It's a lie," Esther said.

"Of course it's a lie. Esther's running a cigar counter, and she kids them all along, but when it comes to—"

"Bunk," the detective said. "She's stringing you along.

Why don't you take a tumble to yourself, sucker? This is the guy that's beating your time. How the hell do you suppose *she* got *here?* She was riding down in the elevator with him. They were headed for her apartment when we picked them up."

The clerk stared from the detective to Esther, then to me. I saw hatred come in his eyes. He shrilled, "That's not true about Esther, but this is the man. I'll swear it's the man."

The detective grinned at me. "How about it, buddy? You the guy?"

"No," I said.

"Well, now, ain't that too bad? Must be a case of mistaken identity. Do you want to help the officers clear it up?"

"Of course."

"Then we'll go over to the hotel and look around."

I said, "No we won't. We'll talk things over right here, or else we'll go see the D.A."

"Oh, no, buddy. You're going to the hotel."

"What do you expect to find there?"

"Oh, we can sort of look around. We'd like to try the blade of your knife and see whether it fits into that little hole in the door."

I shook my head. "If you're going to try and pin anything on me, I'm going to see a lawyer."

"Now listen, buddy, if you're guilty, that's all right. You just go ahead and sit tight. Don't say anything and get a lawyer, but if you're innocent and don't want to have this thing pinned on you, you'd better help us clear it up."

"I'm willing to help you clear it up, but I'm not going to be dragged around the streets."

"Where do you want to go?"

"Out to Ashbury's house," I said.

"Why?"

"I have some work to do out there. That's where my clothes are."

I saw a crafty look on the detective's face. "That's fine," he said. "We'll get a taxi and go out to Ashbury's."

"How about the car you came in?" I asked.

"Well," he said, "that'll be sort of crowded."

He walked back to Esther Clarde and said, "All right, sister, you're at the parting of the ways. Either identify this guy or get hooked as an accessory. Which do you want to do?"

"He isn't the one."

"We *know* he's the man. You're standing right at the forks of the road. Pick your bed, because you're going to have to lie in it."

Bertha Cool, who had walked toward the elevators and paused to listen in on the conversation, said, "Isn't that intimidating a witness?"

The detective looked up at her, an angry flush coming to his face. "Move on," he said. "This is police business." He flipped back the lapel of his coat to show her his star.

Bertha Cool said, "Phooey. That piece of tin doesn't mean a damn thing to me. If I understand what I've heard correctly, you're telling this girl that if she commits perjury, nothing will happen to her, that if she tells the truth, you're going to hook her for being an accessory after the fact."

"Go jump in the lake," the detective said irritably.

"Find one big enough and I will," Bertha cooed.

Esther Clarde remained quietly positive. "He isn't the man."

Markham, the night clerk, said, "You know he's the man, Esther. What are you trying to do? Why should you protect him? What's he to you?"

"A total stranger," she said. "I never saw him before in my life, and neither did you."

The detective who had charge of me said, "Bill, take them out to Ashbury's place. We'll go in a cab. I want to keep this girl and Lam apart, and you'd better keep her from talking to that night clerk."

"Let her talk her head off," the other detective said. "She's just building up a case against herself."

Esther said to the night clerk, "If you'd had a good look at him, Walter, you'd know he isn't the same one. You didn't see him as well as I did. You—"

"You heard what I said," the detective remarked.

"Well, what the hell am I going to do? Am I—"

The detective who had me grabbed Markham by the arm. "You come along with us," he said.

Markham came walking along, his pants flapping around his ankles where the cuffs had been rolled up.

We went in a taxi. The others followed in the police car, clearing the way for the cab with the siren. I never did know how Bertha got there, but she managed to keep right along with the procession. When we pulled up in front of Ashbury's house and got out, the detective looked at her, and said, "You again. Where do you think you're getting in on this party? Beat it."

Bertha said, "It happens this young man is working for me, and I've telephoned a lawyer who'll be here in about ten minutes. Mr. Ashbury wants to see me, and if you try to keep me out of this house, you'll have a damage suit on your hands."

"We don't want any lawyers," the detective said. "All we need is to get things straightened out. Lam can make a frank statement, and that's all there'll be to it."

Bertha snorted.

The detectives held a whispered conference, then we all went in.

"Is Miss Ashbury home?" one of the detectives asked the butler.

"Yes, sir."

"Get hold of her. Get her here right away."

"Yes, sir. Who shall I say is calling?"

The detective pulled back his coat. "The law," he said.

The butler took it on the double quick.

I heard Alta's feet on the stairs—quick, light steps.

Alta paused on about the fourth step where she could see into the room. No one needed to blueprint the situation for her. She stood there staring with eyes that were a little wider and a little rounder than usual, then she came forward with her chin up. "Why, Donald, what is this?"

"A personally escorted tour," I said.

The detective who seemed to be in charge pushed forward and said, "You're Alta Ashbury?"

"Yes."

"You hired this man to get some letters for you, didn't you?"

"I did nothing of the sort."

"What's he doing here?"

"Giving my father physical culture lessons."

"Bunk."

She drew herself up, and there was something about her that put the detectives on the defensive. "This is my father's house," she said. "I don't think he's invited you to call, and I'm certain I haven't."

Bill said, "How about taking his fingerprints, sergeant?"

"Good idea."

They grabbed my hands. I resisted as best I could, but they held my wrists and took fingerprints.

Bill said, "Come on, Lam. What's the use beating around the bush. Your fingerprints check with the ones we found there in the hotel."

"Then someone planted them."

"Yes, I know. You loaned someone your hands for the evening."

I said, "Show me where they check."

The detectives huddled together, began comparing my prints with some photographs they had. I heard the sound of heavy steps in the upper corridor, and Mrs. Ashbury and Bernard Carter came walking down the stairs. He was tenderly solicitous. She was prepared either to make a scene or put on an act, as the occasion might require.

There was something in the ponderous dignity of her appearance that impressed the officers more than Alta Ashbury's clean-cut patrician manner. The officers became deferential.

"What's going on here?" Mrs. Ashbury asked.

"We've caught the murderer," one of the detectives said, and motioned toward me.

"Donald!" she exclaimed in surprise.

He nodded.

I heard quick, pounding steps, and Bob, running up from the billiard room, came to stand in the doorway.

Alta Ashbury moved over to my side and said, "Dad's on his way out here."

He came in while the officers were still in a huddle over the fingerprints. I saw things weren't going to suit them. They shifted photographs around and stared in scowling concentration at the prints they'd taken of my fingers. I was glad I'd remembered to wear gloves there in that hotel room.

Ashbury came over to stand near me.

The sergeant of detectives moved over to talk with Markham, the night clerk. Markham was more and more positive. He kept nodding his head emphatically. They moved over and had a whispered conference with Esther Clarde, and she continued to shake her head.

Ashbury said, "What's it all about, Donald?" Bertha Cool took his arm, pulled him off to one side, and started to whisper.

I said to the sergeant, "It's too bad those fingerprints don't check. You wanted to crack the case, didn't you?"

"All right, wise guy," he said, "go ahead and shoot off your mouth. You'll sing a different tune before we're done with you."

I motioned toward Bernard Carter.

"Why don't you try *his* fingers?" I asked. "See if they match."

"Nuts. The man we're looking for is a man of your build, your complexion— In short, we're looking for *you!*"

"All right," I said, "if you don't try his fingerprints, you have yourselves to thank for passing up a chance of advancement."

At that, I don't think they'd have done it if it hadn't been for the look on Carter's face.

The officer moved over toward him. "Just a routine checkup," he said.

Carter shot his hands behind his back. "What the hell do you fellows think this is? Who do you think you're pushing around? I'll have you busted wide open."

I lit a cigarette.

The officers looked at each other, and then converged on Carter.

He put up quite a fight, first with a lot of threats, and then by trying to break away. They got his fingerprints. It took only one look at the fingerprints and the photograph, a quick consultation, and one of the officers pulled out a pair of handcuffs.

Mrs. Ashbury said, "Bernard, what's the meaning of this? What are they trying to do?"

"It's a frame-up," he yelled. "I'll be damned if I stand for it." He broke loose, and started for the door.

"That's far enough, buddy," the sergeant in charge said.

Carter shot through the door and started to run through the corridor. The officer pulled out a gun. Mrs. Ashbury screamed.

The officer yelled, "I'll shoot! By God, I will!"

We heard Carter's running feet come to a stop. The officer walked toward him.

I said to Ashbury, "That'll just about wind it up," and turned to encounter Alta's eyes.

CHAPTER SIXTEEN

BERTHA COOL FOUND US in the solarium. She looked at me and said, "Donald, lover, I'm damned if I know how you do it, but you certainly reached in the grab bag and came out with first prize."

"Has he confessed?" I asked.

"No, but those fingerprints tally. They found a gun on him that the officers think is the murder gun. They've rushed it to the ballistics department."

Alta patted my hand.

Bertha stood looking down at us. "All right, Donald," she said, "break it up. The rest of it's up to the police. We're going back."

"Back where?" Alta asked.

"Back to work."

"But he's working."

"Not on this case. It's all washed up."

She walked calmly out of the solarium.

"Want to try something?" I asked Alta.

"What?"

I said, "Those letters. There's one place they *might* be."

She looked around in quick apprehension to make certain that no one was listening. "Where?" she asked.

"Got your car out here?" I asked.

"Uh huh."

We sneaked out the back way, got in it, and drove out of the yard. Police cars were arriving, a steady procession of sirens.

"Donald, tell me how did you figure that out?"

"I was dumb," I said.

"*You,* dumb!"

"Uh huh."

She laughed.

I said, "That's the way it figures. It looked like an inside job to me. It had to be. Esther Clarde knew about the switch on letters—everything that was going on here. When the officers took me up to her apartment, she was going to let them in. Then she saw me, and decided to talk in the corridor. I figured someone was in there I knew. It just about had to be Bob. I pegged Bob for the whole business, but it didn't exactly fit. I overlooked the most logical bet."

"What do you mean? You surely don't mean that Carter got in my room and—"

"No," I said. "Your stepmother. Don't you get the picture? You were really the one who made a home for your father. When you went away, and he was left to shift for himself, he got desperately lonely. He wouldn't say anything to you because he thought you had your own life to live, that you'd sooner or later get married and leave him anyway. So he decided to carry on and try to make another home for himself. When you came back, he realized how he'd made a fool of himself. Mrs. Ashbury saw the picture in its true light. Little things you did gave her her clue."

"You mean she got the letters?"

"Yes."

"Why?"

"To involve you in that wife murder and get you thoroughly discredited. She thought it would give her the whip hand."

"And what did she do with them?"

"Gave them to Carter to turn over to the district attorney. Carter turned them over to Jed Ringold because he needed an outside point of contact. Ringold saw a chance to collect twenty grand, and still have enough letters for the D.A. Then he lost his dough gambling and decided to go the rest of the way on the letters.

"Your dad found out you were paying out money. Mrs. Ashbury found it out from him. Carter found out Ringold was double-crossing your stepmother. *She* wanted the D.A. to get those letters. He wanted the D.A. to get some of them. They were prepared for a little delay while Ringold was rigging a plant, but Ringold made the mistake of carrying things too far."

"I still don't see," she said.

"Crumweather, of course, knew about the letters because Lasster told him. When a man gets in jail on a murder rap, he tells his lawyer everything. Crumweather wanted to make certain those letters were destroyed. He supposed, of course, that you'd burned them, but he wanted to make certain.

"Crumweather knew Carter, had business dealings with him, and knew Carter had an entree to your house, so he suggested to Carter that it would be a good plan to make certain the letters were destroyed.

"Then Carter must have passed the word on to Mrs. Ashbury, and she saw a chance to double-cross Crumweather, get you involved in a scandal, and make things so hot for you you'd want to leave the country and never show your face in it again.

"She was the one who got into your room and stole the letters. She gave them to Carter and told him not to let Crumweather have them, but to be certain they got into the hands of the district attorney.

"Carter was willing to double-cross Crumweather if Mrs. Ashbury told him to, but Carter saw a chance to make a little dough out of it. He turned the letters over to Ringold and gave Ringold a nice little fairy story to pass on to you that would account for the letters being offered you in three installments. The plan was that you were to buy two packages of the letters and then the third package was to be turned over to the district attorney. That would give Ringold and Carter a chance to split twenty thousand bucks and still give Mrs. Ashbury everything she wanted, because the letters that reached the district attorney's hands would be the gems of the collection.

"But Ringold decided to double-cross everybody. He couldn't see any reason for turning over that last bunch of letters to the D.A. and getting nothing in return except the thanks of the prosecutor's office which he didn't like anyway.

"Then he realized that Carter would know there'd been a double cross, and Ringold was in a quandary. Finally he hit on a bullet-proof scheme. He'd hocus-pocus you into thinking you had the last bunch of letters. He'd cash your check, and then turn over the rest of the letters to the D.A.

"But Carter didn't trust Ringold, and Mrs. Ashbury couldn't understand the delay. The conversation you overheard between her and Carter was when she was telling Carter to go ahead and show some speed and get you dragged into the case."

"How was the murder committed?" she asked.

"Carter didn't intend to kill anyone," I said, "but he knew you were going to see Ringold. He thought perhaps there was going to be a double cross. He got a room in another part of the hotel, found four-twenty-one vacant, picked the lock with a skeleton key, watched his chance to slip through the communicating door, and hid in the bathroom. He found out all he wanted to know, and wanted to sneak out, but, in the meantime, I'd checked into that room and locked the communicating door. He couldn't get back. Ringold caught him in the bathroom. Carter smoked his way out.

"As a matter of fact, Carter gave himself away. He was so anxious to get you on the defensive by telling you that he'd seen you near the scene of the murder at the time the murder was committed, he entirely overlooked the fact that this constituted an admission he was there himself— Otherwise he couldn't have seen you."

"He hasn't admitted anything. My stepmother's going to get a lawyer for him, and they'll put up a fight," she said thoughtfully.

"Swell," I said. "Let them."

"But won't those letters enter into it?"

"Not unless the D.A. can get hold of them."

"Well, where are they?"

I said, "Look at it this way. Carter doesn't know where they are. Esther Clarde, who was handling the payoff, doesn't know where they are, and Crumweather doesn't know where they are. They've searched the room in the hotel—And I mean *searched* it. Jed Ringold had those letters when he went to the hotel. He didn't leave the hotel, and apparently the letters didn't either."

"Donald, what *are* you getting at? You mean they're concealed in some other room?"

"Perhaps," I said, "but as I size up Ringold's character, I don't think he was that big a sucker."

"What did he do with them, then?"

I said, "We'll find out."

I drove to the post office, walked in to the window which had *Q to Z* over the wicket, and said, "Jack Waterbury, please."

A bored clerk with a rubber finger stall thumbed through a pile of envelopes and handed me one addressed to *Jack Waterbury, General Delivery.*

I handed it to Alta as soon as I got in the car. "Take a look at this," I said, "and see if it's what you want."

She ripped open a corner of the envelope and looked inside. Her face told me the answer.

"Donald, how did you know?"

"There was only one place he could have put those letters. Down the mail chute. He had them with him when he was in the room with you. A few minutes later, when he was shot, he didn't have them. The murderer didn't get them. Crumweather didn't get them. Esther Clarde doesn't know where they are— There was only one place for them to go—down the mail chute.

"The man certainly hadn't acted the part of a gentleman while you were in the room. Yet when you got up to leave, he fell all over himself getting out to the hall to ring the elevator for you. The reason he did that was because the mail chute was right by the elevator. He wanted to drop that letter down the mail chute the minute you had left him."

She said, "I don't understand just how Crumweather fits into it."

"He had me fooled at first," I said. "As Lasster's lawyer, he naturally asked his client about women. Lasster told him about you and about the letters. Crumweather wanted to get them. He approached Carter. Carter told your stepmother, and she promised to get them. She did all right, but she couldn't see any reason why she should let you

216

out of the trap— Well, you know the rest. *She* thought the letters were going to the D.A. Carter and Ringold wanted to get twenty thousand dollars, and *then* turn the last third over to the D.A. Apparently, it never occurred to Crumweather he was being double-crossed until after the murder. Then Esther Clarde got in touch with him by telephone and told him what had happened. Naturally, he was frantic. He wanted to get that last batch of letters before the D.A. did."

She said, "You're a wizard when it comes to figuring things out."

"Not me. I should be kicked for getting off on the wrong foot. I figured Crumweather was in on it all the time. I thought that he saw a chance to sell the letters to you for thirty thousand dollars, and let you burn them up—but evidently he wasn't in on the play. Carter and Ringold were double-crossing him."

"Then why should he agree to represent Carter?"

"Money," I said.

She thought for a minute. "How did you know the name that would be on the envelope?"

"It was Ringold's real name. I asked Esther Clarde what it was last night."

"You mean you'd figured out about the mail chute then?"

"Yes."

"And Carter didn't know Ringold was going to sell me that last bunch of letters?"

"No. Ringold did that on his own. Carter was suspicious, that's all. He didn't dare fall down on the job of putting those letters in the district attorney's hands. Your stepmother meant more to him than Crumweather."

She thought for a minute. "Where are you taking me now?" she asked.

"To the Commons Building. I want to talk with Mr. Fischler's secretary," I said, grinning, "and instruct her to hold out for ten thousand dollars before she surrenders certain certificates of stock and options in a mining company."

Alta said, "Donald, are you going to stick them for that much?"

"All the traffic will bear," I promised.

We reached the Commons Building and went to the Fischler Sales Office. Elsie Brand hastily slammed a desk drawer shut on a magazine as I opened the door. "Oh," she said, "it's you."

I introduced Alta Ashbury. I could see that Elsie was impressed.

"When that salesman comes in," I said, "tell him that Mr. Fischler is in conference out of the office, that he's going to call in in about fifteen minutes, that you can talk with him over the telephone, but he absolutely won't take messages from anyone else, and he doesn't expect to be in the office for two or three days."

She jerked her shorthand notebook out of the drawer on the left-hand side of the desk and made rapid notes. "Anything else?" she asked.

"He'll ask you to call me up and give me a message. Twenty minutes later you can call him back and tell him I'll forget the whole business and surrender the options for ten thousand dollars, that I won't take a cent less."

"Anything else?"

"That's all. Tell him you want the ten thousand in cash, that you'll have Mr. Fischler sign the necessary papers and have the escrow made at Bertha's bank."

Her pencil made a swift flying succession of pothooks. "That's all?"

"That's all," I said to her, and to Alta, "Want to walk into my private office?" She nodded.

We walked on into the private office. As I closed the door, I saw Elsie watching me speculatively. I said, "I don't want to be disturbed."

Alta sat down on the settee across from the desk, and I sat down beside her.

"Is this your office, Donald?"

"Uh huh."

"What did you take it for? I mean what's the idea?"

"Just a little flyer in mining stock."

She looked at me thoughtfully. "You play them awfully close to your chest, don't you?"

"Not particularly."

"And I'm not to say anything about those letters?"

"Not to anyone. Let's see the envelope."

She handed me the envelope, and I burned the letters carefully one at a time, and ground out the ashes in a cuspidor.

I'd just finished with the last of the bunch when I heard a commotion in the outer office, the sound of heavy steps, and then Bertha Cool banged the door open. Henry Ashbury was just behind her.

Bertha said, "Donald, lover, why the hell didn't you tell me where you were going when you left? After all, you're supposed to be working for me, you know."

"I was busy," I said.

Alta jumped up and threw her arms around her father. "Oh, Dad," she said, "I'm so happy!"

He held her off at arm's length so he could look at her. "Everything cleaned up all right?"

"Perfectly," she said, and left a smear of lipstick on his cheek.

Bertha looked me over suspiciously.

Ashbury swung his eyes to look across at me. "Well, young man?" he asked.

"What?" I inquired.

"What's the answer?"

"There isn't any. I did the job I was supposed to do. It's all finished as far as *that* angle is concerned."

"But what about this murder?"

"What about it?"

"Apparently Carter is the one who was in that room, but he won't admit anything, and Mrs. Ashbury rushed to the telephone and got a lawyer for him."

"Who did she get, Crumweather?"

"Yes."

"Crumweather," I said, "should put up rather a good fight. They may have a hard time proving the murder."

"Don't you think you should get that cleaned up a little

more thoroughly?"

"Why should I?" I asked. "It's a police job. Why should *we* get interested in it?"

"So we could see justice done."

"You'd prefer to have your divorce handled very quietly and without any notoriety, wouldn't you?"

He nodded.

I said, "Under those circumstances, Crumweather is a pretty good lawyer for Carter to have."

He stood looking at me for a minute, then said, "You're right as usual, Lam. Come on, Bertha, let's get out of here."

Bertha said, "I want Elsie back in the office."

"You can have her in two or three days as soon as I can wind up the business here."

Bertha looked at Alta, then back at me, then at Henry. She said, "All right, Donald, remember you're working. This is an office, and these are office hours. Break it up."

"Break what up?" I asked.

She jerked her head in the direction of Alta.

Alta Ashbury pushed up her chin. "I beg your pardon, Mrs. Cool," she said, "but as far as I'm concerned, this case isn't finished. There are some other things I want to talk over."

"Well, I've got a detective agency to run, and I'm employing this boy. You can talk to him after hours."

Alta said, "I'll do nothing of the sort. You may not realize it, but we're paying you a hundred dollars a day, Mrs. Cool."

"You mean the—" Bertha Cool heaved a sigh. She took quick stock of the situation, and said to me, "I'm going over to the agency office," and turned to Alta and said, "At that rate, dearie, you can hire him by the month," and jerked open the door of the private office.

Ashbury said, "See you later, Donald," and to Bertha, "Just a minute, Mrs. Cool. I want to run down to your office and check up on a few points."

I heard the sound of Ashbury's chuckle, heard Bertha Cool slam the door shut so hard she jarred the glass partition, and then Alta Ashbury and I went in the office—alone.